The Christmas Vow

Hardman Holidays, Book 4
A Sweet Victorian Holiday Romance

by
USA Today Bestselling Author
SHANNA HATFIELD

The Christmas Vow

Copyright © 2015 by Shanna Hatfield

ISBN-13: 978-1518680618
ISBN-10: 1518680615

Shanna Hatfield
shanna@shannahatfield.com
shannahatfield.com

To those who keep their promises —
no matter what...

Books by Shanna Hatfield

FICTION

CONTEMPORARY

Love at the 20-Yard Line
The Coffee Girl
The Christmas Crusade
Learnin' the Ropes
QR Code Killer

Rodeo Romance
The Christmas Cowboy
Wrestlin' Christmas
Capturing Christmas

Grass Valley Cowboys
The Cowboy's Christmas Plan
The Cowboy's Spring Romance
The Cowboy's Summer Love
The Cowboy's Autumn Fall
The Cowboy's New Heart

Women of Tenacity
A Prelude
Heart of Clay
Country Boy vs. City Girl
Not His Type

HISTORICAL

Dacey: Bride of North Carolina

Hardman Holidays
The Christmas Bargain
The Christmas Token
The Christmas Calamity
The Christmas Vow

Pendleton Petticoats
Aundy
Caterina
Ilsa
Marnie
Lacy

Baker City Brides
Crumpets and Cowpies
Thimbles and Thistles

NON-FICTION

Fifty Dates with Captain Cavedweller
Farm Girl
Recipes of Love

Savvy Entertaining
Savvy Holiday Entertaining
Savvy Spring Entertaining
Savvy Summer Entertaining
Savvy Autumn Entertaining

Chapter One

Eastern Oregon, 1897

Adam Guthry glared across the sea of mourners at his only sibling and vowed his brother would be the next person the community of Hardman gathered to bury.

Unaware of his wrathful stare, Arlan appeared engrossed in the sermon Pastor Chauncy Dodd delivered over the loss of Carl Simpson.

Carl had been Adam's best friend since they were five. A year later, they both fell in love with a hazel-eyed beauty that moved to town to live with her grandparents.

That girl, the one he'd spent the majority of his adolescent years planning to marry, stood near his brother, dabbing at her eyes with a delicate handkerchief while clasping the hand of a little boy.

The sight of Tia Devereux and her son sent relentless pain stabbing through Adam's chest. It was no wonder he'd avoided coming back to his hometown. For him, Hardman held nothing but sad memories and regret.

Slowly shifting his frosty gaze from his brother to the woman who'd effectively destroyed his dreams, he wished Arlan had warned him she was back in town.

The last time Adam had been home was a year and a half earlier when Carl's wife and baby died during a difficult childbirth. He'd rushed to Hardman from Portland to attend the funeral. One night was all he managed to stay before returning to his job as a boat pilot on the Columbia River.

Unable to shake the melancholy threatening to overtake him, Adam focused his attention on the woman leaning against his brother's side. He had yet to meet Arlan's wife, but he'd heard she was brave, strong, and intelligent. The sight of her tall height, black hair, and ruby lips caught him off guard. Alexandra Janowski Guthry had to be one of the most beautiful women he'd ever seen.

A palpable energy exuded from her and Adam wondered how his somewhat bookish brother had captured not only her eye, but also her affections. It was blatantly clear the couple shared a deep and abiding love for one another.

"Let us bow our heads in prayer," Chauncy said. His voice carried over the group, drawing Adam's thoughts to the pastor.

He recalled school days when Chauncy and Luke Granger pulled any number of pranks. Often, they behaved in such a rambunctious manner, the teacher could barely handle them.

Now, Chauncy was a respected pastor. Luke served as an esteemed member of various committees and boards as well as owning Hardman's bank, although he'd made Arlan a partner in it last December.

Chauncy finished the service then smiled at Luke and Filly Granger. "Mr. and Mrs. Granger extend an invitation for everyone to join them at Granger House for refreshments. Thank you all for coming out on this cold December day."

Grateful he'd worn a heavy wool coat and thick scarf, Adam turned the collar of his coat up to block the frigid December wind blowing around them. Snowflakes skittered through the air like dandelion fuzz set free in a summer breeze, making him wonder if the approaching storm might turn into a blizzard.

Snow already blanketed the ground even though it was only the first of December. Piles of it indicated the strong-backed men in town had been busy shoveling it off the boardwalks.

No doubt, Arlan was among those who helped, along with Chauncy, Luke, and Luke's brother-in-law, Blake Stratton.

As the mourners left, Tia cast him a speculative glance but turned away when he frowned. She led her little boy in the direction of the house she'd lived in with her grandmother until the day she'd left town, ripping his heart into tattered pieces.

Arlan had mentioned Mrs. Meyer passed away in September in his last letter. He failed to state Tia had come home for her grandmother's funeral and stayed.

Last he'd heard, the high and mighty Tiadora Elizabeth Meyer Devereux lived in one of Portland's elite neighborhoods. Her father-in-law was a high-powered judge while her mother-in-law was among Portland's most sought-after members of polite society.

Not that Adam paid any attention to those matters, but he made it a point to discover all he could about Tia when he moved to Portland.

Nearly three years ago, he'd read an article in the newspaper that her husband had been killed in a tragic accident with a runaway buggy. He wondered if Tia still mourned the man or if she'd already given her heart to someone new.

Shaking his head to clear his thoughts, he stood with his cold hands in his pockets as the crowd dispersed. Many walked toward the grand home where Luke and Filly Granger resided on the edge of town.

Arlan hadn't seen him lingering at the edge of the mourners, so Adam took no slight in his brother walking away without saying hello.

The scowl on his face turned into a dimpled grin as a hand looped around his arm. The smiling face of Ginny Granger Stratton gazed up at him.

"Goodness sakes, Adam. You spent the entire service looking as if you've sucked a whole lemon," Ginny teased as she squeezed his arm. "Did you just get into town?"

Adam reached out and shook the hand her husband extended. "Blake. It's nice to see you."

"Likewise, Adam." Blake held out his arm to Ginny. She wrapped her free hand around it, sandwiching herself between the two men.

Petite and delicate, she was also feisty and full of opinions. "Will you join us at Granger House?"

"Might as well," Adam said, walking with the couple toward the fancy home her brother owned.

He recalled Ginny and Blake sharing a mutual affection for each other in school. When her family suddenly moved away, she left Blake with a broken heart. It was good to see them together and happy. "And to answer your question, Ginny, I did just get into town. I took the train to Heppner then rented a horse at the livery and rode as fast as I dared to get here in time for the service."

Ginny patted his arm and offered him a sympathetic glance. "I'm truly sorry about Carl. I know he was a dear friend to you."

Emotion clogged his throat, so Adam merely nodded his head.

Mindful of lightening the mood, Blake grinned. "The livery in Heppner didn't give you that ol' flea-bitten bag of bones, did they?"

Adam chuckled. "No, but it wasn't for a lack of trying. I told them I'd need the horse for a month and I didn't fancy that decrepit old mare dying on me three miles out of town."

Ginny turned a hopeful glance to Adam. "Are you really going to stay through Christmas? It's been forever since you've been here for the holiday. Does Arlan know? He'll be so excited. Have you met Alex? Isn't she gorgeous? And she's such fun, too. Do you think…?"

Adam looked over at Blake and caught the man's smirk as he rolled his eyes at Ginny's chattering.

"Why don't you take a breath, Genevieve, and let Adam answer one of those many questions?" Blake suggested.

Ginny giggled. "Sorry. As you both know, I tend to get carried away."

Adam had missed this, missed being around his friends, even if he hated being in Hardman. He looked at Ginny as they approached Granger House. "To answer your questions, I am staying through Christmas, I think. Arlan doesn't know. I haven't met Alex. Yes, she is gorgeous and smart, too. She couldn't have picked a finer man than my brother to wed, although I have a thing or two to discuss with him."

Aware of what had transpired between Adam and Tia, Ginny and Blake assumed Arlan had failed to mention her presence in town to Adam.

The three of them walked around to the back entrance of Granger House. Blake rubbed a gentle hand over the head of Luke's dog, Bart, as they passed by him. Ginny opened the door and stepped inside the warmth of the kitchen while the men stamped snow from their boots. Filly stirred a fragrant pot of spiced cider with one hand while holding a cherubic toddler on her hip.

She glanced over her shoulder and smiled at the three of them. "Welcome back, Adam. It's nice to see you."

"Hello, Filly." Adam shrugged out of his coat and left it along with his hat and scarf on a hook by the door. He walked across the room and touched the baby's hand. She turned to look at him with open curiosity as she rubbed her cheek against the soft sleeve of Filly's elegant dark gown.

From the strawberry-blond curls on her head to the eyelashes fanning her cheeks, Adam thought the little one greatly resembled her beautiful mother.

"Oh, you haven't met our Maura, have you, Adam?" Filly turned so Adam could get a better look at the little girl.

"It's nice to meet you, Maura," Adam shook the baby's foot, making a smile break out on her tiny face. He winked at Filly. "The last time I was here, it was obvious she would arrive soon." He held his hand out in front of his stomach and made a rounded motion, causing Filly to blush.

"Come on, Adam. Let's join the others in the parlor." Blake thumped him on the back as Ginny took Maura and kissed the baby's rosy cheek. Before they left the kitchen, Arlan's wife breezed into the room then abruptly stopped.

A smile wreathed her face as she looked at Adam. "You must be Arlan's brother."

Adam took the hand she held out to him and pressed a light kiss to the back of it.

Alex appeared amused. "You and my husband share a strong resemblance to each other."

"And you must be the angel my brother has bragged about since last December." Adam winked at Alex as he relinquished her hand. "It's a pleasure to meet you. I always wanted a sister. Look what a pretty one Arlan gave me. Do you prefer I call you Mrs. Guthry, Alex, a phantasmagorical magician, or sister dearest?"

Alex laughed. "I can see you're full of charm with a silvery tongue in that handsome head, Adam Guthry. You may call me Alex. I grew up without siblings, so I look forward to finally having a brother." She tipped her head and studied him a moment. Although his hair was a darker shade of brown and curlier than Arlan's, and his eyes were a more vibrant shade of blue, a definite likeness existed between the two brothers. While Arlan was taller, Adam held a brawnier set of shoulders and wider chest than his younger brother.

"Luke and Arlan are in the parlor, Adam," Filly said, ladling hot cider into cups lining two large silver trays.

Alex walked over and started to pick up one of the heavy trays but Adam took it from her. "Lead on, dear lady. Blake and I can carry the trays."

Surprised by his reference to her as dear lady, Arlan's pet name for her, Alex grinned at him as she spun back toward the door. "Right this way, brother."

Upon entering the parlor, Arlan smiled at Alex. When he realized whom she stood beside, he rushed their direction.

Adam handed his tray to Chauncy so he could embrace Arlan in a big bear hug. Amid much backslapping, the two brothers sized each other up with knowing smiles.

"Marriage appears to agree with you, Arlan. My best wishes to you both." Adam held out a hand to his brother in a gesture of congratulations.

Arlan took it in his and gave it a hearty shake. "Thank you, Adam. I had no idea if you received my telegram and would make it in time for the service."

"The past week, I've been out on the river, but a messenger managed to get in touch with me the day before yesterday. I came as quickly as possible. If I'd been ten minutes later, I would have missed it entirely."

"I'm glad you're here." Arlan placed a hand on Adam's shoulder. "Did you meet my wonderful bride, Alex the Amazing?"

"I made her acquaintance in the kitchen. I agree, she is quite amazing."

Alex blushed and moved to help Chauncy disperse the cups of hot cider to those gathered at Granger House.

"Can you stay long?" Arlan asked as he accepted a cup of cider Alex held out to him.

"I might stay for a few weeks, possibly through Christmas, although my plans depend on certain things."

Arlan frowned. "What things?"

A sigh worked its way out of Adam as he pinned his brother with a cool glare. "You could have told me Tia was here."

"I could have," Arlan agreed. "However, if I'd done that, you wouldn't have come, and I missed seeing you, Adam. Haven't you both moved past what happened a decade ago?"

Rather than answer, Adam turned to accept Luke's welcome. The conversation moved to his work and the latest news from Portland.

After partaking of cider, coffee, cookies and cake, those gathered at Granger House bundled into their coats and made their way home before the afternoon settled into dusk.

Tia's absence made Adam wonder if she wanted to avoid him as much as he dreaded speaking to her. What did one say in polite conversation to the woman who took the love he willingly offered and tossed it back in his face without a single word of apology or regret?

Biting back another sigh, Adam smiled at Luke and Filly, thanking them for their hospitality.

"Didn't I hear that your folks returned to Hardman, Luke?"

Luke nodded his head as he walked with Adam toward the door where Arlan helped Alex put on her coat.

"They moved back last year, but they've gone to New York on business. They plan to return in time for Christmas, though," Luke said, grinning at Adam. "You can't miss their house. It's the garish monstrosity two blocks behind the mercantile."

"If Mother heard you say that, she'd have your head," Ginny teased as she approached, carrying Adam's coat, scarf and hat. He'd forgotten he left his things in the kitchen and nodded appreciatively at Ginny as she handed over his outerwear. "Of course, Mother had to have a house even grander than this one, but the outside is quite splendid."

"And the inside?" Adam asked as he pulled on his coat and wrapped the scarf around his neck.

Blake barely suppressed a disdainful snort while Luke coughed to hide his bark of laughter.

Ginny frowned at her husband and brother. "The inside definitely bears Mother's tastes more so than Dad's."

"I can hardly wait to see it." Adam shook hands with Luke and Blake before following Arlan and Alex outside into the cold.

As they moved down the walk toward the heart of town, Adam glared at his only sibling then turned a dimpled smile to his sister-in-law. "If nothing else comes of this trip, I'm pleased to finally meet the woman who won my brother's affections."

Alex laughed. "I'm so glad you came, Adam, but I'm terribly sorry about the loss of your friend. Mr. Simpson seemed like a kind man."

"Thank you." Adam studied her. Alex appeared genuine in her sympathy.

From his experience, beautiful women were often vain, shallow, and self-serving. Tia's lovely face came to mind and fresh pain clawed at his chest.

Purposefully ignoring it, he thumped a hand on Arlan's shoulder as they strolled home. Although Arlan was a few inches taller, Adam towered above most men. The breadth of his shoulders and chest had always intimidated his brother when they'd gotten into scuffles as younger boys.

In truth, they got along well for the most part. Except when Arlan failed to share pertinent information, such as Tia's presence in town.

"What happened to Carl? Would you give me the whole story?" Adam asked as they walked up the steps to the house he had once called home. After his mother died, he went off to Portland to seek adventure and escape his memories. He left Arlan the house, confident he could take care of himself since he had a good job at the bank.

His little brother had done very well for himself, both in his work and with his choice of a bride.

Adam watched Arlan's hand caress the curve of his wife's shoulder as he helped her remove her coat once they stepped inside the warmth of the house.

"While you two settle into the parlor, I'll go make a pot of tea." Alex's smile and eyes held compassion as she disappeared into the kitchen.

Arlan motioned Adam to take a seat in the parlor.

Instead, Adam helped build up the fire then stood before it, warming his hands. He'd forgotten how much colder it could be in Hardman than it was in Portland's milder climate. A pervading chill had hounded him from the moment he stepped off the train in Heppner.

As he lingered by the fire, Arlan took a seat on a sofa and glanced up at him. "No one knows for sure what happened, but the doctor thinks Carl may have been doing something with his cattle. He got a new bull back in October that must have been bred on Lucifer's back forty because it was the most evil animal I've ever seen. Carl couldn't turn his back on that beast for fear it would trample him. A neighbor heard a ruckus over at Carl's place and went over to see what was going on. He found that bull tossing Carl around like a limp rag doll. Doc said he thought a horn punctured Carl's lung. He likely would have died from that even without the other injuries."

Shocked to hear of his friend's horrid, painful death, Adam turned back to the fire and took a moment to swallow down the lump in his throat. "What happened to the bull?"

Arlan sighed. "They had to shoot him to get the body out of the pen."

"Good." Adam nodded his head in approval.

Alex breezed into the room with a tea tray and set it on the low table in front of the sofa. She took a seat next to Arlan and poured three cups.

Adam smiled at her and settled into a chair across from them.

"Would you care for sugar or cream?" Alex asked as she held out a dish with sugar cubes.

"Two sugars, please." Adam watched as Alex placed two sugar cubes on her palm, waved her other hand over them, and made the cubes magically disappear before reappearing in his teacup. She handed it to him along with a spoon.

He grinned. "I hope I get a full demonstration of your magic show while I'm here."

"If you stay until Christmas, I'll do a show on Christmas Eve for the school's Christmas Carnival."

"You don't say." Adam stirred his tea then took a sip. It was rich, sweet, and just the way he liked it.

"I do." Alex handed a cup of tea to Arlan then sat back with a cup. "We really do hope you'll stay, Adam. No one should be alone for Christmas."

Arlan chuckled and pressed a kiss to Alex's temple. "So says the girl who tried to run away last Christmas Eve."

Alex gave him a glance from beneath her long, dark lashes. "That was before."

"Before what?" Adam asked.

"Before your brother professed his undying devotion and convinced me I had to stay." Alex kissed her husband's cheek. "I'm ever so glad he did. I love living here in Hardman, teaching at the school, and being Mrs. Arlan Guthry."

"You should have made Arlan change his name to Janowski. It's got a more colorful ring to it," Adam teased.

"I offered," Arlan said, giving his wife a playful squeeze. "I told her when she put a ring through my nose, she could lead me around anywhere she liked and her wish was my command."

Pretending to be affronted, Alex leaned away from Arlan and pouted. "You never said any such thing. If anyone is led on a merry chase around here, it's me." She leaned closer to Adam and dropped her voice to a whisper. "He played hard to get, since he had two women on the line and couldn't decide which one to court."

Arlan spluttered and sat up straight. "Now, that's not true at all. You know from the moment I saw you outside town with your broken-down wagon, you've owned my heart, dear lady. Don't you dare try to convince my brother otherwise."

Alex laughed and got to her feet. "I know, Arlan, but it's good to keep you on your toes."

The men watched her return to the kitchen to prepare dinner while they remained by the fire.

"I like her, Arlan." Adam took another drink of his tea, giving his brother an approving grin.

Arlan smiled. "Me, too."

Chapter Two

Adam wiped is mouth with a napkin and leaned back in his chair, laughing. "Did you really make the outhouse disappear?"

Alex shook her head. "I'll never tell."

"She won't, either," Arlan said, grinning at his wife. The children at the Hardman School had begged and begged Alex to do a big magic trick. With a little help from Arlan and Luke, she'd seemingly made the outhouse behind the school disappear then reappear while the children had all watched in awe. The students rushed home to tell their parents about the magic Miss Alex executed at school. That was right before Thanksgiving and many people in town still talked about wishing they'd seen it happen.

"Perception is greater than reality," Arlan said, looking at Adam. "That's what my wife tells me when I try to pry details out of her about one of her tricks."

Perplexed, Adam had no idea what that meant but the way Alex looked at Arlan made him think his brother knew more of her secrets than either of them would admit.

"I don't think I've ever met a real prestidigitator before. Wait until I tell the fellas at work my beautiful sister is a conjurer of magic." Adam waggled an eyebrow at Alex as he finished his last bite of bread.

"I'd love to hear about your work, Adam." Alex refilled their coffee cups then regained her seat next to Arlan at the kitchen table.

Although the house once had a formal dining room, Arlan had converted it into an office. Since Adam's last brief visit, Arlan had also knocked out a wall in the kitchen and enlarged the space. In addition, he'd built on a large bedroom and a bathroom at the back of the house.

At the rapid rate progress arrived in Hardman, soon everyone would have those newfangled telephones installed.

Delighted with his brother's apparent success, he looked at his sister-in-law. "What would you like to know?"

"Well, Arlan said you went to Portland to work on a ship then ended up as a captain, but now you pilot other boats down the river. Is that correct?"

"Yep. That's correct." Adam nodded his head. At Alex's expectant look, he grinned. "I suppose you'd like me to elaborate."

Alex offered him a saucy smile. "If you please."

Adam chuckled. "Yes, ma'am." He took a swig of his coffee before he settled back in his chair. "Have you ever heard of the Columbia River Bar?"

"Didn't a ship wreck there last year?" Alex asked as she scooted her chair closer to Arlan. He wrapped is arm around her shoulders and she leaned against his side.

The site of the two of them, so close and in love, made Adam simultaneously happy and depressed. Thrilled his brother was in love with a kind-hearted, lovely woman, Adam couldn't help but wonder if he and Tia would have been that happy had she not turned her back on him.

Intent on pushing the irksome woman from his thoughts, Adam focused on his brother and sister-in-law. "That's right. Two people were killed, one injured, and the ship couldn't be salvaged. It happens all the time on the bar."

"Why? I don't understand what makes it such a dangerous place." Arlan gazed at his brother.

"The Columbia River flows through a narrow channel into the Pacific." Adam held his hands in front of him, moving his palms closer together to indicate a constricted space. "As the water surges toward the ocean, it slows down, dropping sand and silt. Those deposits form a fan-shaped sandbar that extends several miles into the ocean, creating underwater traps and hazards. The conditions can rip ships to pieces and force swells to sheer off, creating a treacherous drop. Pelting rain and heavy fog add into the dangerous mix. Wrecks have been recorded there since 1792."

"My gracious! I had no idea," Alex looked at Arlan then turned back to Adam, eager for him to continue.

"Back in 1846, a group formed to pilot all types of vessels over the bar. The pilots are licensed to captain any type of ship, regardless of size or location." Adam voice held a measure of excitement. "Once the vessels are over the bar, another organization of pilots takes vessels along the Columbia River to various ports. The majority stop in Portland, but some go further up the river or down the Willamette."

"And that's what you do? Pilot the ships down the river?" Alex asked, intrigued by her brother-in-law's work.

"Yes, ma'am." Adam smiled at Alex. "I get called out all hours of the day and night to help navigate ships safely along the river. Although I started out life on a farm back east and then moved here to Hardman, I guess we must have a sailor's blood in our family tree somewhere. There's nothing I enjoy more than being on a boat, driving it down the river."

"Do you ever have free time? How were you able to come for the funeral service?" Alex asked.

"I work four days straight, then have three off, so the days I have off always vary. I often volunteer to fill in for others, so my employer insisted I take time off and not return until after Christmas."

"That's wonderful news, Adam," Arlan grinned at his brother. "It's been too many years since we've spent a holiday together." He glanced at his wife and she nodded in agreement. "We would like nothing better than to have you stay with us to ring in the New Year."

"I'd like that, but how long I stay depends."

"On?" Arlan asked, already knowing the answer. He'd hoped to spare Adam any undue worry by leaving out the fact that Tia Devereux had moved back to town. She'd come for her grandmother's funeral. Instead of selling the house where she'd grown up as everyone expected, she moved in and stayed.

Personally, Arlan thought it was nice to have her back in the community. However, he'd known Adam would bristle at the sight of her. He hated the thought that Adam would let something that happened eleven years ago keep him from celebrating Christmas with his only living relatives.

"What does it depend on, Adam?" Arlan prompted when he failed to answer the question.

"On several factors, none of which I'm in the mood to discuss." Adam's tone held a hint of warning.

Mindful of emotions simmering beneath the surface, Alex stood and began clearing the table. "If you boys help me with the dishes, I think we have time for a game this evening."

Arlan hopped up and carried dirty dishes over to the sink. Alex filled a dishpan with hot water and added soap while Arlan and Adam carried over the remainder of the dishes. The two brothers stored the leftover food in the icebox then helped dry the dishes.

In no time at all, the dishes were put away and the kitchen set to rights. The three of them retired to the parlor where Arlan took a board game down from a shelf and set it on the table in front of the sofa.

"Must we play that one again?" Alex sank against the cushions with a beleaguered sigh. She lifted the lid of the game and held it out toward Adam. "Did he make you play this with him, too?"

Adam chuckled and ran his rough thumb over the lid of the box. "He surely did. I hoped by now he'd have worn out the pieces and could no longer play." He handed the lid back to Alex.

Arlan frowned at them as he set out *Bulls and Bears — The Great Game of Wall Street*. Based on the financial panic of the 1870s, the game promised players they would feel like "speculators, bankers, and brokers."

As a banker exceptionally talented with mathematical figures, Arlan was unbelievably challenging to beat even though much of the entertainment of the game was based on chance.

"To make things fair, I think Alex and I should team up against you." Adam winked at his sister-in-law.

Enthusiastically, she nodded in agreement. "That's a splendid idea. It might give me a slight chance to win. Otherwise, Arlan has to pretend he doesn't notice my cheating."

Adam laughed and sat down on the floor in front of the table while Alex took a seat beside Arlan on the couch.

"I'll even allow the lady to take the first turn," Arlan said, kissing his wife's cheek.

Alex spun the dial and the competition began. An hour later, all three of them laughed uproariously as Alex won the game, thanks to Adam's help.

"On that high note, I'll slice the pie I baked earlier. You two can put the game away," Alex said, rising to her feet and giving Arlan a smile full of smug victory. "Would either of you like more coffee?"

Both men shook their heads. "A glass of milk, please, Alex," Arlan said, then glanced at Adam. He nodded. "Make it two glasses."

"I'll be right back," she said and swept out of the room.

Adam helped Arlan put away the game then added a log to the fire. "Alex truly is amazing, little brother. I'm very happy for you."

Arlan studied him for a moment then broke into a satisfied grin. "Thanks, Adam. I'm glad you like her. It means a lot to me to hear you say that."

Speculatively, Adam narrowed his gaze. "What would you do if I said she was a bad-tempered, homely wench?"

"Blacken your eye and toss you out into the snow." Arlan tugged up his shirtsleeves, lifted his arms in front of him and formed two fists. Playfully, he jabbed one at his brother.

Adam ducked, enjoying their banter. "I see you haven't improved your boxing moves to defend yourself. It's a good thing you don't need to."

Arlan stiffened. "I'll have you know I'm quite capable of defending myself and my wife."

Aware of his brother's ruffled feathers, Adam patted him on the shoulder. "I know you are. I'm just teasing."

"Good. Because I wouldn't want to have to take you out back and beat some sense into you."

The two brothers chuckled. Arlan would be hard pressed to best Adam in any sort of physical exertion and they both knew it.

Arlan sobered and observed his brother for a long moment. "What about you, Adam. Have you met anyone special? You've never once mentioned any females in your letters, other than the crotchety Mrs. Winters who runs the boarding house where you rent a room. Is there a girl who's caught your eye?"

Adam took a seat on the chair closest to the fire, once again feeling chilled. "No, Arlan, there's no one special. My line of work isn't conducive to courting or having a wife, even if I was interested, which I'm most certainly not."

"But, Adam, what happened with Tia is…"

"None of your business." Adam sent his brother a pointed glare as Alex returned to the room carrying a tray loaded with slices of apple pie and glasses of milk.

Once they finished eating dessert, Alex took the tray to the kitchen then bid both of the men a good night.

"You two visit as long as you like, but I've got a classroom full of rowdy youngsters to wrangle in the morning," Alex said, leaning down to kiss Adam's cheek. "I'm so glad you're here, Adam. Welcome home."

Adam gently squeezed her hand and gave her a warm smile. She kissed Arlan and offered her husband a coy glance before walking down the hallway.

Arlan watched her leave then turned his attention back to Adam. "You can sleep in your old room. The bed is made up, ready for you. Did you bring any bags with you?"

"Sure did, but I left them at the livery with Douglas. I'll fetch everything in the morning. I don't need much tonight. If I look, I bet I'll find everything in my room just where I left it the last time I was here." Adam gave his brother a knowing look. "Am I right?"

"No, you aren't. Alex insisted on cleaning the room when we found out about Carl because I was fairly certain you'd come to the service." Arlan walked Adam to his former bedroom and opened the door.

The wood surfaces of the dresser and headboard gleamed from a recent polish and the mirror above the washstand sparkled in the light of the lamp Arlan held in his hand.

"Still looks like my old room, only dust-free and fresh-smelling." Adam took the light from Arlan and patted his back. "Thank you for letting me stay with you."

"You know you're welcome anytime. Alex and I both want you to feel at home here, to stay as long as you like." Arlan backed into the hall. "Rest well, Adam. I'm sorry about Carl. I know how much he meant to you."

"Thanks, Arlan. I appreciate it. See you in the morning." Adam set the lamp on the dresser while Arlan shut the door.

When it clicked shut, Adam released the breath he'd been holding and sank onto the quilt covering the bed. It smelled like sunshine and some unnamed scent he'd quickly associated with Arlan's lovely wife.

The day had been filled with emotion — seeing Tia with her son, meeting Alex for the first time, and dealing with the finality of watching Carl's coffin lowered into the cold, Hardman ground. At least his friend had a proper burial since the ground had not yet frozen beyond the first few inches of topsoil.

If he could avoid running into Tia for the remaining weeks he planned to be in town, he might just survive the visit. Otherwise, he'd have to disappoint his brother and return to Portland much sooner than he planned.

Despite how hard he'd tried to convince himself he no longer had any interest in the woman, he couldn't stop visions of her from floating through his mind. His thoughts spun around how beautiful Tia had looked with the winter wind whipping rosy touches to her cheeks and sending tendrils of hair dancing in the breeze.

Careworn, Adam removed his clothes, blew out the lamp and climbed between the cool sheets. His dreams took him back to his teen years, back to the last time he'd been truly happy.

Chapter Three

Tia sat on the edge of her son's bed, listening to his sweet voice as he recited his bedtime prayers. When he finished, he climbed beneath the covers and looked up at her with unconditional trust and love.

"Mama?"

"Yes, sweetheart?" Tia brushed the cowlick of golden hair back from his forehead. She counted the familiar freckles across his cute little nose then gazed into his bright blue eyes, twinkling with life and a dash of mischief.

"Who was that man today?" Toby reached out, tracing his finger along the embroidered vines decorating the edge of her sleeve.

Confused, Tia wasn't sure which man Toby meant. In the two months they'd resided in Hardman, he'd come to recognize most of the residents of the area through church and living in town. "What man, Toby?"

"The one who stared at you. The big man who looked like this…" Toby worked his face into an exaggerated frown and pushed his eyebrows together until his expression was so comical, Tia had to work to hold back her laughter.

Despite his description, Tia still wasn't sure who Toby had seen watching her, unless it was Adam Guthry. She'd caught him glowering at her more than once.

After what she'd done to their friendship, she couldn't blame him for being less than enthusiastic to see her.

"Was he wearing a dark blue coat with a black hat?" she asked, leaning down and brushing her nose against Toby's, making him giggle.

"Yep. He had a scarf around his neck. He looked mad and sad. Did the mad-sad man know Mr. Carl?"

Tia sat upright and returned to brushing her fingers through Toby's soft hair. At four, he sometimes seemed much more attuned to the feelings of others than many adults.

Adam had looked very sad and angry. It was no wonder. He hadn't expected to see her there and Carl had been his best friend.

Growing up, the three of them were inseparable until Tia and Adam realized they had deeper feelings for each other. Carl had remained a good friend to them both, even after she'd left with no explanation and barely a word of goodbye.

The man had been nothing but kindness since she'd returned to Hardman. It broke her heart he'd lost his wife and baby, and now his own life. They were young, so full of hopes and dreams, it was a shame to see their future cut short.

Tears burned her eyes as memories of all the happy times she'd shared with Carl and Adam flooded through her mind.

Toby tugged on her hand, pulling her back to reality.

"Mama? Did that man know Mr. Carl?"

Quietly sniffling, she nodded her head and forced away her tears. "Yes, baby. He knew Carl. They were the best of friends."

"They were?" Toby looked thoughtful for a moment, weighing her words. "So he was sad that Mr. Carl went to heaven and can't be his friend anymore?"

"Mr. Guthry is sad. Very sad. Just like we're sad that Carl went away." Tia surrendered to her longing to cuddle her son and wrapped him in her arms, kissing the top of his head.

"My father went away like that, too, didn't he?" Toby glanced up at her with eyes full of interest and intelligence.

"Yes, Toby. Your father went away like that, too." Tia absolutely refused to think about the death of her husband with the loss of Carl so painful and fresh.

"Mama?"

"Hmm?" Tia rocked him back and forth in her arms.

"Will you go away like that and leave me all alone?" Toby's voice wavered and tears glistened in his eyes.

"No, baby. Never. I'll never leave you alone. I promise." Tia kissed his forehead and rocked him a few more minutes until they both felt a measure of calm and peace. Gently she tucked him back into his bed and kissed his cheeks and nose. "You close your eyes and go to sleep, Toby."

"Sing me a song, Mama. Please?"

"Only if you close your eyes and go to sleep."

"Okay." Toby closed his eyes, but a smile rode his lips as Tia leaned back and cleared her throat.

As she sang *All Through the Night*, she watched Toby relax, fighting to stay awake, yet ready to succumb to restful sleep.

> *Soft the drowsy hours are creeping*
> *Hill and vale in slumber sleeping,*
> *I my loving vigil keeping*
> *All through the night.*

When air puffed out of his lips, she smiled and switched from singing to humming. Cautiously, she rose to her feet and adjusted his covers one more time before picking up the hand lamp she'd carried into his room and slowly backing into the hall.

After leaving the door partially open, she banked the fires, checked the locks on the doors, and readied for bed.

Tia slid between the sheets and curled up under the layers of quilts and blankets.

The cool temperature of the room and recollections of Adam's frosty glares left her thoroughly chilled.

She assumed Arlan would let his brother know of their friend's passing, but part of her hoped Adam wouldn't be able to make it back to town.

Once she saw him join the group of mourners, Tia was hard-pressed to pay attention to the service.

His presence captivated her, despite his solemn, wounded appearance. Toby was right. Adam did look mad and sad.

The last time she'd seen him, they'd been eighteen. While his shoulders had been broad then and he stood taller than many men, he hadn't been full-grown.

Even though his face still held the same boyish appeal, Adam had filled out his form with the muscles acquired by a hard-working man.

Inconceivable as it was, he'd gotten even better looking as he aged. Dimples still danced in his cheeks when he smiled. That fact might have passed her notice, but she'd caught his smile as he greeted Ginny Stratton with genuine warmth.

Her eyes had lingered on his wide shoulders and solid chest. Memories of being held against that chest, of being encircled by those strong arms, made a sob catch in her throat.

Painfully, Tia bit the inside of her cheek to keep from crying out.

Emotions she'd bottled up threatened to erupt as she dabbed at her tears with the edge of the sheet.

When her husband had died in a freak buggy accident three years ago, Tia mourned his passing much as she mourned the loss of Carl. Patrick had been a friend, but he'd never, not even for one day, possessed her heart.

Sad but true, she'd never been in love with her husband. Patrick was a dozen years her senior when they met the summer she was eighteen. She'd gone to Portland to visit her great aunt and never came back to Hardman.

The day before she planned to leave Portland to return home, she'd taken a walk to the park and bumped into Patrick Devereux.

Handsome, wealthy, and charismatic, he'd swept her off her feet, treating her like a princess.

Infatuated with all a life with him would offer, she accepted his proposal when he asked her to wed just two weeks after their initial meeting.

Even as she committed her life to his, the only feelings she'd ever held for Patrick were those of a friend. It was impossible to give him her heart when Adam Guthry owned her love.

Determined her husband would never know the truth, she did her best to be the wife Patrick wanted and expected. She fulfilled the role of a doting wife, made every effort to be beautiful and charming, and turned his house into a comfortable home.

Patrick was a popular attorney, the son of a high-powered judge in Portland. His mother was a socially sought-after woman everyone vied to please. His brother worked in real estate when he wasn't breaking girlish hearts.

Together, the Devereux family amassed a small fortune and created a name held in high regard.

However, Tia hated the endless parties, the way Patrick's mother politely criticized her every move.

Then Toby arrived and all her regrets about marrying Patrick vanished. The adorable baby boy made everything wrong in her world suddenly right.

She might never have loved Patrick, might spend a lifetime wishing she'd made different choices, but she couldn't regret the path that placed Toby in her life.

Upon his death, Patrick had left Tia a wealthy woman. She could go anywhere she wanted in the world. However, the place she needed to be was in Hardman, back in the house where she'd grown up.

For now, it was the best place to raise her son.

Chapter Four

"Toby, come eat your breakfast while it's hot." Tia set a bowl of oatmeal on the table along with a glass of milk.

"But, Mama, it's so pretty outside. Can't we go out and play?" Toby turned from where he stared out the window. Snow had fallen throughout the night while a coating of frost on every surface created a winter wonderland of glistening white.

"I need to see to several errands this morning, so we'll go out then." Tia smiled at Toby as she wiped her hands on a dishtowel. "First, there's a certain young man who needs to eat his breakfast then comb his hair and make his bed."

"I already made my bed." Toby skipped across the kitchen and climbed onto his chair. He folded his little hands beneath his chin, ready for his mother to ask a blessing on their meal.

"That's wonderful, sweetheart." Tia smiled at him then bowed her head and offered a simple prayer. When she lifted her head, Toby grinned at the boat she'd created in his bowl of oatmeal using an apple slice and raisins.

"Mama! It's a boat! I love boats!" Toby beamed as he picked up his spoon and fished out the apple slice.

"I know you love boats, baby, that's why I made it. Don't dawdle, though. We've got a busy day ahead of us."

Tia watched her little boy enthusiastically eat his cereal and drink his milk.

"I'm all done." Toby started to wipe his mouth on his sleeve, caught his mother's glare, and lifted a napkin to his lips. When he finished, he grinned at Tia. "After I comb my hair, may we go outside?"

Tia reached out and cupped his chin, gazing into his dear face. He looked like a replica of his father. Her heart pinched as she thought of how much she loved her son and how little she missed Patrick and the life she'd lived with him.

"I'll do the dishes while you feed Crabby and give him some attention." Tia tipped her head toward a fluffy white cat with bright green eyes swishing his tail from his box beside the stove.

The feline was cantankerous and ornery on a good day, but Tia put up with the animal because Toby loved it. She'd also seen the cat protect Toby from a stray dog that ran into their yard and almost bit him. From out of nowhere, Crabby sailed through the air and landed on the dog's back in a fury of claws and flying fur.

Although the cat tolerated her presence, it rolled over and purred the moment Toby knelt by his box and stroked a hand over his head. "I started Crabby's motor, Mama."

Tia grinned as she washed the breakfast dishes. "You most certainly did. Do you think Crabby will ever let a grown up make him purr?"

"Nope. He only likes kids." Toby filled the cat's dish with food and poured fresh water into a deep bowl then resumed petting Crabby. "He likes Erin and Maura."

"Yes, he does." Tia had watched the finicky feline let the pastor's little girl and Maura Granger practically maul him with attention. Docilely, he sat and purred, not so much as swishing his tail or cocking an ear. Yet, the moment Chauncy bent over to pet him, Crabby hissed and ran off to hide beneath Toby's bed.

When Tia finished the dishes, she sent Toby off to comb his hair and brush his teeth while she changed her dress and tidied her hair.

After digging through her things at the back of the closet, she found a pair of winter carriage boots trimmed with fur and lined with lamb's wool for warmth. She sat on the end of her bed and pulled them on her feet, tying the black silk ribbons before moving to stand in front of her dresser mirror.

Quickly pinning on a black hat with an emerald plume, she slipped on her favorite wool coat. The dark green fabric accented with hand-painted roses and fur collar had been the last Christmas gift she'd received from Patrick.

One thing she couldn't deny was that he'd possessed excellent taste in fashion. Over the years, he'd provided so many lovely clothes for her, she often wondered if he viewed her as a life-sized doll.

Casting aside her memories and musings, she picked up a pair of gloves and her reticule then hurried down the hall to the kitchen. Toby talked to Crabby as the two of them looked outside.

The cat jumped down from his perch on the windowsill and sauntered to the door. He looked back at Tia once with a narrowed gaze before staring at the door.

"Yes, your highness. The message you'd like out has been clearly conveyed." Tia opened the door. The cat gingerly stepped across the porch and behind the house, disappearing into the bushes.

Toby struggled to button his coat with his mittens already on his hands.

"Here, sweetheart. Let me help." Tia knelt in front of him.

Toby patted her cheeks with his wool-covered fingers as she buttoned his coat then pulled a knit cap onto his head and down over his ears. Before he could run outside, she wrapped a small red scarf around his neck. "Ready to go?"

"Yep! Let's go, Mama. I want to see if Pastor Chauncy let Erin make a snowman in her yard." Toby grabbed her hand and pulled as Tia closed the door. She followed him down the steps and across the backyard to the boardwalk.

She listened to his lively chatter as they strolled toward the heart of town. Some of the industrious men in Hardman had already cleared most of the snow from the boardwalk. Tia wondered if Adam helped since Arlan was often among those who picked up a shovel and cleared away the snow.

Lost in the vision of Adam's muscular arms hefting a shovel full of snow, she and Toby walked around the corner near the mercantile and plowed into a solid form.

Hands reached out to steady her then immediately pulled back, but not before Tia caught the look of distress on Adam Guthry's face.

"Oh!" Tia reached up to straighten her hat as Toby tugged on her sleeve. She looked down at him while he stared at Adam.

"Mama, that's the mad-sad man." His whisper carried loudly through the still morning air.

Adam raised a questioning eyebrow as he glared at Tia. "Mad-sad man?"

Embarrassed by her son's words and unsettled by Adam's proximity, she released a nervous laugh. "Toby noticed you at the service yesterday and asked if I knew the mad-sad man."

Much to her surprise, Adam hunkered down and removed his glove. He held out his hand to her son. "Toby, is it?"

The little boy tugged off a mitten and shook his hand, clearly pleased the big man offered it to him.

"It's nice to meet you, Toby. My name is Adam. I used to live here and knew your mama back then."

"You did?" Toby's voice held a hint of curiosity while his eyes widened with interest. "Did you know Mr. Carl?"

Adam nodded his head. "I sure did. He was my very best friend. I'm sad that he's gone."

Toby took a step forward and placed his small hand on Adam's shoulder, patting it gently. "It's okay. Mama and I are sad he's gone, too. Maybe he and my father will meet each other in heaven. Do you think they'll remember me?"

"I'm sure of it." Adam smiled at the child, unable to resist his innocent, tender spirit. "What are you and your mama doing out on such a cold, frosty morning."

"Mama has to see to errands," Toby said, then leaned closer to Adam. "That means she's going to visit Miss Abby, go to the post office, and the mercantile. I like to go to the mercantile but sometimes Miss Abby lets me stay to play with Erin."

"Is that right?" Adam asked as he helped Toby put on his mitten and pulled his own glove back on his hand. "Well, I best let you get on your way. It was nice to meet you, Toby."

Toby smiled broadly and yanked on his mother's hand again. "Come on, Mama. I want to see if Erin's in the store."

"You run on ahead, baby. I'll be there in a moment," Tia said, watching as Toby skipped partway down the block and opened the door to Abby Dodd's dress shop. She turned her gaze to Adam, taking in the sadness around his eyes and the disappointment bracketing his mouth. "I'm truly sorry about Carl, Adam. I'm sorry about... when I left..." Her voice caught and she found it impossible to speak.

"Just forget about it, Tia. If you think I've spent all this time missing you, what might have been, you're kidding yourself. I left you and all those memories behind a long time ago. You don't mean a thing to me." Adam ignored the pain in her eyes his words inflicted and stepped around her. "I know you cared about Carl, even if you owned no real affection for me. Let's just ignore each other while I'm in town and leave it at that."

He picked up the shovel he'd set aside and marched across the street. Tia stared after him, torn between following after him to give him a piece of her mind or burying her face in her hands and releasing a flood of tears.

Rather than surrender to either desire, she took a deep breath, straightened her shoulders, and hastened into Abby's dress shop.

As she rushed inside, Toby and Erin looked up from where they sat at a tiny table beneath the window. Children's books, a set of wooden blocks, two rag dolls, and a few other toys comprised the play area.

Toby had already divested himself of his hat, scarf, mittens and coat as he gave her a wide grin. "Mama! Miss Abby said I can play with Erin."

"Is that so?" Tia raised an eyebrow at Toby, hoping he didn't plead with Abby to stay. The woman had more than she could handle with the flood of holiday dress orders that had come in as well as taking care of Erin and helping her husband, Chauncy, with church matters. Tia was sure the last thing she needed was an active little boy underfoot.

"I asked him if he'd like to keep Erin company this morning," Abby said, as she set aside the taffeta skirt she embellished with beads and stood. "I'd love to have Toby stay a while. The two of them keep each other entertained and out of trouble, for the most part."

Tia gave the woman a dubious glance, but nodded her head. "Then it's only fair Erin spend tomorrow morning with us."

Abby smiled. "Are you sure? She's quite a handful."

A laugh bubbled out of Tia. "Have you met my son? If your daughter is a handful, then Toby is two handfuls and an extra scoop. I'd love to have Erin visit us."

"It's settled then. Go enjoy your morning and do whatever you need to do. Toby will be fine here with us Dodd women."

When Tia returned to Hardman, she never expected to be welcomed back so warmly and kindly by those who knew her. Old acquaintances such as Carl, Luke Granger, Chauncy Dodd, and Blake and Ginny Stratton made her feel right at home in the close-knit town. She'd also come to know and treasure the friendship offered by Filly Granger, Abby Dodd, and Alex Guthry.

In the years she'd been away, she'd never experienced close relationships like those she'd easily developed with the women in Hardman.

Perhaps it was because Erin and Toby were nearly the same age or it might have been because she and Abby shared a love of fashion, but she appreciated time spent with the talented seamstress.

"If I held any talent with a needle, I'd help you, Abby. The least I can do is keep Erin for a morning or two. If you'd like me to watch her more often, just say the word."

"Oh, Erin has plenty of offers for places to play. On Mondays, she spends the day with Filly and Maura. Ginny and Blake watch her on Wednesdays, and Alex has offered to keep an eye on her Saturday afternoons until I get caught up with my holiday orders." Abby watched as Toby leaned forward until his golden head nearly touched Erin's dark curls. "Our girl isn't suffering by any means. In fact, I worry she'll be spoiled with all the extra attention of her honorary doting aunts and uncles."

"You can't spoil a girl as sweet as that one," Tia said, patting Abby's hand. She walked over to the table where the two children drew pictures on slates with pieces of chalk.

As she knelt down, she settled an arm around each child. "What are you drawing?"

"This is us playing in the snow," Toby said, motioning to two bigger white blobs among smaller white dots.

"I see," Tia said, smiling with approval at her son. She turned to look at Erin. "What about you?"

"I'm drawing a picture of me and Toby and my daddy making a snowman." Erin tapped a delicate finger on her slate.

Tia distinguished two roundish blobs stacked on top of each other and assumed that must be Erin's snowman. "And you're doing such a good job, too."

She kissed Toby on the head then stood. When he gazed up at her, she touched a finger to his nose. "You behave while I'm gone, young man, and mind Miss Abby."

"I will, Mama. Don't hurry back, I want lots of time to play with Erin. Maybe you can talk to the mad-sad man again."

"Mad-sad man?" Abby asked as Tia shook her head and pulled on her gloves.

"Toby keeps referring to Adam Guthry as the mad-sad man. He noticed him at Carl's service yesterday and asked me why the man looked sad and mad. I tried to explain he was sad about Carl going to heaven, which he understands. Yet, I can't explain why Adam is angry at me for something that happened ages ago."

Abby hugged her shoulders as they stood at the shop door. "Didn't I see you talking to Adam when Toby came in?"

"Yes, you did. We ran into each other quite by accident. I'll do my best not to make that mistake again." Tia frowned when Abby giggled. "You can laugh all you want, but that man positively hates me and there's nothing I can do or say to change his mind."

"I wouldn't be so sure." Abby commented as Tia opened the door. "You just never know what might happen in Hardman during the holiday season. Magic and romance float in the air."

"Oh, hush." Tia sailed out the door with a smile and hurried down the boardwalk. She stopped at the bakery and arranged to have cookies delivered to the school as a surprise for Alex and the children the following afternoon. After she left there, she went by the mercantile and left a list with Aleta Bruner to fill. She visited with the friendly woman a few moments, catching up on whatever news the storekeeper had heard that morning.

"You remember Adam Guthry, don't you?" Aleta asked, measuring a length of ribbon Tia wanted. "In fact, weren't you friends with both Adam and Carl before you moved to Portland?"

Tia nodded her head, wondering why Adam seemed to be the only person anyone wanted to talk about that morning.

"I heard he's planning to stay through Christmas. Arlan would never say anything, but I think he really missed having his brother around, especially that first year after their mother passed away." Aleta continued chatting, unaware of Tia's disconcerted state. "Now that Arlan has Alex, it's so nice Adam will spend the holiday with them. Families should be together, don't you think?"

Tia nearly choked at Aleta's words. The last thing she thought she and Toby needed was to spend the holiday with the remaining members of her son's family. With the passing of her grandmother, Tia didn't have a single relative left in the world, except for Toby.

However, the little boy had a set of grandparents and an uncle who continued to remind her they were most eager for her to return to Portland. Judge Cedric Devereux had even gone so far as to suggest she return soon or he'd take measures to ensure a prompt appearance of his grandson, regardless of her wishes.

When Aleta grew silent and stared at her in concern, Tia forced a smile. "Yes, Aleta. Families should definitely spend the holidays together. It's wonderful for Arlan that Adam plans to stay a while. I'm sure it will be good for both of them."

"That's exactly what I think." Aleta waved as another customer entered the store.

Tia took the opportunity to escape the conversation. "I'm in no hurry, Aleta. While you help the others, I'll run down to the post office and see if I've received any mail."

"That's fine, Tia. I'll have everything ready when you get back. If you like, I can have George or Percy deliver your purchases later today. George is out making a delivery south of town and Percy is in school, but one of them could bring it by this afternoon."

"No, I'll pick it up on my way back to get Toby from Abby's shop. Thank you so much." Tia smiled graciously then breezed out the door, letting the winter air refresh her. It wasn't that the mercantile was overly warm, but with her mind buzzing a dozen different directions, she felt overheated and uncomfortable.

Or maybe it was thoughts of Adam that made her temperature rise. Why did he have to be so handsome? And how dare he be so gentle with Toby? It would have been simple to dislike him if he'd ignored her son. Instead, he'd gotten down on Toby's level and made her little boy feel special.

Blast that man!

Suddenly, Tia wished he'd go right back to Portland before he wreaked any more havoc in her unsteady world.

With practice honed from years of feigning emotions she didn't feel, Tia plastered a smile on her face and entered the Hardman Post Office. She spoke briefly with the women gathering their mail and waited her turn. The postmaster handed her a single envelope.

A glance at the return address made her grimace.

"Everything okay, Mrs. Devereux?" the postmaster asked.

"Everything is fine. Thank you for your concern." Tia hurried to open the door. "Have a lovely day, sir."

"Yes, ma'am," he called after her retreating form.

Tia planned to wait until that evening to open the missive from her former father-in-law, but she couldn't do it. A need to know what threats he'd issued drove her around the corner of the newspaper office and into the alley. She leaned against the building and slit open the expensive ecru envelope. The aroma of tobacco and camphor floated around her, assaulting her nose.

Wrinkling it in disgust, she shook out the letter. The single sheet of paper bore Cedric's embossed initials at the top of the page.

Quickly scanning through the message, she read it again then slumped against the wall of the building, devastated. She read it through a third time, just to make sure she hadn't imagined the dreaded words.

Tiadora,

In the event you haven't heard the news, our dear Roland died two weeks past. I won't go into details, but a senseless brawl in an establishment of questionable reputation resulted in his death.

Of course, Catherine and I are beside ourselves. It is such a tragedy to lose both of our wonderful sons. How could they be taken from us in their prime?

In light of this most recent loss, we insist you return to Portland with Tobias. He is our only living heir and as such, we will not tolerate his absence any longer.

When you traipsed off to the wilds of Eastern Oregon with our grandson in tow, it was with the assumption you would return once you settled your grandmother's affairs. That was months ago!

It is long past time for you to come to your senses and bring back the boy.

If you do not return home immediately, I will deem you unfit to provide his care and pursue the appropriate measures to become his legal guardian. After all, you are a woman alone in this world, and incapable of fully meeting our dear Tobias' needs.

It is your choice, Tiadora.

Don't force my hand on this issue. You will not win.

The Honorable Cedric P. Devereux

Livid and on the verge of breaking into a round of sobs, Tia stamped her foot in the snow and rattled the paper in her hand. "Oh! That horrid, horrid man wouldn't know the meaning of the word honorable if it jumped up and bit him on his flabby hin…"

"Tia?"

The sound of a familiar voice drew her gaze to the end of the alley where Adam leaned on the shovel he'd used to move snow all morning.

A shuddering sigh worked free from her chest while a tear rolled down her cheek. She turned away, hoping to spare Adam from witnessing her emotional turmoil, but not soon enough.

Furiously brushing at her tears, she inhaled a sharp breath of bracing air as Adam's hand settled on her arm.

"Tia? Is something wrong?" He pushed the shovel into a pile of snow and reached out to steady her as she swayed.

"I'm supposed to ignore you. Remember?" She shook her head and sniffled. "Besides, everything's fine."

Sarcastically, Adam snorted. "That's why you're hiding in the alley, ranting about someone's flabby hind end? Because everything is fine?"

She looked up at him and couldn't help 'but grin, especially when she noticed the dimples in his cheeks as he smiled at her. With easy movements, he removed his glove, tucked it into his coat pocket then reached up to brush away a lingering teardrop on her cheek. "What's wrong, Tia. Something upset you."

Tired of fighting all her battles alone, Tia held out the letter to Adam. As he read it, she watched the muscle in his jaw clench until she was certain he'd crack a tooth.

"The judge is your father-in-law?" Adam asked, handing the letter back to her.

"Former father-in-law, but yes, I was married to his son." Tia fished a handkerchief out of her reticule and dabbed at her nose.

"And their only other child got himself killed in a saloon brawl?"

Tia nodded her head. "So it would seem."

Although Roland was a bit of a rake and tended to drink to excess, he'd always been kind to her. Frequently, he made the stuffy gatherings she'd endured with his parents less of a tribulation.

"I'm sorry, Tia. Were you close to your brother-in-law?"

"I wouldn't say close, but he was always kind to me. After Patrick died, he made an effort to see Toby and take him on outings. In July, he took Toby to the zoo. Have you been? They have quite a wonderful exhibit of animals on display. You do live in Portland, don't you? You really should make it a point to visit the zoo." Tia rambled, but couldn't stop herself. "Toby loved the bear exhibit best of all. Roland said he..." Her voice caught and tears burned the back of her eyes.

"Come here." Adam opened his arms and she rushed into them, soaking the front of his coat with her tears. For the first time since she'd left Hardman as a girl, she felt at home.

The security and comfort she experienced in the circle of Adam's arms was even better than she remembered. She took a deep breath and inhaled his scent, one redolent of fresh air and sunshine mingled with masculine strength.

The fragrance had haunted her dreams and filled her nose at the most unexpected moments during the last eleven years.

Why she thought happiness could be found anywhere beyond Adam she'd never know.

Home, her true home, was right there in his arms. Due to one impetuous decision as a silly eighteen-year-old girl, she'd destroyed every chance of ever knowing that home again.

Thoughts of all her foolishness had cost her compounded with the grief she felt over losing both Roland and Carl. Tears flooded her eyes and spilled down her cheeks.

Time stilled as she stood in the alley leaning against Adam, enveloped by his care and concern. Finally, she pulled herself together and stepped away from him.

"I'm so sorry, Adam. I shouldn't... I didn't mean..." The soggy, limp handkerchief she held in her hand did little to help with her tears.

Adam took a snowy white square from his pocket and pressed it into her hand. "You never did carry a handkerchief that would get the job done."

The teasing smile he gave her made her want to cry all over again, but she wiped away the remnants of her tears, swiped her nose and stuffed his handkerchief into her coat pocket.

"Thank you, Adam." Tia reached up and straightened her hat, smoothed down her coat then picked up the letter from Cedric Devereux she'd dropped in the snow.

Adam motioned to the letter. "What are you going to do about that? If you return to Portland, will you have to live with them?"

"I still own a house not in Portland, although I've put it up for sale." Tia sighed as Adam walked with her to the end of the alley and then down the boardwalk in the direction of the mercantile and Abby's shop. "I don't want to go back to Portland, at least not because Cedric is threatening me. There is no doubt in my mind he'd make good on it, too. He's a powerful man and most always gets what he wants. However, he doesn't have quite as much pull or power here in Hardman as he does there."

"If I can help you, Tia, let me know. What he's plotting isn't right. From the little I've seen, you're a wonderful mother and your son should be with you." Adam stared at her as they stopped in front of Abby's shop.

Uncertain what to make of his kindness after his harsh greeting when they first met that morning, she studied him as she placed her hand on the knob of the door. "I appreciate that, Adam, but this is my problem. I'll figure something out."

Adam started to offer a comment, but the door opened and Toby launched himself against Tia. "Mama! Come see the pictures Erin and I made. We had the bestest time!" Toby noticed Adam and waved a hand at him. "Hi, Mr. Adam. Wanna see my picture?"

"I'd like to, little man, but I need to get back to shoveling snow. You take good care of your mama."

"I will!" Toby waved again. Tia gave Adam an uncertain smile as she stepped inside and closed the door.

Everything in Adam wanted to storm into Abby's shop, take Tia in his arms and worry her peach-colored lips with the kisses he'd saved up for the last eleven years.

Annoyed that he had so little control over his emotions around the woman, Adam hustled back to where he'd left the shovel. He returned to cleaning off the boardwalk and steps around businesses and residences while his thoughts continued to wander.

After he helped Arlan and Luke shovel around the bank and school early that morning, he told them he had nothing better to do and didn't mind the physical exertion. In truth, he needed the cold, bracing air to keep him from going straight to Tia's house and demanding to know why she'd left him all those years ago.

A desire to hurt her as much as she'd hurt him surfaced when he unexpectedly ran into her earlier.

Instantly, he'd lost himself in the green flecks floating in her hazel eyes, accented by the rich color of her luxurious coat.

She'd styled her tresses in a fashionable updo beneath a wool hat with a jaunty plume. The color of her hair had always put him in mind of the special tea his mother had made at Christmas — glossy brown with hints of red and gold lurking in its depths.

Although she had a wide, square face, Tia's prominent high cheekbones and delicately arched brows gave her a decidedly feminine appearance.

The fact she smelled like rare flowers and decadent spices only encouraged his interest in her.

Even if she hadn't completely captivated him, he'd been unable to resist her lovable son. The little boy had a mischievous twinkle in his eye with the smile of an angel. The combination of those two characteristic no doubt got him out of almost as much trouble as he got himself into.

Adam stopped shoveling and stretched his back. He'd abandoned his hat and coat half an hour earlier as he worked up a sweat.

While his mind played over how beautiful and appealing he found Tia, he'd cleared the snow away from both sides of the street all the way from Granger House to the school.

A hungry pang in his stomach assured him it was nearly time for lunch. He picked up the shovel and headed back to Arlan's house.

Swiftly washing up and changing out of his sweat-drenched clothes, he shrugged into his coat and hurried out the door. He had plenty of time to catch Arlan and take him to lunch at the town's only restaurant.

On his way to the bank, he stopped by the mercantile, interested in finding a little something to give Arlan and Alex as a belated wedding gift.

"Why, Adam Guthry! It's been half of forever since we've seen you." Aleta Bruner stepped around the counter and gave him a welcoming hug. "My goodness, but life on the river must agree with you."

Adam grinned and smiled at the friendly woman. His skin was perpetually tanned from being outdoors most of the time. He rarely wore a hat while he was on the river, so his dark hair held lightened streaks from the sun.

Tall and brawny, he cut quite a dashing figure, even in a simple cotton shirt with his navy pea coat.

"Did you stop by just to say hello or are you looking for something in particular?" Aleta motioned to the aisles of the well-stocked store.

"I need a pair of work gloves and I want to find a gift for Arlan and Alex, since I missed their wedding."

Aleta smiled and led him to a display of work gloves. Adam selected a sturdy pair of leather gloves with smooth palms and tried them on. Pleased with the fit, he removed them and nodded his head. A display of picture frames caught his eye so he strolled over to them.

"Do you think a picture frame would be a suitable gift?" Adam picked up an ornate silver frame and studied it.

"It would be a lovely gift. Would you like me to wrap it for you?"

"That would be great. Thank you." Adam handed Aleta the frame and the gloves. She hurried back to the counter to wrap the frame while Adam browsed through the store. The air inside the inviting shop smelled of cinnamon and leather with a hint of whatever Aleta had cooking for dinner in the apartment overhead. Adam breathed deeply, savoring the pleasant, familiar aromas.

On impulse, he picked up a picture book about boats. He envisioned it being something Toby would enjoy. Irritated that Tia and her son continued to infiltrate his thoughts, Adam set the book down and looked at a selection of rope. He stared at a display of fabrics, focusing on a bolt of soft peach velvet that would set off Tia's complexion and hair.

Angrily growling to himself, he marched back to the counter as Aleta tied a red ribbon around his gift.

"Here you go, Adam. Is there anything else you need?" Adam purchased a small sack of peppermints along with the gloves and picture frame, stuffing everything inside his coat pockets.

"Thank you, Aleta. Your store is always a place I enjoy visiting when I'm in town." Adam would have tipped his hat to her, if he'd remembered to put it on before leaving Arlan's house. Instead, he smiled and started to open the door.

"You know you're welcome anytime, Adam. Don't be a stranger," Aleta said. She glanced down at a box on the counter then turned back to him with a sly grin. "I don't suppose you'd be willing to make a delivery for me? It's right here in town."

"I'd be happy to help out. What do you need me to deliver?" Adam returned to the counter.

"Just this box." Aleta tapped her hand on the edge of a large wooden box filled with flour, sugar, spices, a tin of tea, and a few cans of peaches.

"I'll take it right now. I'm meeting Arlan for lunch, but I've got time to deliver this. Where does it need to go?"

"To Mrs. Devereux's house. You do know where she lives, don't you?"

Adam clenched his jaw. "Yes. I know."

"Wonderful. Tia was supposed to stop back in earlier this morning to pick this up, but she must have forgotten or had something arise that kept her from returning. Please let her know she can pay for her purchases the next time she stops by." Aleta offered Adam a reassuring smile.

Not only was the storekeeper a friendly gossip, she was also a scheming, conniving matchmaker in the making.

He'd have no part of it. None at all.

"On second thought, maybe I better get on over to the bank. Arlan might be ready to go and…"

Aleta bustled around the counter and opened the door then proceeded to give Adam a nudge outside. "Go on. It will just take a moment to drop off that box for Tia. It's practically on the way to the bank, anyway. And I do so appreciate your assistance, Adam. You and Arlan always were such nice boys. Why your mother used to…"

Adam rolled his eyes and strode outside. "Goodbye, Aleta."

"Bye, Adam." She waved at him. "Thanks again."

Peeved, Adam walked to the end of the block then around a corner and down a few blocks until he reached the old Meyer place. Recently painted, the house looked clean and fresh, but the roof appeared as though it could use a few repairs before a windstorm loosened several shingles.

He stepped onto the porch and opened the screen door. With his fist, he tapped on the wooden door.

The door swung open almost instantly and he gazed down into the happy face of Toby Devereux.

"Hi, Mr. Adam! Did you come to visit us?" Toby stepped back so Adam could enter.

Before he answered, Tia breezed into the entry, wiping her hands on an apron. "Toby, did I hear you talking to... Oh, Adam. What are you doing here?"

"Aleta Bruner said you forgot to pick up some things this morning. She mentioned you could settle the bill the next time you stop by the mercantile." Adam held out the box in front of him, eager to set it down and be on his way. The longer he lingered in Tia's presence, the harder it was for him to resist the temptation to taste those sweet lips.

Tia blushed. It painted a rosy hue on her cheeks, causing an insane desire in Adam to kiss each one.

"I completely forgot about going back to the mercantile. I'm so sorry she asked you to bring this over. It could have waited until George returned this afternoon." Tia started to take the box from Adam but he held onto it.

"It's heavy, Queenie. I'll take it into the kitchen for you." Adam grimaced as the pet name he used to call Tia slipped out unbidden.

Tia hurried into the kitchen. Adam followed close behind her, admiring the swish of her skirts and the bob of the apron bow at her waist.

She pointed to an empty space on the counter. "Please, if you'll leave it there, I'd appreciate it."

Adam set down the box and looked around the kitchen that appeared much as it had the last time he'd been in the house years ago. The stove was new and the sink now had running water instead of a pump, but for the most part, everything was the same.

He glanced at the scarred wood of the kitchen table. Many afternoons after school, he and Carl had sat there with Tia enjoying a snack of milk and cookies before they went home to do their chores.

Flooded with memories of the past, Adam spun around, intent on escaping the pain it resurrected. He nearly plowed over Toby. He stopped and lifted the little boy, tossing him into the air and making him giggle.

Like vines climbing around a post, Toby's innocent laughter twined around Adam's chest.

"Do it again, Mr. Adam!"

Adam tossed him into the air three more times before setting the boy on his feet. He dug into his pocket and handed the child a peppermint drop.

"You save that for after your lunch, Toby, if it's okay with your mama for you to have it."

Tia nodded. The sight of Adam making her son laugh squeezed painfully at her heart. While Patrick had loved both her and Toby, he'd always been somewhat reserved. He'd never played with Toby like Adam had just done.

"How come you called my mama, Queenie?" Toby asked as he walked with Adam to the front door.

Adam should have known the bright little boy would notice his blunder. He hunkered down so he didn't tower above Toby and tweaked the child's freckled nose. "Way back when your mama and me and our friend Carl were young, she used to boss us around all the time. Carl and I called her Queenie because she acted like a queen, expecting us to follow her orders."

Toby sighed and leaned against Adam's thigh. "She still does that."

To keep from laughing at the long-suffering look on the boy's face, and the humor of his words, Adam chewed the inside of his cheek. To commiserate with Toby, he gravely nodded his head. "I didn't really think she'd outgrow it."

Adam glanced up and winked at Tia then rose to his feet and ruffled Toby's hair.

"You two stay out of trouble."

"Bye, Mr. Adam. Thank you for the candy and playing with me." Toby waved with unbridled enthusiasm as Adam stepped outside.

"Yes, thank you, Adam." Tia placed a hand on Toby's shoulder as they stood in the doorway.

Adam lifted a hand in parting, calling himself an idiotic ignoramus for letting both Tia and Toby get under his skin.

If he had a brain in his head, he'd pack his few belongings and ride out of town before he found himself in too deep with both members of the Devereux household. At the rate he was going, he'd be wrapped around both Tia's and Toby's fingers before the week was out.

Chapter Five

Tia pushed the rolling pin against the piecrust with more force than she intended and tore a hole in the delicate pastry.

Aggravated, she slammed the pin onto the counter and wadded the crust into a ball then started all over again. At this rate, she might as well use old shoe leather to cover her canned cherry pie. The crust would be tough and tasteless if she had to roll it out too many more times.

"May I help, Mama?" Toby ran into the room and dragged a kitchen chair over to the counter.

Tia wasn't in the mood for his help, but she tamped down her temper and smiled at her son. She pinched off a piece of dough and set it in the edge of the counter as Toby climbed onto the chair and stood on it. He pushed up the sleeves of his shirt then flattened the dough with his fingers.

"Are you making pies, Mama?" Toby poked holes into the dough with his index finger, creating eyes and a nose. He giggled at the silly face then worked the dough back into a ball before repeating the process.

"I am making pies, sweetheart." Tia finished rolling out the crust and carefully laid it over a sweet, thick cherry filling. "You like pie, don't you?"

"Mmm, hmm." Toby rolled the dough into a long tube then trailed it back and forth along the counter. "I like pie and cake and cookies and pudding and..."

"Everything sweet." Tia grinned at him as she placed two pies inside the oven. When she finished, she leaned over and kissed his nose.

Toby swiped at his nose, rubbing it on his arm in an attempt to wipe away her kiss. "Aw, Mama. You can't do stuff like that. I'm a big boy now, you know."

Tia schooled her features to look properly contrite. "Oh, I'm sorry. I forgot again, didn't I?"

"Yep." Toby jumped off the chair, dough clutched in his small hand. "Can I play outside?"

"I don't know. Can you?" Tia lifted an eyebrow his direction.

Toby shot her an oppressed look as his shoulders slumped forward. "May I play outside?"

"Yes, you may, but stay where I can see you from the window. Do you need help with your coat and boots?"

"Nope. I'll do it myself." Toby ran out of the room and returned a few minutes later with one arm shoved into his coat sleeve and his scarf held in his teeth.

Tia caught him before he rushed out the door. She wrapped the scarf around his neck, buttoned his coat, and tugged a knit cap down over his ears. "Where are your mittens?"

He fished them out of his coat pocket. Tia helped him put on one. When he held out his hand to put on the other, the glob of pie dough squished between his fingers.

Repulsed by the gray color it had turned, Tia took it from him. "I think you've played enough with the dough." She slid his mitten on his hand and opened the door.

Toby ran outside and flopped back in the snow, waving his arms and legs as he made an angel.

Tia watched him for a moment before shooing Crabby outside. She felt better if the cat kept watch over Toby. Even though he played where she could keep an eye on him, she worried about her son. With Crabby on guard, she held a measure of peace no one would disturb the boy.

Quickly cleaning up the mess from making pies, she stirred the stew that simmered on the back of the stove then made herself a cup of tea.

Weary, she sank down at the table and released a sigh. She'd hardly slept the past several nights, ever since the letter from Cedric arrived.

She refused to take Toby to Portland and relinquish him to the control of her former in-laws. He belonged to her, not them, and she'd decide the best way to raise him. Maybe it would be in Portland, maybe in Hardman, but that was her decision to make.

Distraught over what measures Cedric would take when she didn't soon return to town with Toby, she wondered if she could buy some time by saying she wanted to stay through the holidays in Hardman. Surely, he'd understand both she and Toby needed to spend Christmas surrounded by their friends.

After making a mental note to send Cedric a telegram, she took a sip of her tea and glanced outside. Toby packed snow into a ball and rolled it across the ground, attempting to form a snowman. She laughed when he made a move to pick up Crabby and the cat darted beyond his reach. The two of them kept up their game and Tia relaxed.

Admittedly, it wasn't just the idea of the judge taking Toby that had kept her awake, tossing and turning long into the night.

Thoughts of Adam Guthry disrupted her sleep and left her anxious. The intensity of her feelings toward the man hadn't diminished in eleven years. In fact, if anything, they'd multiplied.

Despite his surly tone and the hurtful words he'd spoken when she first ran into him the other day, he'd been extraordinarily kind — like the Adam she remembered — when he found her crying in the alley.

She couldn't believe he'd called her Queenie. Carl had been more likely to refer to her as "your highness" or a "bossy know-it-all."

Adam was the one who called her Queenie. As teens, he'd often bowed before he like she was royalty in a teasing gesture. However, the light in his eyes when he'd looked at her made her feel cherished and loved.

Tia smiled as she thought of how much and yet how little Adam had changed over the years.

He'd always possessed a thick thatch of dark, unruly hair. When they were twelve, she'd shown him a picture book in the mercantile about a family of bears. Laughingly, she told him his hair made him look like a grumpy bear.

After that, Adam deliberately left it mussed. Oh, he kept it cut, but the top of his head always looked like he'd rumpled it instead of combed it.

That edge of wildness and rebellion was one of the things she'd admired most about him.

He never worried about conforming to what others thought was proper. He tended to march to his own tune, whether anyone else liked it or not.

Yet, with his good looks and a dimpled smile guaranteed to melt female hearts, rarely did anyone take offense to his actions.

In truth, Adam Guthry was one of the most attractive men Tia had ever encountered. Rough and rugged, tall and commanding, Adam owned a tender spirit and a healthy dose of humility.

Bright blue eyes that sparkled with mischief or softened as they glimpsed into the depths of her soul coupled with that lopsided, playful smile made her wonder, again, why she'd ever left Hardman.

Tia breathed deeply and her traitorous nose conjured up Adam's scent. No matter how hard she tried to remove it from her mind, every whiff of him smelled like a precious memory of her past she didn't want to forget.

Curious why he'd never married, she was glad he'd remained single. If he'd been happily wed with a family of his own, she would have eventually forced herself to stop thinking about him, pining for him.

Through the years, her grandmother kept her updated on Adam's whereabouts and marital status. When he moved to Portland, Tia had vainly hoped to run into him. A dream of walking down the street and bumping into him kept her studying every dark-headed brawny man she encountered.

The folly of her actions often left her convicted. Even if she had run into Adam, she wouldn't have done more than engage in polite conversation. She might not have loved Patrick, but she never would have betrayed him.

Once Patrick passed away, she'd frequented a park along the banks of the Columbia River. While Toby played, she covertly watched the boats on the water, hoping for a glimpse of Adam. Most likely, she wouldn't have been able to discern if one of the men was Adam anyway, but being there made her feel closer to him somehow.

In the process, Toby had fallen in love with the water and boats. The little boy didn't seem to care if the boats were large or small, ships or barges, he held a fascination for them all.

Of course, Cedric and Catherine did all they could to discourage his interest, calling it beneath him.

Secretly, Tia encouraged him, buying him toy boats and picture books. She'd even had Abby sew him a little pea coat she planned to give him for Christmas. Toby would be thrilled with anything that made him think of boats and sailors.

Movement outside drew Tia's gaze to her son and a burly man in a navy pea coat helping him build a snowman.

As though her thoughts had conjured his presence, Tia studied Adam's broad shoulders as he lifted the head onto Toby's snowman and settled it into place.

The look of unmistakable joy on her son's face made Tia's heart catch as the two loves of her life worked together outside the kitchen window.

Suddenly recalling the pies she'd placed in the oven, Tia hurried to check on them. They weren't quite done, so she shut the oven door and stood at the window, watching Adam play with Toby. Crabby supervised from his spot on top of a box Toby had set near the snowman, tail swishing back and forth.

Tia's jaw dropped when Adam leaned down and picked up the cat, cradling it on one arm as he brushed a hand along its white back. To her knowledge, no other adult besides her had been able to get close to Crabby.

Rooted to her spot, she stared in shock as Adam and Toby sauntered across the yard. Fearful of being caught watching them, she hurried to pour milk into a saucepan on the stove. While it heated, she took out a square of baker's chocolate and finely grated it then added it with a few spoons of sugar and hot water to another saucepan.

Quickly stirring the melting chocolate, she smiled over her shoulder as Toby and Adam trooped inside, stamping snow from their boots before entering the warmth of the kitchen.

"Mama! Did you see me and Mr. Adam make a snowman?" Toby asked as he jerked off his hat and tugged on his scarf.

"I did, sweetheart." Tia glanced at the cat still cradled on Adam's arm. "Good afternoon, Adam. I see you've made a new friend."

"Toby tells me Crabby isn't too fond of people." Adam rubbed a hand over the cat's head. A loud purr filled the kitchen and made Toby laugh.

"Crabby seems to like you just fine." Tia raised an eyebrow at her little boy. "Why don't you take Crabby and go wash your hands, sweetheart. I'm making hot chocolate for you boys and I think there are a few cookies left."

"I should be going." Adam set Crabby down and turned toward the door, but Toby grasped one of his big hands in both of his.

"Please, Mr. Adam? Won't you stay and have hot chocolate with me? Mama makes it really good." Toby looked up at him with pleading eyes.

Unable to tell the child no, he agreed. "Okay, I'll stay for a cup of chocolate." Adam cast a glance at Tia and she nodded her head in agreement. "But then I need to be on my way."

"Hooray!" Toby shouted as he whipped off his coat and tried to kick off his boots.

"Here, little man, let me help." Adam squatted down and settled Toby on one solid thigh while he helped the boy remove his boots. "There you go."

"Thank you, Mr. Adam!" Toby wrapped his arms around Adam's neck and gave him a tight squeeze before racing off down the hall to the bathroom.

Tia had hired a crew of workers to add a bathroom soon after she decided to stay in Hardman. She couldn't bear the thought of using an outhouse after she'd been spoiled with indoor plumbing for so long.

Adam watched Toby disappear before rising to his feet and removing his coat and gloves.

In Hardman for less than a week, he'd already grown stir-crazy. He'd shoveled the boardwalks twice, mended a broken pew at the church, fixed a squeaky door at Arlan's place, and repaired a leak in Filly's kitchen sink.

With nothing to do that afternoon, he'd attempted to settle down in Arlan's parlor and read a book. Both Alex and Arlan recommended *The Island of Doctor Moreau* by H.G. Wells.

Adam read the first chapter with interest. The danger of shipwrecks was all too familiar to him.

Although he'd not mentioned it to Arlan, he'd survived a brutal shipwreck in the spring. A large scar across his shoulder and down his back along with an occasional stiffness in his left hand reminded him that life was fleeting at best. They hadn't lost anyone in the wreck, but it had been so close, Adam had nightmares about it for weeks afterward.

By the third chapter of the book, Adam's thoughts drifted to Tia and Toby. He'd seen them at church Sunday, but managed to be polite, though aloof. Now, he wished he'd been a little friendlier.

Picturing Tia all alone in that old house, he questioned whether she had enough wood cut for her fireplace and stove. Did the shingles blow off the roof in storm they'd had yesterday morning? Had she decided what to do about her father-in-law threatening to take Toby?

The Tia he remembered would have sent the man a scathing note telling him what she thought of his high-handed behavior in no uncertain terms.

The grown-up Tia, though, seemed more inclined to suggest demurely she didn't appreciate the judge's plans.

Adam wondered when Tia had lost her fire or if being part of the proper and snobby Devereux family had just banked the embers.

Annoyed that he cared, he set the book aside and got to his feet. In need of physical exertion, he'd gone outside for a walk.

Without conscious thought, his feet carried him past Tia's house. When he saw Toby outside struggling to make a snowman on his own, Adam stopped to assist him. The next thing he knew, he'd agreed to stay for a cup of hot chocolate.

"Is there anything I can do to help?" Adam asked, stepping behind Tia as she mixed the melted chocolate into the hot milk.

"If you wouldn't mind taking down the mugs, I'd appreciate it. You'll find them in that cupboard, there." She jutted her chin in the direction of a cupboard near the sink. Adam lifted out three mugs. One he recalled from when they were kids because Tia always wanted to drink out of it.

Creamy white with a chip in the handle, a pattern of deep pink roses decorated the side of the cup. It appeared Tia valued the sentiment of the piece more than she did having a cupboard full of matching dishes.

Adam set the mugs on the counter and watched as Tia filled them with the steaming hot chocolate. She added a dollop of cream to one and stirred it in as Toby raced back into the kitchen with his hair combed and hands scrubbed.

Tia placed the mug with the cream in front of Toby then grabbed the rose-emblazoned mug, handing the last one to Adam.

Nearly as quick as she took a seat, she popped back up, arranged cookies on a plate, and set it in the center of the table along with three napkins.

She handed Toby a cookie then held the plate out to Adam. He accepted one of the sugar cookies and took a bite before sipping the hot chocolate.

Toby was right. His mama did make really good hot chocolate. Unlike many people who scrimped either on the chocolate or sugar, this drink was rich and sweet.

Rather like the woman who made it.

Adam groaned inwardly and redirected his thoughts away from how enticing Tia looked with her hair in a loose bun and a smudge of flour on her cheek. His fingers itched to reach out and brush it away, so he finished his cookie and wrapped them around the cup of hot chocolate.

Toby filled the silence with his chatter. When Adam mentioned that he piloted boats down the river, the little boy scurried to his room and returned clutching a book in his hand. He set it down next to Adam and climbed on his lap without hesitation.

Page by page, Toby went through the different types of boats, pointing out which ones he liked best and why.

"I see you've got a sailor in the making on your hands," Adam observed, offering Tia his dimple-cheeked grin and a wink before returning his attention to Toby.

Flabbergasted by Adam's easy manner with her son, Tia's tongue felt tied in knots. She studied the dark-haired man bending over to peruse her golden-headed child's book.

"That's a steam schooner." Adam pointed to a picture then to another. "And a sternwheeler."

"Have you been on a schooner, Mr. Adam?" Toby asked, turning his gaze from the book to the man who intrigued him.

"I sure have, Toby, and a sternwheeler. If it travels on the water, I've probably piloted it at some point. Most often, I pilot big ships coming inland from the sea to Portland and barges carrying wheat. Did you know that a large portion of the nation's wheat crop, and even a percentage of the world's wheat, is grown right here in Oregon?"

"It is?" Toby's voice held a note of wonder as he gazed at Adam.

"It sure is." Adam watched as Toby returned his attention to the book and pointed to a canoe.

"Have you ever been in one of those?" Toby tapped his tiny finger on the picture.

"I have," Adam said, leaning back in his chair. Toby propped an elbow on the table and studied Adam with a mixture of awe and excitement.

"Was it fun?"

"It was fun," Adam agreed. "There's this old Indian named Charlie Two-Teeth. He paddles his canoe along the shore, catching fish in traps. One day we stopped nearby, so I walked over to Charlie and asked him if I could sit in his canoe. He shrugged, so I wasn't sure he understood me. When I held out a fifty-cent piece, he grinned and handed me the oar. I don't know what happened to ol' Charlie's teeth, but all he's got is one here," Adam pointed to one of his top teeth, "and one here." He touched a bottom tooth.

"Golly!" Toby said, eyes wide. "Where did you take his canoe?"

"I paddled it across the river and back again." Adam made a rowing motion with his arms. "Luckily for me, it was at a narrow spot."

Tia smiled and watched Toby relax against Adam as they finished looking through the book.

Her son missed having a father figure in his life. When Patrick died, Roland had tried to stop by weekly to give Toby some special attention. Although Cedric and Catherine claimed to dote on the boy, they seldom spent time with him. She couldn't fathom why they'd want to take him away from her.

Neither of them had any interest in the day-to-day care of a child. The thought of them hiring a nanny and ignoring Toby made Tia even more determined to keep it from happening.

"Look, Mama." Toby pointed to a photo of a houseboat. "That's like the boat I want to have someday. I'm going to marry Erin Dodd and we'll have our very own boat."

Adam chuckled and Tia smiled. She reached out and caught Toby's chin in her hand, turning his face to hers. "Those are some big plans, young man. I'm glad to see you're thinking ahead."

"I am, Mama. Erin and I will live on the big boat and you, and Pastor Chauncy, and Miss Abby, and Mr. Adam, and everyone can come visit us. We'll have lots and lots of room."

"I'll look forward to seeing that big boat, Toby." Adam patted the boy on his back, drinking the last of his chocolate.

He set Toby on his feet then rose to his own. "Thank you for allowing me to help with your snowman and showing me your book. Maybe I can show you how to make a sailor's knot or two sometime."

Animated, Toby grabbed Tia's arm and shook it. "Can he, Mama? Can he show me how to tie a real sailor's knot?"

"Of course, as long as Mr. Guthry has time and you behave yourself." Tia grinned at Toby, pleased by his enthusiasm.

"The one thing I've got the next few weeks is plenty of time," Adam said as he pulled on his coat and wrapped a scarf around his neck. He'd once again forgotten to wear his hat, although he didn't really care. He opened the door but turned back to Tia before he stepped outside. "I noticed there are some loose shingles on your roof. It wouldn't be any trouble to fix them for you."

Tia pushed past him out the door and rushed down the steps, walking backward across the yard until she could see the roof. As Adam said, she could see several loose shingles. The two men she usually hired to do odd jobs around her house were already overextended with projects. They let her know before Thanksgiving that they wouldn't be available to do any work until after Christmas.

While she hated to accept help from Adam, she didn't want to lose any shingles in the next windstorm.

Crossing her arms over her chest, she marched over to where he stood with Toby at the door. "I'll purchase all the necessary supplies and pay you for your time."

"You've probably already got all the necessary supplies and you won't pay me for my time. If you insist on it, I won't do it at all. I might take a pie as payment. However, I'd prefer one without a blackened crust."

"Oh, gracious!" Tia raced inside the house and pulled the pies from the oven. Enthralled with Adam and the affectionate interaction between him and Toby, she'd completely forgotten about her pies.

The crust was darker than she liked, but at least they weren't black, as Adam had suggested.

His chuckles floated back to her as he strode outside and down the porch steps.

Chapter Six

A knock at the front door caught Tia by surprise as she slid a chicken into the oven to roast for dinner.

Swiftly wiping off her hands and removing her apron, she hurried to the door as someone knocked a second time.

An impeccably dressed man stood on the front step, holding his hat in his hand as she opened the door.

"Mrs. Devereux?" He smiled in a seemingly friendly manner.

"Yes?" Tia had no idea who the man was as she took in his stocky, short build. A hint of foreboding settled like a lump of unpalatable mush in the pit of her stomach.

Although his clothes were expensive, the man appeared out of place in them, like an actor playing a part. In spite of how he looked, Tia had no problem picturing the man as a ruffian.

"I'm Edward Nivens. The Honorable Cedric Devereux retained my services in the matter of guardianship of his grandson."

"What?" Tia took a staggering step back and bumped into Toby as he ran to the door to see who had arrived.

The little boy sensed her fear and clung to her hand. "Mama?"

Tia forced a smile to her face and turned to her son. "Sweetheart, would you run into the kitchen to make sure we have enough cookies for today? If we have additional visitors, we might need to bake more."

"Okay," Toby said, dragging his toes and staring at the strange man over his shoulder as he shuffled to the kitchen.

When he was out of earshot, Tia returned her attention to the man who lingered in her doorway. "What is the meaning of this?"

"Judge Devereux is concerned about his grandson's wellbeing. Since he did not receive a reply to the letter he sent, he began proceedings to seek guardianship of the child. I'm to serve these papers to you and, if you're in agreement, bring the child back to Portland with me."

"Of course I'm not in agreement!" Tia hissed, refusing to take the thick envelope Mr. Nivens held out to her. "Has Cedric lost his mind? The only way he'll get guardianship of Toby is over my cold, dead body."

"I believe he's willing to consider that as a possibility." Mr. Nivens leered at her and stepped inside the house.

The cold gleam in his eyes sent fear slithering along Tia's spine. "Get out of my house and don't ever come back!"

"I'll remain here until the boy is in my keeping. You might as well get his things because whether you willingly send him today or I take him by force, he's still going."

"I won't allow it! I won't!" Tia regulated the volume of her voice so it wouldn't carry to the kitchen and frighten Toby. However, her tone clearly conveyed her disgust and dismay. "I insist you leave this instant or I'll…"

The man grabbed her wrists and pinned them behind her back. "Or you'll what, missy? Seems to me you don't…"

A blur of white fur launched across the room and latched onto Mr. Nivens' leg. He howled in pain as Crabby dug in his claws and rapidly climbed upward. Screeches rang through the house as Mr. Nivens attempted to shake off the enraged feline while the cat snarled and spat, furiously inching toward the man's head.

Bits of white fur floated like fluffy snowflakes in the air as the man tried to grab the writhing feline. Sharp teeth sunk into his palm, drawing blood. Mr. Nivens waved his bleeding hand in the air as he gaped in utter disbelief at Crabby.

"Get this demented beast off me!" he shouted, panicked as the cat continued his ascent.

Unaware of the danger, Toby ran into the room and sank onto the floor with laughter, watching the man spin in circles as the cat clung to his chest.

Tia took advantage of the intruder's distress to give him a hard shove out the door. She locked it behind him then stood at the window, watching as the cat raised a paw and clawed a deep scratch across Mr. Nivens' chin. Crabby jumped down and pranced through the snow toward the back of the house.

With a look of shock and anger on his face, the man swiped at the blood dripping down his chin, shook his fist toward the house, and stomped off.

Relieved he'd gone, Tia sank onto the sofa, trying to gain control of her shaking limbs.

Stunned that Cedric would hire a thug to do his dirty work, she tried to think of the best course of action.

Perhaps she should pack a bag and steal away in the night to protect her son. She had a few friends in Pendleton that might help her. Maybe it would be best to head south to California, toward a warmer climate.

Lost in her worries, she jumped to her feet as Toby tried to open the door.

"Toby, no! Don't open the door!" She rushed to his side and dropped to her knees, pulling him into her arms.

"But, Mama, Mr. Adam's out there." Toby pointed to the door as another knock sounded. "I want to tell him about Crabby climbing all over that man."

Tia stood, still holding Toby, and unlocked the door. Adam took one look at her and stepped inside, placing a hand on her arm as he closed the door. "What's wrong, Tia? What's happened?"

She gave Adam a cautionary glance then rested her cheek against Toby's forehead. "I think you might need to check on Crabby, sweetheart. Why don't you get your boots and coat and go outside? Just long enough to check on the kitty. And make sure you stay where I can see you."

"Okay, Mama." Toby started squirming before she set him down and raced into the kitchen. In no time, the sound of the kitchen door opening and closing carried back to where Adam and Tia stood by the front door.

"You're shaking like a leaf, Tia. What's wrong?" Adam took her hand in his and led her to the kitchen. He eased her down into a chair where she could watch Toby in the backyard while he pulled the kettle toward the front of the stove to heat the water for tea.

Tia needed something to steady her nerves yet he doubted she had anything stronger than coffee in the house.

"What happened?" Mindful of her agitated state, Adam took her favorite mug from the cupboard and located the tea and sugar.

"Toby's grandfather sent a man here to take him back to Portland, by force. If it wasn't for that crazy cat, he might have done it, too."

"Was he a stocky, short man in a gray coat with shredded trousers?" Adam asked as he leaned against the counter.

"Yes. Did you see him?" Tia started to rise when Toby disappeared from her sight then sat down when he ran into full view.

"Sure did. He was holding a handkerchief to his chin and dripping blood down the street, muttering curses with every step." Adam's look held shock and a hint of amazed wonder. Dimples popped out in his cheeks as he snickered. "The cat did that to him?"

Despite the fear threatening to swamp her, Tia grinned. "Yes. Crabby took offense to his plan and let him know we wouldn't go down without a fight."

Chuckles rumbled out of Adam as the kettle whistled. He made a cup of tea and set it in front of Tia.

"What are you going to do?" He hunkered down beside her, placing a warm hand on her shoulder and giving it a gentle squeeze.

"I don't know, but I won't allow that awful man to take my son." Tia sipped the tea, sweetened just the way she liked. Surprised Adam remembered, she glanced down and realized he'd handed her the mug she always favored.

"I'm going to work on the roof for a while and keep an eye on Toby. You just sit here and try to relax. I don't think the judge's man will return today, at least not if he knows what's good for him." Adam stood and walked over to the back door. "Don't worry, Tia. We'll figure something out."

Soon after he stepped outside, she heard Toby's giggles as Adam tossed him in the air. She listened to the sound of the ladder being set against the house then footsteps thudding overhead as Adam made good on his promise to repair her loose shingles.

Her thoughts spun around and around in her head, making her dizzy as she tried to decide the best thing she could do to protect her son.

Frustrated by her own sense of inaction, she smacked the top of the table with both hands, got to her feet, and marched out of the room.

With each nail Adam pounded into the roof, he pondered Tia's situation. Each time he set a new shingle in place, he sent a prayer heavenward for wisdom.

Below him, Toby played in the snow while the cat sat nearby, swishing his tail and keeping watch.

Adam wished he'd been around to see Crabby in action. He'd never heard of a cat attacking a man before. Based on his shredded trousers and multiple scratches dripping blood, Adam doubted Tia would have any more trouble with Cedric Devereux's hired thug that particular day.

In his work, Adam had seen plenty of men like the one who'd terrified Tia. No matter how nicely they dressed or how fine their manners upon first meeting, they were all the same — all heartless bullies who lived to strike fear in others while making a little money on the side.

As he worked to repair Tia's roof, Adam realized he could no more turn away from Tia and Toby now than he could cease his need for air to breathe.

He'd never intended to speak to her again, let alone open his heart to her. Not a single doubt lingered in his mind that she'd rip his heart to pieces a second time if given the opportunity.

Even in light of that knowledge, Adam couldn't force himself not to care about her and her son.

Toby was the most intelligent, adorable child Adam had ever encountered. He understood why the judge and his wife wanted him, but that didn't make their actions acceptable.

The little boy belonged with his mother, wherever she decided to raise him.

"Mr. Adam, watch me!" Toby waved to get his attention.

Adam leaned over the edge of the roof and smiled. "I'm watching."

Toby tumbled across the snow-covered yard in a somersault then hopped a few paces on one foot before falling into a pile of snow with a giggle. "Did you see me?"

"I did see you, Toby. That was very good."

"Mama taught me to do summersalls." Toby pointed up at Adam. "Can you do a summersall?"

Adam wondered if Tia taught Toby by executing a few somersaults of her own or just giving him instruction. A picture of her trying to do one with her long skirts and petticoats made him grin.

"Stay right there, Toby, and I'll show you something." Adam maneuvered around until he sat on the edge of the roof with his back to the ground. He set aside his tools and made sure he didn't have anything sharp in his pockets. Relaxing his muscles, he placed his hands on his knees, leaned back, and rolled off the roof. He spun around in a perfect circle before landing on his feet in the snow.

"Oh, Mr. Adam, do it again! Please, do it again!" Toby ran over to him and tugged on his hand, excitedly hopping up and down. "Can you teach me to do that?"

"I'm fairly certain your mother would skin me alive if I taught you to do that. Don't you let me catch you trying. You have to be a full-grown size before you can try that trick. Understood?"

"Yes, sir." Toby nodded his head solemnly but a smile quickly brightened his countenance. "But will you do it again?"

"Once more, then I need to finish my work."

"Hooray!" Toby clapped his mitten-covered hands and watched as Adam hurried up the ladder to repeat his performance.

The door opened and Tia stepped out just as he rolled off the roof a second time. She gasped and placed a hand to her throat. "Adam Guthry!"

He landed with a lopsided grin and flourish of his hand as he bent toward her. "Yes, Queenie?"

"Good heavens! Have you lost your mind? What if you injured yourself?" Tia stood on the back step with her hands fisted on her hips. "What were you thinking?"

"That it would make Toby smile," Adam said and glanced down at a beaming little boy who leaned against his leg. "Besides, I do it off boats all the time in the summer and this way, I don't have to worry about anything sucking me under the water. It's just a matter of balance."

"Well, cease from balancing that matter off my roof. What if someone much smaller than you takes a notion to emulate your careless behavior?" Tia looked pointedly at Toby.

Adam reached down and ruffled the boy's hair. "Toby knows he can't try this until he's as big as me, isn't that right?"

"Yep. Mr. Adam already said I couldn't try it, Mama. Did you see him roll right off? Boom!" Toby clapped his hands together. "I wish Erin could have seen it. Will you do it again, Mr. Adam, if I go fetch her?"

"No, he will not, young man." Tia marched over and took Toby's hand in hers, leading him toward the door. "You've been out here long enough. Let's get you inside and warmed up."

"But, Mama, I'm not cold and Mr. Adam…"

"Inside, Toby." Tia nudged him up the steps. Although he didn't argue or disobey, he dragged his feet as he went. When Toby was inside the kitchen, Tia took a step back and glared at Adam. "You should know he'll try to copy everything you do. He already talks about you like you're a hero."

"He does?" Adam stopped halfway up the ladder and pinned her with his mesmerizing gaze. "There's no possible way for him to set up this heavy ladder and

Toby's a good boy. If you tell him not to do something, he minds, doesn't he?"

"Yes, but that's not the point." Tia fought the urge to stamp her foot in frustration.

Toby wasn't the cause of her worry. When she told him not to do something, her son most always obeyed.

No. Her fear was for the big, loveable lunk who'd scared her half witless when she saw him tumble off the roof.

"I believe that's exactly the point." Adam's lopsided grin revealed his dimples and made her mouth water for want of his kiss.

Aggravated with herself, Tia aimed her fury at Adam. "The point is your recklessness might get you or someone else horribly injured." She turned around and strode toward the kitchen door. "I insist you…"

A snowball caught her square in the back. Mouth hanging open in surprise, she spun around and gaped at him.

Adam worked to form another snowball, ignoring her scowl.

Incensed, Tia surrendered to the need to stamp her foot. "How dare you!"

"Just like this." He grinned and lobbed another snowball at her, catching her on the shoulder. Bits of snow sprayed into her face and hair.

"Oh! You are in for it now, Adam Guthry!" Tia bent down and hastily formed a snowball. With unmistakable precision, she threw it at Adam, hitting him on the chin.

He spluttered and returned fire, barely grazing her arm as she twisted away at the last second.

Peals of her laughter filled the quiet December afternoon and drew Toby outside as she and Adam continued to throw snow at each other.

"Mama?" The little boy's lip quivered. "Did you send me inside so you could play without me?"

"No, baby. I'm sorry. We didn't intend to leave you out. Adam tossed some snow and I threw some back. That's all." Tia cast a reproachful glare at Adam. "Why don't you both come inside and have a snack? I just took molasses cookies out of the oven."

"With milk?" Toby asked, tugging on Tia's hand.

"Of course, with milk." She swung Toby up into her arms and kissed his cheek.

"You gots snow in your hair, Mama." Toby reached out and brushed at it. "And your ear."

"So I do." Tia looked at Adam as she tipped her head and dislodged the snow. "Are you coming in?"

"I'll finish this first. It shouldn't take me long." Before he scurried back up the ladder and finished nailing on the last of the shingles, Adam watched her brush snow from her dress and walk inside the house with Toby.

A smile lingered on his face as he thought about how much fun it was to play with Tia. It had been years since he'd formed a snowball. Yet tossing them at her had been just like old times when they'd engaged in snowball fights with Carl.

When he finished the roof repairs, he returned the tools to the shed behind her house and stored the ladder on hooks where Toby couldn't reach it.

Hastily brushing off his clothes, he stuffed his gloves inside his coat pocket and tapped on the door before stepping inside.

The house was quiet and Toby was nowhere around, but the sight that greeted him made him stop mid-button as he removed his coat.

Tia sat at the kitchen table cleaning a double-barrel shotgun with a degree of calm that unnerved him.

"What are you doing?" Adam asked as he removed his coat and left it hanging on a peg by the door.

"What does it look like I'm doing?" Tia swabbed a cloth down one barrel and pulled it out. "I don't think this gun has been shot since the last time Gramps used it and he's been gone fifteen years." Tia swabbed the other barrel before Adam lifted the gun from her hands and set it on the table.

"Have you shot a gun since the last time you went hunting with me and Carl?" Adam used a clean rag to wipe off the outside of the shotgun.

"No, but I bet I could shoot well enough to fill Mr. Nivens' backside full of lead." Tia tossed down the dirty rag in her hands and walked over to the sink. She scrubbed her hands then turned back to study Adam as he finished cleaning the gun.

He lifted his brilliant blue gaze to hers. "Tia, I don't want you trying to shoot that man. What if he wrestled the gun away from you? What if Toby ended up hurt?"

Deflated, she slumped against the counter and pressed the palms of her hands against her eyes. "I don't know what else to do, Adam, other than run away."

He set down the gun, wiped his hands on a rag, then moved until he stood in front of her.

"Tia?" He reached out and pulled her hands away from her face. Tears filled her eyes and her lower lip quivered, much as Toby's had earlier. "Promise me you won't run away. That won't solve anything, at least not in the long-run."

Slowly, she nodded her head.

Adam pulled her against his chest. He felt her stiff posture relax and held back a sigh. The closer he got to Tia, the more it would hurt when she left him again. Except this time it would be twice as hard since he'd come to care for Toby, too.

"Where's Toby?" he asked as he rubbed a hand over her shoulders and along her back.

"Sleeping. He won't take a nap for days then all of a sudden, he'll run out of energy and need one." Tia rubbed her cheek against the soft flannel of Adam's shirt and breathed in the comforting familiarity of his scent. "He'll probably sleep for an hour or so."

"Good." Adam kissed the top of Tia's head then took a step back, ignoring the bereft feeling he experienced without her in his arms. He lifted his coat from the hook and slipped it on while Tia studied him.

"Where are you going?" she asked as he wrapped his scarf around his neck.

"I'm going to get the sheriff so you can tell him what happened. After that, I want you to walk over to the attorney's office with him to discuss your options while I stay here with Toby." Adam took Tia's hands in his and bent his knees so he could look her square in the face. "I promise you, Tia, I won't let anything happen to you or Toby."

"It's not your battle to fight, Adam. I don't want you to…"

Adam brushed his hand along her jaw then trailed a finger across her cheek, causing her to snap her mouth shut. "I want to help you, Tia, and I will. I vow to see you through this." His finger caressed the curve of her cheek before he dropped his hand and pulled on his gloves. "While I'm gone, keep both doors locked. And put that gun away before Toby sees it. You're likely to scare him half to death if he happens to catch you handling it."

Tia nodded and locked the door behind Adam when he left. Instead of moving the gun, she leaned against the door, skin tingling from his soft touch. Every part of her ached to lean into Adam, to pull his head down for a kiss, and confess her soul-deep love for him.

She knew he vowed to help her out of some misplaced sense of duty based on their old friendship, not because he held any true affection for her. Although he hadn't been gruff with her again, she caught the wary looks he cast her way when he thought she wasn't watching.

At a loss to set things right between them, Tia sighed and returned the gun to the spare bedroom closet where she'd found it.

In the event Adam did bring the sheriff back with him, Tia made a pot of coffee as well as one of tea, using her grandmother's best china to fill a heavy silver tray. When Adam knocked on the front door, Tia hurried to open it and welcomed him and the sheriff inside.

"Mrs. Devereux." The sheriff tipped his head to her as he removed his hat and coat. "Adam told me you had a little trouble this afternoon. I'd best get the story straight from you."

"Yes, sir," Tia said, smiling at the lawman. "Would you care for some coffee or tea?"

"Coffee would be appreciated," he said, draping his things over the hall tree by the front door.

"Adam?" Tia asked as he removed his outerwear and left his coat by the sheriff's.

"Coffee's fine." He turned to look at her. "Do you need any help?"

"No, thank you." She breezed back to the kitchen and retrieved the tray she'd already prepared, carrying it into the parlor and setting it on the table in front of the sofa. She handed the sheriff a cup of coffee and a plate with two molasses cookies then did the same for Adam before she sat down on the sofa.

Adam took a seat next to her while the sheriff settled into a chair by the fire. After taking a sip of the coffee and a bite of a cookie, he set the refreshments on the table next to his chair. He pulled a small notebook and pencil from inside a vest pocket.

"Why don't you start at the beginning and tell me what led up to the man coming to see you today?" The sheriff offered her an encouraging smile.

Tia began to pour herself a cup of coffee, but her hands shook so badly, she nearly dropped the pot. Adam took it from her. Instead, he poured her a cup of tea, hoping it would calm her jangled nerves.

Anxious, she took it from him and sat back against the cushions. Slowly drawing a deep breath, she relayed the story of receiving the threatening letter from her father-in-law up through the cat chasing off Mr. Nivens earlier that afternoon.

The sheriff choked on his coffee as she told about the cat climbing up the man's leg and clawing his chin.

"I saw him walking through town, Sheriff. His trousers were in tatters and he looked like he'd wrestled a wild animal." Adam grinned as the sheriff fought to control his urge to laugh.

"And you say he brought some papers, Mrs. Devereux?" the sheriff asked, taking notes while he finished the last bite of his cookie.

"Yes, I forgot about them until now. He dropped them by the door." Tia jumped up and hurried to the front door, returning with a thick envelope bearing the embossed initials of the judge.

"May I?" the sheriff asked, holding out his hand.

Tia handed him the envelope. He extracted the papers, mostly filled with a plethora of legal terms that wouldn't make sense to the average person.

"I could be mistaken, but I believe the man is seeking guardianship of your son based on the fact you are a widow of questionable means living on your own in a house that may not be suited for the adequate care of his grandson." The sheriff held the papers out to Tia, but Adam snatched them and quickly scanned the details.

When he finished, Tia took them from Adam. A frown laced with warning settled over her face as she read them. She'd often read Patrick's paperwork and understand most of what the papers said. The sheriff was correct, though. It boiled down to Cedric putting together a case based on the fact Tia was alone in the world.

"That judge is… is…" Tia struggled to find a word to convey her feelings that wouldn't shock both men senseless. Finally, she gave up and looked to the sheriff. "Would you mind accompanying me to Frank Carlton's office, sir? I'd like to discuss this matter with him, since he's an attorney. Adam volunteered to keep an eye on Toby."

"Certainly." The sheriff and Adam rose to their feet when Tia stood. Adam held her coat while she slipped it on. As the sheriff pulled on his coat, Tia pinned on a hat, tugged on her gloves, picked up her reticule and the correspondence from the judge. She promised Adam she wouldn't be gone long then rushed out the door with the sheriff.

Adam took the tea tray back to the kitchen, inhaled the delicious scent of the roasting chicken, and carried in more wood for the fires.

By the time he'd washed the dishes and dried them, Toby wandered into the kitchen, sleepy-eyed, dragging a stuffed bunny behind him that had seen better days. Crabby glanced up from his box by the stove and watched Toby before closing his eyes.

"Where's Mama?" Toby asked as Adam squatted down and let the boy lean against his chest.

"She had to run an errand, but she'll be back soon enough. Do you suppose you'd keep me company until she returns? Maybe we could sit in that big rocking chair by the fire. Is that a good place to wait?" He lifted Toby in his arms and carried him to the parlor.

Adam sank into the chair and the child nestled against him, holding tightly to his stuffed toy. "What's your rabbit's name?" Adam asked as he set the chair into motion, unhurriedly rocking back and forth.

"Bunny." Toby yawned and his eyelids drooped.

Lazily closing his eyes, Adam continued rocking the chair. The crackling of logs on the fire added to the cozy atmosphere of the room. "Bunny's a good name," he whispered as Toby released a soft breath, falling back asleep.

Unaware how long he slept, Adam awoke to a cool hand on his cheek and looked up into Tia's smiling face. A finger to her lips indicated he should be quiet as she lifted Toby and carried him out of the room.

Groggy, Adam got to his feet and waited for her to return.

"You two looked so peaceful sleeping, I hated to wake you, but I was afraid you'd get a crick in your neck."

Adam rolled his neck to one side then the other and grinned at her. "I didn't mean to doze off, but it was hard to keep my eyes open sitting by the fire."

"I do the same thing," Tia admitted. "Thank you for your help today and keeping watch over Toby. Would you like to stay for dinner?"

"No, I need to get going, but I appreciate the offer. Did you have a good conversation with Mr. Carlton?" Adam asked as he grabbed his coat from the hall tree and shoved his arms into the sleeves

"It was enlightening," Tia said, turning to straighten a pillow on the sofa.

"How so?"

Tia couldn't force herself to meet Adam's gaze. "Mr. Carlton is of the opinion that the judge's petition to gain guardianship wouldn't hold up in any court if, by some happenstance, the status of my widowhood altered in the immediate future." Nervous, she fiddled with the button on the sleeve of her dark blue woolen gown.

Adam observed her nervous movements. "Just spit it out, Queenie. What did Mr. Carlton say?"

Embarrassed, she turned to stare out the front window. Frost already rimmed the edges of the glass as afternoon gave way to a cold evening.

Humiliation sent heat creeping up her neck and into her cheeks. "He said if I'd wed someone immediately, then Cedric would have no chance at getting Toby."

Air whooshed out of Adam. More than once in the past few days, marriage had crossed his mind as a solution to Tia's troubles. If he cared to admit it, which he didn't, the thought held a great deal of appeal to him.

"What are you going to do? Do you have someone in mind?"

"Good heavens!" Tia spun around and glared at Adam.

You. Only and forever you.

She huffed in feigned irritation. "Of course not. Don't be ridiculous. I'll figure something out that doesn't involve a man sacrificing his freedom to save my son."

Uncertain what to say in response, he offered her a curt nod and rushed out the door.

Tia watched him in the light from the street lamps as he hurried down the street in the direction of Arlan and Alex's place.

She couldn't blame him for his abrupt departure. Any man with a lick of sense would run far and fast when a woman found herself in desperate need of a husband.

Chapter Seven

"You... you what!" Arlan stammered as the knife in his hand clattered onto the table. The bite of mashed potatoes Alex held on her fork halted mid-air, halfway to her mouth.

Both of them turned astonished looks to Adam. He pushed food around on his plate instead of eating the meal Alex hurried to put on the table when she arrived home from teaching school.

"I said I'm thinking about asking Tia to marry me." Adam scowled at Arlan as his brother continued to gape at him.

Alex set her fork on the edge of her plate while Arlan cleared his throat and gathered his thoughts. "Are you sure that's a good idea, Adam. I mean... after all... the last time you..." The memories hung heavily between them.

"He proposed to her before?" Alex asked, glancing from her husband to Adam. "Tia turned you down?"

"No. I never got the opportunity to ask her. She left town before I worked up the nerve and that was the last time I saw her until Carl's funeral."

"Oh." Alex lifted a dark eyebrow Arlan's direction and he shook his head in some unspoken communication Adam had no hope of interpreting.

"Based on the painful situation that occurred the last time you considered marrying the girl, I'm concerned you might be rushing into this." Arlan sat back in his chair and eyed his brother.

Adam had always been the bold one, full of mischief and fun, along with an eagerness to experience every adventure available.

After Tia broke his heart the first time, Adam embraced an entirely new level of reckless abandon that frightened his younger sibling and eventually led to his job as a pilot on the Columbia River.

Arlan cleared his throat and rapidly fired out questions. "Have you thought things through? Where would you live? Could she put up with your demanding work schedule? Are you prepared for the possibility she'll never love you? What if she leaves you?"

Disconcerted, Adam rocked back in his chair and blew out a long breath. "Yes, Arlan, I've thought things through. Truthfully, I've thought of little else since I discovered her former father-in-law wants to take Toby away from her. She still has a house in Portland, but she did say she plans to sell it. We could live there or buy a house close to the river. I make a good wage at my work and am capable of supporting a family. However, I'm under the impression her husband left her well cared for upon his death. Tia or Toby aren't lacking money. At any rate, I love my work on the river, so Tia would just have to get used to the idea of my schedule."

"But you'd be gone often, wouldn't you?" Alex asked, placing a hand on Adam's arm. "No wife wants to consider her husband being gone for days on end, especially when he might be in a perilous situation and never return."

"I know. It's not perfect, but we could make it work if we're both willing to try." Adam turned to Arlan. "I'm not saying I'm pledging my heart to Tia. She destroyed it the first time she left. Regardless, I'm vowing to keep her and Toby together by offering a marriage of convenience. I wouldn't expect anything from her. In fact, if she wanted to stay here in Hardman, that might be for the best. As for her leaving me high and dry, I assume she could have the marriage annulled any time it suited her purposes. I once loved her with every bit of emotion an eighteen-year-old boy can give, but I'm not a boy any longer."

Adam studied the food growing cold on his plate before he spoke again. "This isn't about reuniting with a long lost love. Not in the least. It's about saving Toby from the clutches of a cruel, manipulative man. Tia and her son aren't my problem or my responsibility. But if you had the opportunity to keep a little boy from being separated from the one person in the world who loves him completely, wouldn't you do everything humanly possible to help?"

Slowly, Arlan nodded his head. "I suppose I would, but what about your heart, Adam? You can lie to yourself all you like, but you still have feelings for Tia."

Adam growled and ran a hand over his head. "I didn't realize it was that obvious."

"It isn't, only to those who know you well." Arlan grinned at Alex. "And those who've just met you. Perhaps to a stranger walking down the street."

Alex winked at her brother-in-law. "From what I've observed, Tia cares about you a great deal. Probably as much as you care about her. She seems like a very nice person and I can't see her backing out of a vow to you once it's made. Nevertheless, aren't you cheating yourself out of the opportunity to fall in love with someone by marrying her now?"

"Like I said, Tia drained every bit of love out of my heart the summer we were eighteen. I'm not ever going to fall in love again, so it matters little to me if I tie myself to Tia and Toby. If marrying her ensures Toby's safety, then I'll do it without a moment of regret." Adam shifted his gaze from Alex to Arlan. "As for you, that's enough teasing and sarcasm for one night."

The playful shove he delivered to Arlan nearly knocked him from his chair, but both brothers chuckled as they picked up their forks and returned to their meals.

"Did the cat really tear up that man's clothes?" Alex asked as Adam sliced a bite of roast beef.

A snort escaped from him. "He sure did. If I hadn't heard it was the cat that had gotten to him, I'd have assumed he'd wrestled with a spool of barbed fencing wire or encountered a cougar."

Arlan chuckled. "Remind me to take a wide berth around ol' Crabby. I knew the cat didn't care for people, but I had no idea Tia had trained it to attack."

Humored, Adam shook his head. "I don't think she had any idea he'd attack, either. She seemed as surprised as anyone did by the cat's behavior. On the other hand, Toby appeared impressed and entertained by the cat's antics."

"I'm sure he was." Arlan smiled. "For being such a handful, he really is a good boy."

"Yes, he is," Adam agreed.

"Are you sure you're ready to become a father? You wouldn't just be marrying Tia. You'd also be taking on responsibility for her small son." Arlan set down his knife and fork, waiting for his brother to consider his words.

Finally, Adam nodded his head. "I know I haven't spent much time around children, but Toby and I get along with no trouble. He's bright and inquisitive, yet he minds well and truly does have a tender little spirit."

Surprised by his brother's observations, Arlan nodded his head. "It sounds like you've got it all figured out."

"If Tia will agree to marry me, we should do so right away. She can send word to the judge she is no longer a widow alone and any attempts on his part to take Toby are pointless." Adam buttered a slice of bread. Alex passed him a dish of strawberry jam and he slathered it over the entire surface before taking a bite.

"If Tia does agree to wed, would you give us a few days to prepare? The ladies of Hardman would be terribly disappointed if they lacked the opportunity to make a true celebration out of the event." Alex offered Adam an innocent smile, belying the impishness twinkling in her eyes.

A groan escaped Adam. "Can't we just have Chauncy marry us in a quiet little ceremony?"

"Most likely," Alex grinned at him, "but where's the fun in that? Besides, the women of Hardman are quite good at throwing together a wedding reception on a moment's notice."

"The ladies in town had a nice spread for Luke and Filly's wedding and that was with less than a week's notice. Ginny and Blake got married with only a few hours to plan, although it was a Christmas Eve wedding, so the church was already decorated," Arlan commented. He reached across the table and squeezed Alex's hand, sharing a look full of love. "I thought we might have a second Christmas Eve wedding last year when I begged this gorgeous woman to marry me with as much speed as possible, but she insisted we invite you to the wedding and wait for your reply."

"I wish I'd been here. By the time I received the telegram, it was a week old and I didn't want to hold things up any longer than necessary." Adam waggled his eyebrows at Arlan. "I suppose I should have asked you to wait while I arranged to take time away from work and then traveled halfway across the state. However, I assumed you'd much rather marry your bride and have your way with her in all due haste."

Alex blushed and Arlan choked on the bite he'd just swallowed. Adam thumped him on the back and winked at his sister-in-law. "In the event I failed to mention it before,

I'm so glad you two have each other. I'm thrilled to see you both so much in love."

"Thank you, Adam." Alex turned back to her meal, although a pink hue persisted in coloring her cheeks.

After dinner, the three of them gathered in the parlor where they continued discussing Adam's plans.

When they retired for the evening, Adam hugged Alex and shook Arlan's hand. "Even though marrying Tia isn't what you believe is best for me, I appreciate knowing you'll support me no matter what I decide to do."

"Of course, Adam. That's what family is for." Arlan squeezed his shoulder then disappeared with Alex into their bedroom.

As they readied for bed, Alex sat in front of the mirror at her dressing table, brushing her long, dark hair and smiling at Arlan in the reflection of the glass. "Do you really think Adam will work up the gumption to ask Tia to wed?"

"Yes. Once he's decided on something, there's usually no changing his mind." Arlan moved behind Alex and took the brush from her hand, running it gently through her hair, admiring the way her midnight tresses gleamed in the lamplight. "Adam never stopped loving Tia and she hasn't gotten over him, either. It's about time the two of them finally do what they should have done years ago."

"Why, Arlan Guthry! You are a matchmaker in disguise." Alex grinned at her husband as he continued to brush her hair. "What was all that falderal about his plans to wed Tia being a terrible idea and suggesting he was rushing into things?"

"Generally, Adam does the opposite of what I suggest just to show he can. He might be the oldest, but he's also the most obstinate and stubborn. I learned a long time ago if I wanted Adam to do something, I had to tell him he couldn't or shouldn't. The more I emphasize it's a bad idea, the more determined he'll be to prove me wrong." Arlan gave her a smug smile. "By noon tomorrow, he'll be an engaged man."

"I had no idea I'd married such an underhanded schemer." Alex's eyes held amusement and invitation as she gazed at Arlan in the mirror. "I kind of like seeing this side of you."

Arlan set down the brush and placed a warm, moist kiss to her neck. "I've got a few more things I can show you, Mrs. Guthry. Are you interested?"

She turned and pressed her lips to his in a heated exchange. When she pulled back, desire glowed in her eyes. "You bet I am."

Chapter Eight

Nerves unlike anything Adam had ever experienced made it impossible for him to swallow any of his breakfast the following morning. He refused the coffee Alex offered him, eventually agreeing to a cup of tea.

He left the house with Arlan and Alex, accompanying them to the point where they headed toward the school. For a few minutes, he watched them walk together. Arlan would help Alex get a fire going at the school and bring in more wood for the stove before he went to the bank for the day.

Leisurely strolling through town, Adam admired the festive pine garlands and bright bows several businesses had put out to decorate their storefronts in the last few days. The effect was appealing and cheerful — a reminder Christmas would soon be upon them.

Thoughts of spending the holiday with Tia and Toby made him consider what would be appropriate gifts for the two of them. An idea for a gift for Toby came to mind and Adam decided whether Tia wed him or not, he'd make the present for the boy.

He veered toward the mercantile, intent on finding the necessary supplies, then decided he needed to ask Tia the question weighing heavy on his mind before he lost his nerve.

As he meandered toward her home, he waved to people he'd known most of his life, pleased by their smiles and words of greeting.

The friendly atmosphere of the town was one thing he missed living in Portland. No one in the neighborhood where he lived waved from their porch or invited him to stop in for a cup of coffee. For the most part, people didn't even make eye contact as they hurried down the street, intent on their errands.

Adam stopped at the end of Tia's front walk and stared at the snug little house. With the roof repaired, it appeared to be in good shape, although he was sure he could find a few things to work on if Tia let him.

"Might as well get this over with," he muttered as he trudged down the walk and up the porch steps, shoving his gloves into his coat pockets.

Prior to his hand connecting with the wood of the door to knock, he inhaled a deep breath.

The loud rap reverberated in the still of the morning. At least the day hinted that it would be one full of sunshine as streaks of gold gradually filled the sky.

The door swung inward and Tia smiled at him through the screen door. "Good morning, Adam. What brings you by so early in the day?"

"I um… there's a matter I…" Adam struggled to hang onto his thoughts as Tia's enticing scent ensnared his senses while his eyes lingered on the luxurious depths of her hair. It fell to her waist in a cascade of finger-tempting waves.

As children, he'd tugged on her hair plenty of times. He'd dipped the end of her braid into an inkwell just to see what color it would turn, and even threaded flowers into it one spring day when she declared she'd wanted a crown for her head.

Captivated, he wondered if the strands would feel as soft and silky now as they did then. Before he voiced his thoughts, Tia pushed open the screen and stepped back, allowing him to enter.

"Now, tell me what's got you on my doorstep before the school bell has even rung." Tia motioned for him to take a seat in the parlor.

He waited until she sat on the sofa then settled himself in a chair by the fire. The steady increase of his temperature caused by Tia's lovely presence forced him to shed his coat and scarf. Absently, he wondered if he'd taken ill with some malady. His stomach churned, his throat ached, and if he touched his forehead, he was sure it would be as clammy as his palms.

Briskly wiping his hands along the legs of his trousers, he inhaled another calming breath and met Tia's questioning gaze.

The sight of her smile, of those apple cheeks dusted with a light hue that put him in mind of summer peaches, sucked all the moisture from his mouth. As his tongue cleaved to the roof his mouth, he awkwardly swallowed.

"Tia, I..." Adam faltered, uncertain how to word his proposition. He cleared his throat and swallowed again. "This might sound a little strange... perhaps entirely daft, but I've come to care for Toby a great deal in the short time I've been back in town. The thought of his grandfather raising him, of taking him away from you, makes me angry. Toby belongs with you."

Tia sniffed and dabbed at the tears that suddenly filled her eyes. "Thank you, Adam. I appreciate your kind words."

"It's not just words I want to offer, Tia. It's me."

Confused, she cocked her head to one side. "You?"

Adam moved from the chair to sit beside her on the sofa, taking one of her delicate hands in his. "I'm saying this badly, but I've done little else than think on what Mr. Carlton said about a marriage being the simplest way to ensure the judge can't take Toby. Will you marry me, Tia? For Toby's sake? To keep him safe and here with you?"

Tia sat back, staring at Adam as if he'd begun speaking gibberish. Her gaze dropped to the hand he held between his. She'd always liked the way he held her hand, so gently, yet possessively. The roughness of his skin against hers felt so familiar and so right.

The one thing she'd wanted more than anything in her life was for Adam Guthry to ask her to be his wife. In fact, the entire last year they attended school, she hoped every single day would be the day Adam proposed to her.

When summer arrived with no hint of plans for a future together, Tia grew restless. Tired of waiting for him to get around to asking for her hand and fearful he never would, her grandmother insisted Tia go to Portland to visit her great aunt for a few weeks. Only she never came back.

Now, all these years later, Adam had finally asked the question she'd longed most of her life to hear.

And she had to tell him no.

"I can't marry you, Adam." Tia pulled her hand from his and slid back on the sofa, putting space between the two of them.

"Why?" Adam asked, taking her hand in his again, meshing their fingers together. Memories of all the times they'd sat with their fingers entwined made fresh pain arc through his chest.

"Because..." Tia scrambled for a reason. She couldn't verbalize a single one with Adam sitting so close, filling her nose with his manly scent and her heart with his willingness to sacrifice his freedom for her son.

"That's not a reason, Queenie." The teasing smile he gave her did great justice to the dimples in his cheeks while wreaking havoc on her ability to reason. "Please, Tia, will you please marry me?"

"I can't." She pulled her hand away again and rose, turning to stare out the window at the serene, snowy scene of her front yard. Chickadees pecked at the birdseed she'd helped Toby set out in a flat pan. The fluttering of vermilion wings added a splash of color to the blanket of white as two cardinals darted from the fence to another dish holding seeds.

Finally, she turned to face him. "It wouldn't be fair to you to accept your proposal of marriage for the sake of getting me out of this predicament." A sigh escaped her. She glanced down, brushing at a speck of lint clinging to the front of her deep green and navy striped gown. "It's a mess of my own making and I'll figure out how to deal with it. I could always take Toby and agree to live with Cedric and Catherine. At least that way, I know we'd be together."

"Until they kicked you out or found some other way to torment you." Adam got to his feet and moved until he stood so close to her, the toes of his boots touched the tips of her shoes beneath the hem of her skirt.

When she continued staring at her feet, Adam cupped her chin in his hand and lifted her head. He looked into her face and noticed the gown made her eyes look more green than blue — like the color of the river in deep autumn.

He'd always been fascinated with the shifting colors of her eyes. The hues ranged from gray to brown and everything in between, depending on her mood and what she wore.

"Look, Tia, I have no desire to marry anyone for love. Not today, not ever. Originally, I'd planned to remain a bachelor and become the doting, amusing uncle to any children Arlan and Alex may have."

A smile hovered on Tia's mouth and Adam sighed. "You'd actually be doing me a favor by marrying me. There's a bevy of misguided women trapped in the delusion they'll one day catch me. If we wed, they'd have to give up trying." The smirk he gave her followed by a rakish wink was pure male flirtation.

Pretending to be affronted, she took a step back and he dropped his hand. "It's nice to see you're as conceited as ever, Adam Guthry."

"Be that as it may, please think of what's best for your son. He'd be safe under my protection, and so would you. I'm not asking for a traditional marriage, Tia. Think of it as more of a business venture. You're providing assistance with my problem, and I'm helping with yours. No strings attached. No expectations. A marriage in name only."

The two of them stood quietly for several moments, studying each other.

"Where would you live?" Tia asked unexpectedly.

The fact she hadn't refused him again stirred his simmering hope. "Until I return to Portland after Christmas, I can stay at Alex and Arlan's home, unless you want me to stay here. My presence might deter the judge's hired thugs. You've got a spare room, don't you?"

The almost imperceptible nod of her head nearly missed his observation.

Fretfully, her fingers plucked at the thick green lace on the cuff of her sleeve. "What about after Christmas? You plan to go back to Portland. Would we stay here or go with you?"

"That's up to you and Toby. If you choose to stay here in Hardman, I'll make it a point to visit a few times a year. Not that I care one whit about what people say, but I wouldn't want anyone to think I'd abandoned you. If you'd rather come with me to Portland, that's fine, too. I live in a boarding house, but I've saved enough money to purchase a home. We could look for something near the river." Adam took both of her hands in his. "I vowed I'd take care of you, Tia, of you and Toby, and I mean to see it through. If you meet someone and fall in love and decide you want out of our farce marriage, you can always have it annulled."

Wounded he'd think she wouldn't take their marriage vows seriously, she frowned. She'd given him no reason to trust her, to trust she wouldn't run off and marry the first man who asked her despite how much she loved him. That was the very thing she'd done eleven years ago and it stood to reason he'd be wary of history repeating itself.

"Why would you do this, Adam? Why would you sacrifice yourself for a woman who doesn't deserve it? And don't give me any more nonsense about women chasing after you."

Adam looked long and deep into her eyes, wondering if she could see the love he still felt for her shining in his. "I'm not doing this for you. This is about keeping Toby where he belongs, and that's with you. He's already lost his father. That little boy deserves to grow up with the one person who loves him more than anything in this world. There's not a single thing the judge can say or do to convince me his reasons for wanting Toby are unselfish. From where I stand, this is about him flexing his power and proving he can run roughshod over people."

"You never did cater to bullies." Tia gave him a knowing glance. "If I agree to this, Adam, and that's a very questionable if at this point, I want you to rest assured I wouldn't make a vow to you unless I plan to keep it. If we wed, there'll be no request for an annulment from me." Not when marriage to Adam was what she'd always wanted. Nearly every girlish dream she'd ever had centered on being Adam's wife. "That's why I want you to be sure you won't regret doing this in a week or month or year from now."

"No, Tia. I won't regret it." Adam couldn't help himself. The need to touch her overrode common sense. His thumb traced over her cheek and along her jaw. "I'll ask one last time: Tiadora Elizabeth Meyer Devereux, will you please marry me?"

"If you're absolutely, without a doubt sure you want to be saddled with a wife and four-year-old son, then yes, Adam Gilbert Guthry, I'll marry you."

With a mischievous twinkle in his eye, Adam took a step closer and bracketed her face with his hands. "Shouldn't we seal the deal with a kiss?"

"I don't think that's a..." Whatever words she planned to say were lost when Adam touched his lips to hers in a kiss so sweet and gentle it made tears puddle in her eyes.

The look on his face as he raised his head and smiled at her made longings she'd forgotten existed swirl to life in her mid-section.

"Was that so bad?" Adam whispered, brushing his thumb across her lips.

Tia thought she might die from the bliss of knowing his touch again. Goose bumps broke out over her arms and a shiver of delight started at her head, working its way down to her toes.

A giggle from the doorway drew their attention to Toby.

"Hi, there, little man. How are you today?" Adam hunkered down and Toby ran straight into his arms. He lifted him up and gave him a hug.

"Are you gonna marry my mama?" Toby asked, leaning back in Adam's arms and staring at him.

"I sure am. Is that okay with you?"

"Mmm, hmm." Toby reached out to Tia. She took his hand in hers, kissing his fingers as the little boy grinned at Adam. "Can I marry you, too?"

Adam chuckled and tossed Toby into the air. "How about I take you both to the restaurant for breakfast? Have you eaten yet?"

"As a matter of fact, we have, but I'm more than happy to make you something, Adam." Tia moved toward the kitchen but looked back over her shoulder with a saucy smile. "Come in here while I fix you something to eat and we can discuss the terms of your surrender."

Chapter Nine

People strolling through town watched Ginny Stratton sprint down the street with her skirts flapping around her knees. Curious if some tragedy had befallen the Granger family, they stared as she made haste toward Luke and Filly's home.

By the bright smile on her face, though, it was evident whatever sent her racing pell-mell from one end of Hardman to the other was a happy occurrence.

Ginny slid on the ice and almost took a tumble before she regained her balance and ran toward the kitchen door of Granger House.

Luke's dog, Bart, lounged across the back porch steps. Ginny nimbly jumped over him and opened the door, slamming it shut behind her.

Wide-eyed, Filly glanced up at the sound from where she cut a pan of toffee into squares.

Swiftly removing her outerwear, Ginny walked across the kitchen and snitched a piece of the candy.

"Mmm. That is so good, Filly. What would we do without you to ply us with delicious treats?" Ginny leaned against the counter.

Filly grinned. "Not have nearly as many sweets to enjoy. I don't know how your brother has a tooth left in his head for all the candy and desserts he eats." Filly returned to cutting the candy. "Admittedly, I'm quite partial to his white-toothed smile."

"And the dimple in his chin and the sparkle in his eyes," Ginny teased. The adoration Luke and Filly shared for each other wasn't a secret to anyone in town.

"What brings you noisily into my house in the middle of the afternoon?" Filly set aside the knife and began placing pieces of the toffee into small tins.

Ginny helped herself to another piece of the candy. "I heard the most exciting news a few minutes ago. I'm waiting for Alex to let classes out for the day so we can start making plans."

Filly's hand stilled and she looked to Ginny. "Plans? Plans for what? You've already planned the skating party for next week and the week after that is Christmas. Alex has all the committees lined up for the Christmas Carnival on Christmas Eve. We're all helping with the program at church. What other plans are there? I'm not sure I can handle too many more unexpected activities and still bake all the treats you gluttons have come to expect."

Giggling, Ginny motioned for Filly to finish filling the tins as she hurriedly stuffed candy inside the one closest to her. "Blake and I were making furniture deliveries when Adam stopped us. He asked Blake if he could use some of his tools for a special project for Toby Devereux. Casually, Adam mentioned that he and Tia plan to wed. He wants to make something he thought the little boy will love."

"What? Adam's getting married? When did this happen?" Filly wiped her hands on a dishtowel and pushed Ginny toward the kitchen table. Hastily, she poured two cups of tea then sat down beside her. "Start from the beginning."

"That's all I know. Adam said he and Tia had, and this is his phrasing, 'come to an understanding,' and they planned to wed this Thursday."

"This Thursday?" Filly rocked back in her chair, shocked by the sudden nuptials. "Well, good gracious!

That doesn't give us much time to pull everything together."

She hurried across the room to a drawer, extracted a paper tablet and pencil then returned to the table. "Let's make a list."

"You can do the cake," Ginny suggested. "Put that at the top of the list."

Filly rolled her holly green eyes. "Cake, baked by me. What else? Do you suppose Abby has a gown in her shop that would fit Tia? Then again, Tia has so many lovely clothes, she probably already has something suitable." Filly laid down the pencil and let out a breath of air. "Oh."

"Oh? Oh, what?" Ginny nudged Filly's arm with her elbow. "Keep going."

"Well, don't you think before we get too carried away, we might want to speak with the bride-to-be? See what plans she's making?"

"You're right." Ginny's smile melted and her lips formed into the pout she'd perfected as a child. "It sucks all the fun out of it, but you're right."

"Why don't we round up Alex the minute school is out and visit Tia? The three of us can offer to help and listen to what she already has planned. After all, it is her wedding so we should let her decide what she wants."

"I agree." Ginny glanced at the clock on the wall and jumped to her feet. "I'll go fetch Alex since school will be out soon. Is Maura sleeping?"

Filly nodded her head. "She is, but she should awaken any moment. I'll bundle her up and leave her with her daddy at the bank. Luke won't mind. I'd ask Mrs. Kellogg to watch her, but she's gone to visit family for the holidays."

"I'm sure she's having a wonderful time, although that means more work for you around here. Are you finally going to cave to Mother's insistence you hire 'full-time domestic help,' as she puts it."

"I am not. I like taking care of my own home and doing my own cooking, although having help with the laundry and some of the other tasks a few days a week is nice. Mrs. Kellogg will be back after Christmas. I can muddle through that long." Filly carried their cups to the sink and cleaned up the last of the toffee mess. "You hurry to the school to let Alex know, and I'll see if Abby can join us after I stop by the bank. I'll meet you at Tia's."

"See you there." Ginny yanked on her coat and left in a flurry of swirling skirts.

Filly washed her hands, removed her apron, and hurried up the back stairs to the expansive room she shared with Luke. With fast movements borne from always being in a rush, Filly changed into a fresh dress and tidied her hair before entering Maura's nursery and finding the baby sleepily rubbing her eyes.

"Are you awake, Maura, love?"

The baby smiled at her mother and waved her hands, wanting picked up.

Filly changed Maura's diaper and gown before carrying her downstairs where she dressed them both in warm coats. She tugged a knit hat over Maura's curls and kissed the baby's perfect little nose, making her giggle.

"Shall we go see Daddy?" Filly asked, wrapping a knit blanket around her daughter before picking up a tin of the toffee from the counter and tucking it into a basket along with the tablet and her reticule.

"Dadda! See Dadda!" Maura bounced in Filly's arms.

"Off we go, sweet girl." Filly sailed out the door. As she stepped over Bart, she cautioned him to stay home and keep an eye on the house while she was gone.

When she opened the door to the bank, Luke stood and hurried around his desk, taking Maura in his arms while kissing Filly's cheek.

"What are my two best girls doing out and about today?" Luke removed Maura's cap and nuzzled her curls, inhaling the marvelous scent of his baby girl's head.

Maura patted a hand against his face, smiling and chattering in her own language.

"Your sister and I heard about Adam's upcoming nuptials and wanted to pay a visit to Tia, to offer our assistance with any wedding plans." Filly smiled at Arlan as he escorted a customer to the door then turned back to join the conversation.

"Adam stopped by earlier to share the news." Luke grinned at his wife. "I had a meeting with one of the silver mine supervisors for lunch today, or I'd have told you earlier. It doesn't surprise me at all that you and Ginny have somehow managed to become privy to the news and deemed yourself in charge of the plans."

Filly huffed. She would have swatted Luke on the arm if he hadn't been holding Maura. "Adam told Blake and Ginny. Of course, she came to tell me so we could offer to help. In fact, I need to hurry along so I can meet her at Tia's."

Arlan smirked. "Tell my wife she doesn't need to worry about dinner tonight. Adam insisted on taking us out to the restaurant to celebrate."

"How did you know Alex would be there?" Filly asked, setting the basket on Luke's desk. She removed her things and left the basket that contained diapers, extra pins, a tin of soft crackers, and a few toys for Maura. She kissed the baby's cheek then backed toward the door.

Arlan grinned. "Because you three come up with more schemes and nonsense together than you'd ever dream up on your own."

Filly scowled at Arlan, and then Luke when he barked with laughter. She shook a finger at him. "I'll not be gone long, so don't stuff our daughter so full of candy she won't want a bite of her dinner."

"Yes, ma'am." Luke winked at her then helped Maura wave goodbye as Filly rushed out the door.

Unable to believe Adam Guthry had shown up on her doorstep that morning and practically insisted she marry him, Tia didn't know whether to be elated or heartbroken.

On one hand, she couldn't be happier at the prospect of marrying Adam. It's what she'd always wanted. The moment she'd set eyes on him at Carl's funeral, all the love she'd held for him resurfaced, bubbling up to fill the empty caverns of her heart.

The sound of his voice, the warmth of his touch, the sight of that dimpled smile destined to weaken women's minds and resolve made her realize how much she'd missed him.

Other than keeping Toby safe by her side, there wasn't a single thing that would please her more than marrying Adam.

However, it devastated her tender heart to hear him admit the only reason for the proposal was to protect Toby. She'd hoped some little part of Adam still cared for her, still loved her.

Evidently, she'd done such a thorough job of destroying his love, not a smidgen of it remained, if he'd ever loved her.

Tia couldn't quite reconcile how she would marry Adam, knowing he'd never love her, never truly want her as his wife. Because he'd made a vow to keep her son safe, it seemed as if she'd be stealing his freedom, shackling him to her and Toby.

Adam was one of the few men who would keep a promise no matter the personal cost. He'd been that way when they were children. Apparently, his sense of loyalty and honor had grown nearly as big as the man himself.

For as long as Tia could remember, Adam had been dependable and trustworthy despite his drive to experience adventure. He'd never once let her down. She was the one who'd faltered, who'd failed them both so miserably.

In light of the second chance she'd been blessed with that morning, Tia intended to utilize everything in her power to do right by Adam.

He might be sacrificing his freedom for her son, but she'd sacrifice everything she was, every possession she owned, to bring him a measure of peace and happiness.

Determined to make the marriage work, despite Adam's refusal to love her, Tia sat down at the kitchen table.

Adam thought it would be nice to have a simple ceremony at the church with their closest friends and family followed by a small reception. He suggested they wed that Thursday, just three days away. After the wedding, he would send a telegram to Judge Devereux, letting him know he no longer had any chance of taking Toby.

Dazed by the sudden and unexpected proposal, Tia agreed to Adam's plans. Now, though, she wished she had more time to prepare for a wedding.

Even though she'd wed once before, it had been a quiet ceremony without a hint of celebration. For reasons that befuddled her at the time but later made complete sense, Patrick had insisted no one but Roland attend their wedding.

They'd stood before a judge at the courthouse and exchanged vows with Roland as their witness. Tia didn't have a fancy gown or a wedding cake, although Patrick had produced a small bouquet of yellow tulips for her to carry.

Overwhelmed by memories, Tia closed her eyes and took a deep breath. In need of a few quiet hours to gather

her thoughts and composure, she was grateful Adam took Toby with him for the afternoon.

She'd just filled the kettle to make a cup of tea when a knock sounded on the front door.

As she rushed to answer it, she pushed in a few loose hairpins and whipped off the apron covering her gown. She peeked around the edge of the drapes in the parlor to make sure the detestable Mr. Nivens hadn't returned.

The three women standing on the front step made her smile. She almost tripped over her skirts in her haste to open the door.

"What a treat to see all of you." Tia stepped back and motioned them inside. "Please come in."

"Hi, Tia!" Ginny breezed inside and hugged her enthusiastically. "We heard the news and came right over."

"The news?" Tia asked, confused.

"You did agree to marry Adam, didn't you?" Alex asked, removing her gloves and setting them along with her coat and hat on the hall tree.

"Well, yes, I did." Tia looked at each of them then laughed. "I forget how fast news travels in a small town."

Filly grinned and took Tia's hand in hers. "We're all so happy for you, Tia. Thrilled. We came to offer our services. If you need any help with wedding plans, we're happy to do whatever we can."

"And if you'd rather we mind our own business, you can show us to the door." Alex said, smiling at the woman who would soon be her sister-in-law. Alex had always wanted a sister. Now she'd have one who was sweet, kind-hearted, and fun.

Tia looped her arm through Alex's and led the way into the parlor. "I'd love some help. I was just sitting here, pondering how I'd pull together even a small wedding on such short notice. Any ideas you ladies would like to share, I'm open to suggestions."

Alex hugged Tia's shoulders as they sat together on the sofa while Filly and Ginny settled into side chairs. Filly set the tin of toffee on the table in front of her then took out the tablet she'd started making notes on at the house.

"Abby would have joined us, but her shop was full of customers and she couldn't get away. She did say if you need a dress, she will figure something out," Filly said, offering Tia an encouraging look.

"Oh, that's so kind. With the abundance of dresses I own, I'm sure something will suffice. In fact, before you ladies leave, perhaps you could help me choose the best one to wear for the wedding."

Ginny excitedly wiggled in her seat. "We'd love to. Filly volunteered to bake a wedding cake and I know some of the other women from church would be happy to contribute to a meal. We could have a nice luncheon after the ceremony if you wed in the morning or dinner if you decide on an afternoon exchange of nuptials."

"I think a late morning wedding would be best. That way, no one is out in the dark or cold if they are traveling from outside of town." Tia smiled at her friends. "I haven't done this before, so I'm not sure of the best thing to do."

"Didn't you have a big wedding when you married Mr. Devereux?" Ginny asked, leaning forward in her chair.

"No. We wed at the courthouse with only his brother present. Patrick didn't want his parents to know. I should have realized then that..." Tia swallowed back a sigh of regret. "Anyway, this is my first wedding in a church and the last time I'm getting married, so I'd like to make it special for Adam."

Tia glanced around at the women she considered dear friends. "I'm at your mercy. Tell me what you ladies have planned."

Ginny giggled and clapped her hands. Filly rolled her eyes and Alex grinned. "Well, what do you think about…?"

Chapter Ten

Adam stood at the front of the church with Arlan and Chauncy Dodd.

The pastor grinned and thumped him on the back. "Are you ready to do this?"

"If I wasn't, I sure wouldn't be standing up here letting Arlan choke the life out of me with this tie." Adam scowled at his brother as he adjusted the knot in the ascot tie around his neck, tightening it ever so slightly.

"I'm not choking the life out of you. You'd think a sailor, of all people, could execute a respectable knot for a tie." Arlan stood back and admired the deep green tie Adam wore. It looked festive against the white of his shirt and the dark gray wool of his suit.

Adam sighed and glanced down the aisle, wishing it would make Tia appear. The faster she made her way to him, the sooner they could exchange their vows and he could step out of the limelight.

He had no idea how Alex, Ginny, Filly, and Abby had managed to decorate the church with enough garlands and bows to please any bride. Someone had fastened a sprig of mistletoe tied with a red ribbon directly above where he would stand with Tia.

A wry grin touched his face as he glanced upward. Amused by the subtle prompt for him to kiss his bride, the addition of mistletoe to the décor was unnecessary. He could hardly wait to touch her lips again.

What he really needed was something that removed the consuming desire he felt for the woman. Every moment he spent in her presence made it multiply until Adam thought of little else but making her his own.

Thinly stretched, his self-restraint wouldn't last much longer. He had no idea how he'd live in the same house with Tia and refrain from touching her, loving her.

As people filed inside the church and settled into the pews, Adam glanced at Arlan. His brother offered him an encouraging nod.

Tia had left Toby in Abby Dodd's capable hands as she readied for the wedding. Alex would serve as her matron of honor while Filly and Ginny rushed around making last minute adjustments to their preparations.

Toby looked up from where he and Erin studied a picture book and waved at Adam. The little boy didn't seem to understand what would take place that morning between his mother and the man he continued to refer to as Mr. Adam.

"You'll be a good father to him, Adam," Arlan whispered as the last of the guests found seats. "It's in your nature."

"Thank you, Arlan. That means a lot coming from you. I have no idea what to do, but I figure Tia will let me know if I'm not doing what I should."

Arlan chuckled. "That she will." He tipped his head toward the back of the church. "Speaking of Tia..."

Adam turned his gaze to where the doors opened and Alex walked up the aisle in a deep red gown that accented her dark hair and the lively light in her eyes. Her gaze focused on Arlan, no doubt recalling their wedding that had taken place at the beginning of the year.

"Your bride is amazing and gorgeous, little brother." Adam cast a quick glance at Arlan.

"So is yours," Arlan said, watching the bride begin her walk down the aisle on the arm of Luke Granger.

Emotion clogged Adam's throat as he thought of all the times he'd imagined marrying Tia when they were young.

In his dreams, he'd never pictured her looking that beautiful. The light streaming in the church windows refracted from the rhinestones strewn across her cream silk gown. The delicate embroidery of white and silver threads made it appear as though snowflakes floated across her skirt and bodice with a rhinestone set in the center of each one.

A modified Elizabethan ruff gave her a regal air, although the layers of airy tulle ruffling around her neck and lining the top of her bodice were undeniably feminine.

Dazzled by her appearance and the gleam of her brown tresses caught in a loose bun at the back of her head, he noticed a thin shimmering band of rhinestones in her hair.

Adam glanced down as she lifted the bouquet of red and white roses she carried, offering him an appreciative smile.

Alex suggested Tia might like a bouquet so Adam sent a telegram to a hothouse in Portland and had the roses sent on the train. One of Alex's older students rode into Heppner to pick them up. Adam had no idea how Tom Grove got the bouquet back to town without the blossoms freezing, but the flowers looked like they'd just been plucked from a summer garden.

Adam glanced over at Toby when the child leaned close to Erin.

"My mama looks like a pretty doll," Toby declared. His loud whisper carried throughout the church. Adam agreed with the boy's assessment.

Entranced with his bride, she stole his breath away. When Luke placed her hand on his arm and offered him a teasing grin, Adam barely registered it.

Although he continued staring at Tia, mesmerized by the sparkle in her eyes that appeared almost golden in hue, he listened as Chauncy asked who gave Tia to be wed.

Luke cleared his throat and waved his hand around, to encompass everyone. "Her friends and I do."

Chauncy smiled and nodded his head, motioning for Luke to take a seat next to Filly and Maura.

The ceremony was simple and brief, but Adam took each word to heart. He didn't lightly make a vow to Tia. For as long as she'd allow, he would cherish and protect her.

After all, a vow was much more than a promise, far deeper than a commitment. It was a pledge, a troth to another, and Adam intended to honor every word.

Even if Tia never felt another ounce of love for him, he would shelter her from life's storms, encourage her dreams, and offer her a safe haven in his arms.

A broad grin covered Chauncy's face as he pronounced them husband and wife then instructed Adam to kiss his bride.

Heedless to those watching, Adam bracketed her face with his hands and slowly lowered his head to hers. He thought he heard Tia whisper his name in the moment before his mouth brushed against hers, softly, reverently. Love poured from his lips to hers at the tender connection.

When he lifted his head, Tia's eyes held such a look of longing, Adam almost ravaged her mouth right there, but a slap on his back from Chauncy disrupted the intimate moment.

"May I present Mr. and Mrs. Adam Guthry? If you'll please join us over at Granger House, a luncheon is ready for the enjoyment of all."

Adam secured Tia's hand around his arm and started down the aisle. He stopped and picked up Toby, giving the little boy a warm hug before the three of them made their way to the back of the church. They shook hands and accepted the well wishes of friends as people made their way out of the church and down the street to Luke and Filly's home.

Abby took Toby with her and Erin while Chauncy closed up the church.

Adam glanced at Tia's gown with the silk train shimmering in the midday light. "You look like a snow princess today, Tia. That's a beautiful gown."

She looked down at her skirt as it sparkled in the sunlight. "Thank you. I wore it to a holiday ball a few years ago. It seemed a shame not to wear it again, so I'm glad I saved it."

Adam studied her from head to toe. "Can you pick up your train?" he asked.

Tia gave him a curious glance, but leaned back and lifted the train, securing it with a hook so it didn't drag on the ground. When she finished, Adam winked at her and swept her into his arms, carrying her down the church steps and through town.

"Adam! You shouldn't carry me like this! Put me down!" Despite her fussing, Tia thrilled at the opportunity to be in Adam's strong arms.

When she'd first walked into the church with Luke, the sight of Adam in his finery caused her knees to wobble.

He was handsome on any given day, but the dark gray frock coat, double-breasted waistcoat, dark pants, snowy white shirt and dark green tie caught her by surprise. She'd never dreamed he'd appear so dashing dressed up.

Evidence of an attempt to subdue his hair into some semblance of order made her smile. Tia's fingers itched to reach up and muss it before Chauncy began the ceremony.

How she longed to be loved by Adam, to freely give her love to him, but that wasn't meant to be.

Nonetheless, accepting the crumbs of his affection seemed better than feasting on another's love. From experience, she knew no one would ever fill the place Adam had laid claim to in her heart. Too late, she realized she didn't want anyone else to try.

Part of her hoped Adam would return to Portland and agree for her to stay in Hardman. She couldn't fathom living in the same house with him, sitting across from him at the table every day, and not admitting how much she loved him, wanted him.

As he carried her through town to Luke and Filly's home, Tia glanced up and caught Adam's gaze. The brilliant blue of his eyes twinkled with humor while dimples popped out in his freshly shaven cheeks.

It would be so easy for her to steal a kiss, but she didn't. Instead, she grinned at him. "If you're not careful I might get used to this."

"It would be my pleasure, Queenie, to carry you anywhere you want to go." Heat turned Adam's eyes into liquid warmth as he stared at her.

Unnerved, Tia glanced at the bouquet she still held in one hand. "Thank you for the flowers, Adam. They're lovely, and so thoughtful. I didn't expect to have a bouquet."

Adam smiled, revealing his dimples again. "I know you didn't, that's why I ordered them. I'm glad you like the flowers. Alex thought they'd be festive, like Christmas."

"They are festive, and I love roses."

As they turned down the walk to Granger House, several people on the porch cheered as Adam carried her up the steps and inside the house. He set her down in the parlor where Toby ran over and gave her a hug.

Once Chauncy arrived, he asked a blessing on the meal and the group indulged in the lunch prepared by the women of the church who each contributed a dish.

After everyone had eaten, Filly brought out a multi-layered white cake embellished with frosting scrolls and one of the roses from Tia's bouquet.

"It's too pretty to cut," Tia said as Filly handed her a silver cake knife. The blade and handle bore etchings of hearts and vines. "You went to so much work, Filly. How can we thank you?"

"By cutting this cake, and having a happy ever after." Filly patted Tia's arm and stepped out of the way as Ginny nudged Adam next to Tia.

"You two share the first bite," Ginny said, giving Adam a sassy smile.

Adam placed his hand over Tia's as the knife glided through the cake. Carefully, she lifted out a small slice and fed him a bite then he gave one to her. The symbolic promise to provide for each other made an ache throb in Tia's heart. She knew Adam would honor his vows, would provide for her and Toby.

Regardless, what she really wanted was for him to love her. Even with just a smidgen of the love she thought he once held for her.

Swiftly tamping down her disappointment over what she couldn't have, she focused her attention on the guests. As a parting gift for all those who attended the celebration, Ginny and Filly stood at the door handing out paper cones full of spiced nuts.

When everyone had left, except for those Tia considered family, Luke ushered a photographer into the parlor.

The man had traveled from Heppner. He planned to stay a few days and take photos of any families who'd like to set up an appointment with him. Mrs. Ferguson at the boarding house had agreed he could use her parlor for the photograph sessions if he took one of her with her beloved cat.

As he set up his camera equipment in Filly's parlor, Tia turned to Adam with an expectant look.

"Did you do this?" Tia asked.

Adam nodded his head. "I thought it might be nice to have a photograph. We'll send one to the judge along with a copy of our marriage certificate. There will be no doubt, legal or otherwise, that you are now a married woman."

Taken aback by his thoughtfulness, Tia didn't know what to say. Before she'd adequately gathered her thoughts, the photographer moved her and Adam into position and took three photos, then he took a few of them with Toby.

Adam insisted Arlan and Alex join them for a photo, and one included them with the Granger, Stratton, and Dodd families.

Toby begged to have one with just him and Erin, so Adam agreed and asked the photographer to make two copies of it.

Adam paid the man and arranged to pick up the photographs from him Monday afternoon at the boarding house.

After the photographer left, Adam turned to Luke and Filly. "Thank you both for opening your home to us this afternoon. We appreciate your kindness and generosity."

"It was our pleasure, Adam." Luke thumped him on the back. "It's not every day there's a wedding in town. Besides, my sister and my partner's phantasmagorical wife joined forces with Filly, insisting this is the way things had to be."

Alex cocked an amused eyebrow at Luke. "Are you ever going to grow weary of saying phantasmagorical?"

Unabashed, he grinned. "Nope. Most likely not. In fact, someone needs to make sure it's engraved on my headstone." Luke straightened and slapped a hand to his chest. "'Here lies Luke Granger, a phantasmagorical wonder of a banker, husband, father, and friend.'"

Everyone laughed and Ginny tossed her gloves at him. "You forgot egotistical brother."

Luke handed her gloves back to her and reached out to muss her hair. Expertly, she ducked away from him.

"Now, Ginny Lou, that's no way to talk about your favorite sibling," Luke goaded her, using the nickname she hated.

"I'm fortunate you're my only sibling because I don't believe I could handle two of you." Ginny slipped her arms into the sleeves of the coat Blake held for her.

Alex and Arlan donned their outerwear while Chauncy and Abby put on their coats. Erin and Toby played with Maura in the foyer among the adults gathered there.

"Thank you all for everything you did to make our wedding so special and memorable," Tia said, ready to go home. The evening shadows had started to lengthen, chasing away the sun that warmed the December air earlier in the day.

"You're welcome." Alex hugged her shoulders and stepped outside with Arlan. The rest of them followed.

As the cold nipped at her cheeks and made goose bumps break out on her skin, Tia remembered she'd left her coat at the house, not wanting to wrinkle her gown before the wedding.

Now, she wished she could wrap up in its warmth.

Adam stepped beside her on the porch, recalled she'd not had a coat earlier, and swept her into his arms again.

"Adam, you can't carry me all the way home." Tia wrapped one hand around his neck, since the other held her bouquet.

"I can and I will. Those shoes you're wearing aren't fit for this kind of weather, although they are mighty fetching." Adam's eyes twinkled in the light from the street lamps as they reached the end of the walk. Toby skipped ahead of them with Erin, blissfully ignorant to anything else going on around him.

"Toby, it's time to go home, sweetheart," Tia called to him as they approached the Dodd family.

"We'd be happy to have him spend the night with us," Abby offered with a hopeful nod at Tia.

"No, that won't be necessary. You've done so much already. He'll be fine coming home with us." Tia smiled at her friend.

Toby scuffed his toes as he slowly moved to stand beside Adam. Erin's little lip puckered in a becoming pout.

"Maybe he can spend the night with you another time, Erin," Adam suggested.

Both children brightened and Chauncy winked at Adam. "I think that would be a great idea. You just let us know when. Toby's welcome anytime."

"Thank you. I better get my bride and boy home since she's trying to turn into an icicle out here." Adam smiled at the pastor and his wife. "Come on, Toby. Let's see how fast we can get back to the house."

The little boy trotted beside Adam as he hastened his pace, anxious to get Tia out of the freezing temperatures before she caught cold.

He also needed her out of his arms. The warmth of her body pressed against his chest while her scent invaded his senses made any number of thoughts flit through his head that would cause her to blush to the roots of her hair.

In record time, they hurried up the front steps of their home. Adam set Tia down long enough to unlock the door then swept her up again, carrying her over the threshold.

Reluctant to let her go, yet also relieved, he set her down in the parlor. While she helped Toby remove his coat and boots, Adam built a roaring fire in the fireplace and added wood to the stove in the kitchen.

Earlier that morning, he'd dropped off his things. Now, Tia showed him the room that would be his for the remainder of his stay in Hardman. While he'd much rather share the bed in her room, he knew that line of thinking would only get him into trouble and cause more heartache.

"Will this be comfortable for you, Adam?" she asked, waiting in the doorway as he stepped into the simply furnished room.

In addition to the bed, there was a washstand, a chest of drawers with a mirror, and a rocking chair beneath the window.

"It'll be fine, Tia. I don't need much more than a place to rest my head at night and the bed looks plenty comfortable."

She nodded and backed into the hallway. "If you need more blankets, let me know."

"I'll be fine. I sleep warm most of the time and end up tossing off my covers."

The vision of a tousle-haired, bare-chested Adam in her bed entered her head and made her step back so fast, she tripped on her skirt.

He reached out to steady her, and the touch of his hands on her arms seared her skin. From the way he dropped his hands and fastened his gaze on the floor, she wondered if he felt it, too.

Desperate to escape before she acted on her surging emotions, she cleared her throat. "I think I better change out of this gown. If you'll please excuse me…"

She'd taken one step down the hall when Adam's hand pulled her to a stop.

When she glanced back over her shoulder, she couldn't tell if mischief or longing made his eyes such a vibrant shade of blue. The reaction it stirred created a trembling in her knees and a quivering in her stomach that made her wish he'd take her in his arms and kiss her senseless.

For what seemed like half an eternity, his gaze held hers. Finally, he stepped back, breaking the spell they both seemed to be under. "Need any help?" he asked, flashing his dimples.

"No, sir. I do not." Marching down the hall, she shut her bedroom door with a firm click.

Adam chuckled as he returned to his room and removed his finery, changing into a soft flannel shirt and a pair of denims. He made his way back to the kitchen where Toby sat on the floor by the stove, petting Crabby and telling the cat all about the wedding and reception.

When Adam pulled out a chair at the table and took a seat, Toby wandered over and leaned against his leg. "Mr. Adam? Can I ask you a question?"

"Sure, Toby. What's on your mind?" Adam asked, lifting the boy to sit on his thigh.

"You married my mama today, didn't you?"

"Yep, I did." Adam glanced down at Toby's earnest little face. "Is that okay with you?"

Enthusiastically, the child nodded his head. "Mmm, hmm. My mama gets all moony when she sees you."

"Moony?" Unsure what Toby meant, Adam kept his expression amicable. "How does she get all moony?"

"Well..." Toby wiggled one foot and pulled a string from his pocket, wrapping it around two fingers. "When Mama sees you she's happy, and smiles, and she looks like this." Toby fluttered his eyelashes and affected a smoochy face that made Adam hold back a laugh.

A grin lifted the corners of his mouth upward as he bounced Toby on his leg. "Is that so?"

"Yep!" Toby giggled as Adam added a few wild movements to the bounces.

"What do you think it means — your mama being all moony over me?" Adam stopped bouncing his leg.

Toby quieted and crooked his finger, motioning for Adam to bend closer.

Adam leaned over until Toby's mouth was close to his ear. The little boy smelled of sunshine and sugar, most likely from the two pieces of cake he'd eaten.

"I think Mama loves you." Toby sat back and smiled at Adam. "Almost as much as I love Erin."

Adam lifted the string from Toby's hand and leaned over on one hip while balancing the little boy on his leg.

After taking a knife from his pocket, he cut the string in half then tied it into a reef knot. Intrigued, Toby watched his movements then took the string when Adam finished.

"Golly, Mr. Adam! Can you do that again?" Toby held the string out to him.

"I sure can. How about you call me Adam without the mister attached? Since I'm going to be living here with you and your mama, you don't need to be so formal."

Toby tipped his head thoughtfully to the side and studied the large albeit friendly man as he tied another knot in the string. "I forgetted. Why are you gonna live here?" The little boy liked the idea of this overgrown playmate staying at his house permanently.

"Because I married your mama today, it's my responsibility to take care of both of you." Adam tweaked Toby's nose, making him giggle.

"Are you my daddy now?"

Adam turned his attention from the Carrick bend knot he tied to the child on his thigh. "Would you like me to be your daddy?"

"Oh, yes! I would!" Toby wrapped his little arms around Adam's neck while wrapping himself around the sailor's heart.

Adam wrapped Toby in a loving embrace and held him for a long moment, thinking he'd never experienced anything quite so unabashedly superb as the youngster's hug.

The sound of a sniffle near the doorway drew their gazes to Tia as she dabbed at her eyes with a lace-trimmed handkerchief.

Adam and Toby both grinned at her.

"Hi, Mama!" Toby jumped down from Adam's lap and ran over to her, throwing his arms around her waist. "Adam showed me how to tie knots and he's gonna stay with us and take care of us and be my daddy!"

"My goodness. You two had quite a conversation while I changed my clothes, didn't you."

Adam expected Tia to be upset or disapprove of Toby's eagerness to have him fill the role of a father.

The ability for him to speak fled when Tia picked up Toby and winked at him. "I think that's grand, Toby. Why don't you call him daddy from now on?" Tia looked to Adam for agreement. "If that's okay with you?"

He nodded his head.

Occasionally, he'd imagined what life would have been like if Tia had married him instead of running off to Portland and marrying the attorney. In his dreams, he pictured them having a son, but nothing lived up to the reality of the sweet little boy Tia so willingly shared with him. Touched by her kindness, his heart ached with what might have been, what might still be.

Perhaps she'd never love him, but she had married him. That fact alone gave him hope.

"From now on, Toby, you can call me daddy or papa, if you like." Adam stood and ruffled the boy's golden hair.

"Hooray!" Toby cheered. "I have a new daddy!"

"You certainly do, baby." Tia kissed his cheek again then set him down. When she raised her eyes to Adam's, they held gratitude, warmth, and something else he was afraid to define.

The dark purple dress she wore brought out almost violet flecks in her ever-changing eyes. In the years he'd been away from her, he'd forgotten his fascination with the varying hues of her eyes.

Subconsciously, Adam leaned toward her, drawn to the amethyst color. Tia sucked in a gulp of air and stepped back, bumping into the wall. "I, um... I suppose I should fix something for supper, if you boys are hungry."

"I'm not hungry," Toby said, flopping down by the stove to pet Crabby. He puffed out his tummy, making it look full and causing Adam to chuckle.

Lighthearted and full of devilish charm, Adam moved closer to Tia. "I'm starving, but not for dinner."

Shocked by his implied suggestion, her eyes widened. While her heart encouraged her to explore his meaning, her head overruled. She playfully smacked his arm and stepped around him to make a cup of tea.

Adam let her go, wondering how much effort it would take on his part to woo his wife.

Later that evening, after Tia made popcorn for them to munch while they played a simple guessing game with Toby, Adam watched as she tucked the boy into bed. She read the little boy a story from *Granny's Wonderful Chair* by Frances Browne. He recalled his own mother reading the book to him and Arlan when they were young.

Leaning against the doorframe, he listened as Tia read one of the adventurous tales. Toby's eyes grew sleepy and drifted closed.

Softly humming a lullaby, Tia set aside the book, kissed her son's cheek, and adjusted his covers.

"Night, Mama," Toby whispered.

"Good night, baby. Have wonderful dreams." Tia rose to her feet from where she'd sat on the bed.

Toby opened his eyes and smiled at Adam. "Night, Daddy."

A lump lodged in Adam's throat as he pushed away from the doorframe and stepped across the room. He bent down and brushed his hand over Toby's head. "Good night, son. Sleep tight."

"I will." Toby's eyes fluttered closed and Adam started to stand, but a pair of little arms latched around his neck, hugging him tightly.

"I'm glad you're my daddy now."

Adam hugged the child then settled him back beneath the covers. "I'm glad I am, too, Toby. Rest well."

Content, Toby released a sigh and shut his eyes, rolling onto his side.

Adam studied him for a moment before silently walking across the room to join Tia in the hall. She partially shut Toby's door then motioned for Adam to follow her into the parlor.

"I need to thank you, Adam." Tia squeezed his hand as she sank onto the sofa.

Puzzled, he took a seat beside her. "For what?"

"For marrying me. For making it difficult for Cedric to take Toby away. Most of all, for being so kind to my son. He often mentions his longing for a father. He's chattered non-stop about you since the day the two of you met. You can't begin to know how much it means to him — to both of us — for you to allow him to think of you as his father." Tia's eyes burned as she spoke, overwhelmed by the emotions of the day and her love for the gentle giant of a man holding her hand so tenderly in his own. "If you never do another kind thing in your life, Adam, you've filled the quota today."

Warmed by her gratitude, Adam lifted the back of her hand to his lips and pressed a kiss to her soft skin. "I'm just getting started, Mrs. Guthry."

Tia sat back and sighed. "It might take me a while to get used to hearing that."

Adam stiffened, thinking she preferred the name of Devereux. As though she read his thoughts, she placed a hand on his arm and smiled. "I meant that I've been Tia

Devereux for such a long time and this has happened so fast, I've hardly had a moment to think about anything."

Reflective, she stared into the flames of the fire before the flicker of firelight in the stone of her wedding ring captured her interest.

She held out her hand and studied the rose-gold band set with a stunning oval opal. She'd never seen one so perfect and admired the delicate scrolls encircling the stone.

"It's a beautiful ring, Adam. Where did you find such a lovely one on short notice?"

Adam lifted her hand and stared at the ring for a moment, pleased by how right it looked on Tia's finger, how perfectly it fit, as he knew it would.

He brought her hand to his lips and kissed the ring, then the tips of each finger, fastening his gaze to hers.

Heat pooled in his belly and he fought to maintain his control, but he didn't let go of her hand.

After delivering a moist kiss to her palm, he gently set it on her lap and slid back against the cushions of the sofa. Before he surrendered to his longing to take her in his arms and never let her go, he needed to put some space between them.

"I've had that ring since a month before we graduated from school."

"What?" Tia sat up straight, seeming to shake off the trance Adam had so easily put her under. "You mean to tell me you've had this ring for eleven years?"

"Yes, ma'am." Adam leaned further into the cushions and settled an arm along the back of the sofa, turning slightly to look at her. "Remember when Arlan and I went to Portland with Mother the spring before we graduated?"

"Yes, I recall the two of you going. Arlan came home with a terrible cold and missed the spring dance, not that I think he minded terribly."

Adam chuckled. "No, he never minded missing out on dancing, although he did like to play his trumpet with the band."

"I've heard him play in the community band. He's still quite good."

Slowly, he nodded in agreement. They remained silent for several uncomfortable minutes until she spoke.

"Why, Adam?" Tia gazed at him imploringly while her heart thundered in her chest, afraid of his answer, afraid to hear the truth. "Why did you buy that ring?"

"I bought it for you, Tia."

Caught off guard, she swallowed hard and stared at the beautiful ring again. If she could have picked any ring in the world, it would have been that one.

For years, she'd hated the large gauche ring Patrick forced onto her finger the day they wed. She'd been relieved to remove it after his death. Not once had she ever admired it the way she did the ring currently on her finger.

Lit from within, the stunning opal reflected the glow of the fire, as if it held a shimmering mystery. The notion that Adam had not only purchased it for her more than a decade ago but also kept it made her heart as soft as butter in the warming oven.

"I don't understand, Adam," Tia said, unable to look at the man she so dearly loved. "It wouldn't have been an appropriate graduation gift, and even so, you didn't give it to me."

Unsettled by the prospect of baring his heart, Adam's foot jiggled nervously. "I didn't purchase it as a graduation gift. I bought it to slip on your finger when I asked you to marry me. In case you've forgotten, I loved you, Tia. I loved you with every ounce of love a boy that age could possess. I dreamed of spending my life with you, of building a future together."

Tia's head snapped up and she stared at Adam. Spluttering, she gaped from him to the ring. "But you never... you didn't... I would..."

Adam sighed. "I planned to ask you the summer after graduation. All of a sudden, you got it into your head to traipse off to Portland to visit your great aunt. You never came home." With nonchalance, he shrugged. "It was probably all for the best anyway. Obviously, we outgrew the childish infatuation we shared back then."

Devastated by his words, Tia slumped against the sofa cushions while all the color drained from her face. If she'd just waited another week, even another day before she left for Portland, she might have spent the last eleven years loving Adam instead of longing for something she'd never have.

Woozy from the unexpected and complete understanding of how deeply she'd hurt him, how stupidly she'd altered the course of her future, she felt sick to her stomach.

"Here, take a sip of this." Adam held a cup of tea out to her.

Tia took it with a shaking hand and sipped the lukewarm brew.

When Adam placed the back of his hand against her forehead, he frowned. "You feel a little warm, Queenie. Do I need to fetch the doc?"

On the verge of breaking down into uncontrollable sobs, Tia set the cup on the nearby table, got to her feet, and glanced down at Adam's bewildered face. "I'm fine, Adam, but thank you. It's been a tiring day. If there's anything you need to settle into your room, please let me know. Good night."

Perturbed by her abrupt departure, Adam watched her scurry out of the parlor.

With a dejected sigh, he stared into the fire, wondering how he'd manage to survive the remaining weeks until he could head back to Portland.

What he'd said to Tia was true. It probably was for the best she'd run off to Portland. If she hadn't, he'd most likely never have moved and found a job he loved so much.

It wasn't just the adventure of piloting a different boat every day. He loved being out on the river, riding the motion of the craft moving through the water. There was nothing like the sounds of the river whooshing by or the warmth of the sunshine on his face as he guided a vessel through the Columbia River Gorge.

Besides, if Tia hadn't run off to Portland and married the fancy pants attorney, she wouldn't have Toby.

No matter what had transpired, the little boy was a precious, precocious gift to his mother and, Adam admitted, to him. Although he'd only known him a few weeks, Toby had already taken a spot in Adam's heart, right next to the huge portion Tia unwittingly owned.

His words about outgrowing their childish infatuation rang with truth, as well. Oh, he'd loved Tia then. Absolutely, undoubtedly loved her. He would have married her, cherished her, and done his best to make her happy.

But what he felt for her as a boy maturing into manhood was nothing compared to what he felt for her now.

All the love he'd locked away poured out in a vast flood the moment he'd set eyes on her again. He'd tried to ignore it. To fight it. To shove his feelings back down into the empty black hole she'd left behind in his heart.

No matter how hard he tried, though, his love pulsed stronger and more insistently each time he encountered the woman and her adorable son.

The possible outcomes, the probable consequences of his brash decision to marry Tia to thwart the judge's despicable plans didn't concern him. Not nearly as much as the thought of leaving Hardman without staking his claim on the woman he loved.

Officially, legally, and undeniably married to her, Adam had no idea what to do with his bride.

Ruefully, he shook his head as he got to his feet and viciously poked at the fire. He knew what he wanted to do with her, but she held no interest in his amorous notions.

He had to make it through three more weeks before he could return to his job. In light of how distraught Tia seemed at the realization she was his wife, he planned to leave her in Hardman.

If she'd never open her heart to him again, he might as well put as much distance between the two of them as possible. Otherwise, he might lose the iron grip on his self-control and confess the depths of his love while ravaging her with kisses.

He'd greatly enjoyed the one they shared during the ceremony and had stupidly considered the many more he longed to lavish upon her.

Vaguely recalling his promise that it was a marriage in name only, Adam released a frustrated breath.

It would be pure torture to get through the holidays, trapped as he was with a woman he'd wanted to make love to since he was sixteen.

Toby served as a good buffer between him and Tia while the boy was awake, but how could he endure evenings alone with her if they all went as badly as this one?

After washing the few dirty dishes and putting them away, Adam banked the fires and moved with a weary tread to his bedroom.

The heart-wrenching sound of muffled sobs coming from Tia's room drew him to her door. He raised his hand to knock then thought better of it.

Convinced she still mourned her husband, Adam assumed her tears came from the hasty marriage she'd entered into with him.

Determined to harden his heart where she was concerned, he returned to his room and closed the door.

Chapter Eleven

Tia's hands shook so badly, she could barely unfasten the hooks of her dress. Once she finally yanked it off, she removed her underthings and slipped on a warm flannel nightgown then slid between the cool sheets of her bed.

Overcome with regret and longing for the man who'd never love her again, she turned her face into her pillow and sobbed.

The entire day had seemed like a dream. A wonderful dream that somehow made her feel seventeen again, just like the summer she'd spent running wild and free with Adam and Carl, secretly pondering what it would be like when she and Adam wed.

At that point in her life, she held no doubt that one day her last name would be Guthry and she'd be Adam's wife.

The entire last year of school, as she fell deeper and deeper in love with Adam, she kept waiting for him to propose.

Oh, she knew it was silly when they both were so young, but Adam was intelligent and hard working. When he wasn't at school or with her and Carl, he worked for a nearby rancher.

As a memory from the spring they graduated from school hit her with brutal force, she sat up in bed and lit the lamp.

Hugging her knees to her chest, she rocked back and forth, assailed by the past.

"Queenie! Come to the mercantile with me," Adam begged, tugging on her hand as she hung clothes on the line behind her grandmother's house.

"I can't, Adam. I've got to finish hanging the wash then Grandma wants me to weed the flower beds." Tia snapped a pillowcase and hung it on the line.

Adam handed her a clothespin and met her frown with a dimple-cheeked grin. "Aw, come on. I promise it won't take long. If you're worried about getting in trouble with your grandma, I'll ask her if you can go. I'll even help you with your chores."

Tia lifted the end of a sheet from the basket and handed it to Adam. She took the other end and together they hung it on the line.

When he smiled at her with those dimples, she couldn't tell him no. "I'll go, but we have to finish this first."

Adam helped her hang the laundry on the line then the two of them snuck out of the yard and ran down the street to the mercantile. When they entered the busy store, Adam maneuvered her over to a display case of jewelry.

As they waited for Aleta Bruner to help the customers already in line, they studied all the jewels sparkling in the case.

"That one's the prettiest," Tia said, pointing to an opal brooch.

Adam bent down and studied it. "Why do you like that one best?"

Tia shrugged. "I read somewhere opals symbolize hope. Wouldn't it be something to wear a little piece of hope every day?"

"It sure would, Queenie." Adam kissed her cheek and handed her a licorice whip before paying Aleta for the candy and walking her home.

Tia held out the ring on her finger and studied it.

Milky white, the opal almost looked like the polished surface of a tooth until she moved it into the light from the lamp on her bedside table. A rainbow of colors glistened in the shadows of her room.

Iridescent flecks reflected and refracted the light like a magical stone. Tears began anew as she thought about telling Adam an opal held hope all those years ago.

Now that she owned such a dazzling gem, she was utterly bereft of hope.

Long into the night, Tia cried out the disappointment she'd held in check, letting her tears soak her pillow until she had no more left.

Finally, she rose from her bed and moved on silent feet to check on Toby. Assured he slept peacefully, she brushed a lock of hair away from his forehead then left his room.

She made herself a cup of tea and took it to the parlor where she stoked the fire.

Curling into the rocking chair by the fireplace, she tucked her feet under her and draped a throw over her lap before turning to lift her cup from the table by the chair.

She nearly jumped out of the seat and barely suppressed a startled squeal when Adam handed her the cup.

"What are you doing up?" she whispered in a reproachful tone. Unsettled by his presence, she watched firelight play over the muscled contours of his bare chest.

Grateful he'd at least pulled on his pants before he scared her half witless, she ogled his form despite her intention to look away.

"I heard you up. Since I wasn't sleeping, I thought I'd check on you and Toby." Adam smirked as he took a seat in the chair on the other side of the fireplace and stretched out his long legs. "That boy is a sound sleeper."

"He always has been, even as a baby." Tia stared at Adam's bare toes, wondering how a man as big and brawny as him could always appear so graceful.

Like most boys, Adam had gone through a gangly stage in his teens when he was all long arms and big feet, but he'd grown out of it.

Entirely too well, if the swirling warmth in her midsection was any indication of the attraction he had the power to stir in her with his shirtless appearance.

"I'm fine, Adam. You should get your rest." Tia took a sip of her tea, hoping it would calm her fluttering nerves.

Adam had never made her nervous when they were younger. He'd always been her best friend, the one person in the world she could always count on.

However, the fidgety, invigorated feelings he inspired were undeniably new.

"I'll sit up with you for a while," Adam said, crossing his ankles and placing his hands behind his head as he leaned back in the chair. "I've been in there tossing and turning for a while anyway."

"Is the bed uncomfortable? Do you need more blankets? A different pillow?" Tia started to rise but Adam waved a hand at her, motioning for her to remain seated.

"No, Queenie, everything is fine. The bed's comfortable. I guess my mind just doesn't want to rest after everything that happened today." He glanced at the clock and grinned. "Well, technically, I guess it was yesterday. It's not every day a man finds himself married with a son."

Tia glared at him. "It's not every day a man takes on the burden of responsibility for a woman and child."

Adam dropped his hands to his thighs and leaned forward as his look turned from amicable to scolding. "You and Toby aren't a burden, Tia. I don't ever want to hear you say that again and I certainly don't want you to think it. If I didn't want to marry you, I wouldn't have asked. It's not a burden when you view something as a privilege. Do you think I woke up yesterday morning expecting that sweet little boy of yours to decide he wanted me to be his daddy? That's a blessing, Tia. A pure, unequivocal blessing."

Stunned, she gaped at Adam, unable to form a reply. Uncertain whether he spoke from his heart or just said words he thought she wanted to hear, something deep inside her soul whispered that she knew Adam. Knew him well enough to know he was honest and true. He'd never once given her a reason to doubt his words or his sincerity.

Finally, she found her tongue. "Thank you, Adam. Thank you for accepting Toby and making this sacrifice for him — for us."

Rather than give his longing to hold her free rein, Adam leaned back in his chair once again.

"Do you remember the time Carl decided we should build a raft and float it down the creek until we found a river?"

Tia relaxed and smiled. "Of course! We spent weeks gathering the material to make the raft and build it down by the creek. When we finally launched it, we made it what… a dozen or so yards before it capsized. We all took a dunking in the water with nothing to show for our efforts but some soggy ol' boards and snapped rope."

Quietly, Adam laughed. "At least now I could tie a knot that would hold." He sighed as his smile faded. "Carl always came up with the best plans for adventure."

Tia shook her head. "No. You were the one who typically led the tomfoolery. Carl and I would have blindly followed you anywhere."

"You both came up with plenty of ideas, too."

"You were the ringleader of our little band of hooligans. Ask Arlan if you don't remember correctly."

Tia thought back to the first time she met Adam. After her parents died when she was six, she came to live with her grandparents. The first Sunday she was in town, she walked into church, holding tightly to her grandmother's hand. They slid into a pew and the boy sitting in front of Tia turned around and grinned at her with a gap-toothed smile. His dark hair was a tousled mess, but he held out a peppermint drop to her and she took it with a grin. In that moment, she'd met her first friend in Hardman and the boy she'd love with all of her heart.

She watched Adam shiver in the midnight chill that settled over the house. "Would you like some hot tea, Adam? I could make you some hot chocolate or even warm up some broth. You're probably hungry, since we didn't have any supper."

"I wouldn't object to some hot chocolate and cake. It was nice of Luke to bring over several pieces." Adam rose to his feet and held out his hand to Tia. He wasn't really cold or hungry, but he liked the lighthearted conversation they'd had and didn't want it to end too soon.

"I think Filly and Ginny talked him into coming to check on us. The cake provided a good excuse," Tia said, wrapping the throw around her shoulders when she realized she'd left her robe draped across the end of her bed.

"Do you really think those two women would do that?" Adam waggled his eyebrows at her, making her laugh.

"I do. Although Ginny has changed significantly from her childhood years, she is still a very busy body." Tia poured milk into a pan and started to add wood to the stove, but Adam beat her to it. She offered him a nod of appreciation as she set about making the hot chocolate. As it warmed, she took out a platter with several slices of cake she'd tucked into the cupboard. She set one piece on a small plate and placed it on the table.

"Don't you want a piece?" Adam asked as Tia handed him a fork.

"No. I'm not hungry, but I will have some hot chocolate." She stirred the melting chocolate and watched as Adam waited for her to come to the table before he sat down to eat his cake.

Distracted by the sight of his half-naked form, she dropped the spoon into the pan and reached in to grab it out.

The chocolate mixture was hotter than she thought and she yanked her fingers out, blowing on the tips.

"Careful, Queenie." Adam's presence surrounded her as he took her hand in his and blew on her fingers.

The breezy warmth of his breath on her hand combined with his enticing scent caused goose bumps to break out on her skin while her legs trembled.

When Adam brought each fingertip to his lips and licked away the chocolate clinging to them, Tia thought she might collapse in a heap right there on the kitchen floor.

Her gaze shot to his but Adam kept his focus on her fingers, thoroughly licking each one before turning on the faucet and letting cool water run over her hand.

Without saying a word, he picked up a fork and fished the spoon out of the pan, stirring the contents and pouring it into the hot milk. He turned back to Tia and studied her as she remained at the sink with her fingers beneath the running water.

In truth, she hadn't burned them, but Adam's seductive attention to each finger left her so thunderstruck, she couldn't have told anyone her age, address, or even her name at that moment.

Certain he teased her with his flirting, she had to get her thoughts concerning him straightened out in her head. If she didn't, her heart would never survive until Christmas.

Women she'd once considered her friends when she lived in Portland would no doubt find Adam too rugged for their tastes. However, Tia thought he couldn't possibly appear any more appealing than he did at that moment.

Her perusal started at this thick dark hair and traveled down to his broad shoulders. She made note of the angry scar running down his back, wondering how he'd gotten it. The wound didn't offend her. Rather, it made Adam's past more mysterious.

While he stirred the chocolate, she studied the fit of his pants over his firm seat and the length of his legs, imagining the muscles the denim material covered.

Bewitched by his raw masculinity, she felt lightheaded. Then she made the mistake of glimpsing into his vibrant blue eyes. He winked and offered her a bow with a grand flourish.

"Milady, please be seated and I'll offer you a cup of refreshment." Adam affected an accent that sounded quite similar to Blake Stratton's.

Tia smiled and curtsied, mindful that Adam grew infinitely more alluring with every passing minute. At the rate things were progressing, she'd be on the floor at his feet, begging him to love her.

The vision that created caused her to stifle a giggle, although Adam heard it and turned from pouring hot chocolate into mugs toward her. "What's so funny?"

"You, us, this…" Tia waved a hand around the kitchen, unwilling to admit what truly made her laugh. "I just never pictured you serving me hot chocolate in the middle of the night while I'm such a mess."

"So you pictured me serving you hot chocolate in the middle of the night while you wore a ball gown?" Adam grinned as he set a mug in front of her and took his seat at the table.

"No, you nut." Tia giggled then clamped a hand over her mouth to muffle the sound. The last thing she needed was to awaken Toby. Even though the boy was a sound sleeper, as much noise as they'd made, she wouldn't have been surprised to see him stumble into the kitchen.

Adam cut a bite of the cake and ate it, closing his eyes as he enjoyed the treat. "Filly sure knows her way around the kitchen. She and Luke have had us over for dinner a few times, and I have to admit, I ate with all the restraint of Chauncy Dodd."

Unable to hold back her mirth, Tia laughed. "Surely not, Adam. No one is as bad as Chauncy when it comes to Filly's cooking."

"So I've heard, and even witnessed it one evening." Adam took another bite of cake. "Do you remember Filly from our school days?"

Tia offered him a befuddled glance. Filly was a few years older than she was, but Tia recalled all her fellow students. She couldn't remember a single girl named Filly.

"She went by Philamena back then," Adam said, holding out a bite for Tia.

Lost in her thoughts of trying to place her friend, Tia accepted the bite before she realized what she'd done. Adam smirked at her with a look of smug victory and licked the fork before plunging it back into the cake.

"Wasn't there a girl named Philamena Booth?" Tia asked.

"That's Filly. Her father imprisoned her on their farm right after her mother died until Luke rescued her not long before they wed. Arlan gave me the particulars, but Luke doesn't like folks to know about Filly's past because her father was the town drunk for several years. He's afraid people will judge her for that instead of love her for the sweet woman we all know."

Tia stared at him a moment. "I had no idea. Of course, I remember Alford Booth, but I had no idea what happened to Philamena. She just sort of disappeared and since she was older than us, I never gave it much thought." Tears filled Tia's eyes. "How horrible for her. Oh, I feel so bad I didn't realize... that I didn't..."

Adam settled his big hand on top of hers as she traced the pattern of the cloth covering the table. "No one knew, Tia. Oh, a few people, like Chauncy, knew Filly lived out on the farm, but no one knew Alford kept her imprisoned there. If we'd known, realized what she'd endured, I like to think some of the men in town would have taken action. The sheriff would have done something, I'm sure. He's a good man."

Tia nodded her head as she fought for control of her emotions.

Adam patted her hand and returned to his cake. "Besides, Filly seems perfectly happy with life now. I bet if you asked her, she'd tell you she wouldn't trade the past for anything because it brought her the gift of the present."

Mindful that Adam tried to take her mind off what must have been a horrific experience for their friend, she let him. "Aren't you turning philosophical in your old age?"

"Old age?" Adam slapped a hand to his impressive chest. "How dare you call me old when you're older than me by twelve days?"

"Then we're both bordering on ancient," Tia teased, sipping her hot chocolate and wishing there was some way to preserve the spirited exchange with Adam for days when her heart weighed heavy.

"I refuse to accept either title. I much prefer to be lumped in with the youngsters."

Tia raised her eyebrows and shook her head. "That isn't going to happen, my friend." There wasn't a single possibility of anyone confusing the spectacular man Adam had become with a boy.

As they drank hot chocolate and ate cake, they recalled more funny stories from their childhood.

Finally, Tia let the fatigue she'd fought for hours settle in. When she yawned, then yawned again, Adam offered her a sympathetic look.

"It's been a long day, Tia. Go to bed. I can wash the dishes." Adam stood and carried their mugs to the sink.

"Oh, just leave them until morning. I'll wash them with the breakfast dishes." She rose to her feet and returned to the parlor where she left the throw over the end of the sofa and banked the fire while Adam attended to the one in the kitchen.

The clock above the mantle chimed twice and Tia sighed. Toby would be up and ready to face the day in four short hours.

"You better get some sleep while you can. I have an idea that little man of yours is an early riser." Adam's voice near her ear made Tia jump. She pressed a hand to her throat in a vain effort to still her pounding heart.

"You almost scared the dickens out of me, Adam Guthry."

He chuckled and put a hand on her back. The heat of his touch gave her a moment of concern, sure he'd burn a hole right through her nightdress with just his fingers and the palm of his hand.

Sensations she'd never experienced made her arms and legs completely languid, like she trudged uphill through a stream of molasses.

Discombobulated, she tripped on the hem of her gown. Adam wrapped his arm around her waist, pulling her back against his chest and preventing her fall.

Teetering on the edge of panic, Tia took a deep breath and nearly drowned in Adam's beguiling scent. She'd never, in her life, felt anything as tantalizing as Adam's chest pressed against her back. The hard contours of his solid frame scorched her skin through her nightgown.

Quickly sucking in a gulp of air, she somehow mustered the strength to step away from him. "Thank you, Adam. That surely would have awoken Toby if I'd fallen."

"You're welcome. Do you need me to tuck you in?" Although his voice held a teasing tone as they spoke in hushed whispers, Tia could see an intense glow in his eyes from the light of the small lamp she carried in her hand.

Miraculously, she hadn't dropped it when she tripped.

With the conclusion she'd tested her luck and self-control enough for one evening, she hurried down the hall to her room.

Adam followed behind her, stopping in his doorway as she turned back to him. "Thank you, again for everything. Rest well."

Tia shut her door and leaned against it for several minutes before she moved to the bed and fell into an exhausted slumber, dreaming of her new husband.

Chapter Twelve

"Hi, Daddy!" Toby said as he raced into the kitchen the following morning.

Surprised the boy remembered their conversation from the previous day, Adam set down the newspaper he'd been reading and opened his arms to his new son. "Hi there, Toby. Did you have good dreams?"

"Yep," the imp said, settling himself on Adam's thigh. "I dreamed you were my daddy now. Then I woked up and you are!"

Adam chuckled as he tweaked the child's button nose. "I sure am." Despite Tia's predictions her son would rise early, the boy had slept until well past seven.

Gulping the remainder of the coffee in his cup, Adam jiggled Toby on his knee. "What do you think of starting the day with breakfast at the restaurant?"

"Really?" Toby asked, wide-eyed.

"Really. Let's get you dressed and we'll go eat while your Mama sleeps. So be very, very quiet. We don't want to wake her up."

Adam set Toby on his feet then stood, hiding a grin as the little boy tiptoed down the hall with exaggerated movements to his room.

Quickly helping the child dress, Adam escorted him to the bathroom where Toby made use of the facilities.

Bleary-eyed from lack of sleep, Adam leaned against the door and watched as the boy washed his face, brushed his teeth and combed his hair unassisted. He figured Toby's hair appeared more tamed than his did, even before the child ran a comb over his golden locks in a haphazard fashion.

As they walked past Tia's bedroom door, Toby looked up at Adam and touched his index finger to his lips, indicating they should be quiet.

Adam nodded in agreement.

Back in the kitchen, he helped Toby on with his coat and boots then shrugged into a chore coat he'd purchased after the first day of shoveling sidewalks in his pea coat.

The realization that Tia would be frantic if she awoke to find Toby suddenly gone sent him hurrying to the small writing desk in the parlor. He located a sheaf of papers along with an inkwell and a pen.

The delicately carved desk chair groaned beneath his weight as he sat down to scribble a note to Tia.

He left it on the kitchen table, setting his coffee cup on it to keep anything from blowing it off.

After tugging on Toby's mittens, Adam opened the back door and the child rushed outside. He glanced at the cat, curled in his box by the stove. "Come on, Crabby. Time for you to get some fresh air and sunshine."

Lazily, the cat stood and stretched out his front paws, arched his back, and wiggled his hind end before stepping out of the box and sauntering to the door. He glanced up at Adam and meowed once on his leisurely jaunt across the floor.

"I see we're going to have to work on your ability to hustle out the door, Crabby." Adam grinned as the cat stopped in the middle of the doorway and sat down to lick his paw.

When he used the toe of his boot to scoot the cat outside, Crabby scowled at him. The feline stalked down the steps and minced his way through the snow to the bushes behind the house.

"Mama says Crabby likes to do things his way," Toby said as he ran up to Adam and grabbed his hand.

"I'm starting to see that," Adam said, smiling down at the boy. "Are you hungry?"

"Yes, sir!" Toby jumped off the porch step and skipped along, staying close to Adam.

"What are you going to have for breakfast? Do you like pancakes?"

Toby stuck out his tongue and licked his upper lip with wide blue eyes. "I love pannacakes."

"Me, too." Adam grinned as the little boy tugged on his hand to hurry up. Lengthening his stride, Toby jogged beside him, eager to reach the restaurant.

The child almost ran out into the street in front of a wagon, but Adam kept a firm grip on his hand. "Whoa, there, little man. Let's wait for the wagon. Your mama would lock me out of the house if I let you get smashed before we can even eat breakfast this morning."

The boy gazed up to him with such trust and unfiltered love on his face, it made Adam's heart skip a beat.

He'd never spent much time around children, yet he enjoyed being with Toby. Unable to discern if part of that was because the boy belonged to Tia or because of his own unique personality, Adam just knew his heart felt lighter when he was around the rascally little fellow.

When they entered the restaurant, a waitress nodded at Adam to acknowledge his presence. She set down the plates of food she carried at a table with three men.

Toby balanced on one foot then the other as they waited for a seat.

Once the waitress showed them to a table, Adam helped Toby remove his mittens, coat, and hat before he took off his own coat and scarf, realizing he'd left his hat at Arlan's house. He'd stop by and fetch it on his way back to Tia's.

The waitress placed a padded wooden block the width and depth of the seat on a chair. Adam set Toby on it before he scooted in the child's chair.

Toby grinned and picked up his napkin, draping it across his lap with great care.

Adam hid his smile by studying his menu. He read off the selections to Toby but the little boy remained firm in his decision to have pancakes.

The waitress returned to their table, bringing Adam a cup of coffee and Toby a glass of milk. "What would you two men like this morning?" she asked.

"Two orders of pancakes, make mine a double order, please, and a large side of bacon with eggs." Adam handed the waitress his menu and winked at Toby. "You think that will hold us until lunch, Toby?"

"Yep!" Toby grinned at the waitress and Adam watched her visibly soften. She reached out and ruffled the child's hair before hurrying back to the kitchen with their orders.

"What do you and your mama do to pass the time?"

Toby gave him a confused look.

Adam realized he needed to be more mindful of how he worded things. Although Toby had an expansive vocabulary, he was only four. "How do you and your mama spend the day?"

"Oh, I understand." Toby took a gulp of his milk and set down the glass, politely wiping his mouth on his napkin.

With self-mockery, Adam decided he could learn a thing or two about manners from the child.

Toby smiled at his new father. "Mama and I have breakfast then I take care of Crabby." Toby leaned closer to Adam. "Can you keep a secret?"

"I sure can," Adam whispered back to the boy.

"Mama doesn't make very good pancakes. She thinks I don't like them, but I just don't like the way she makes them." Toby wrinkled his nose. "She makes lots and lots of other good things, though. It's important for a mama to make good food for a daddy, isn't it?"

Adam nodded his head, forcing himself not to chuckle. "It is important. I'll remember not to request pancakes, though. Once in a while, you and I can eat breakfast in a restaurant and have pancakes. That way, we won't hurt your mama's feelings. It's very kind of you, Toby, not to tell her you don't like the way she makes them."

Toby beamed at Adam's praise. "My mama tries hard. I don't want to make her sad."

"Me neither."

Toby gazed around the restaurant then rubbed a little finger across his chin as he studied the other patrons. "I'm glad you married us and like my mama. She cries a lot when she thinks I'm asleep, but I know you can fix her."

Under the assumption he'd made things worse instead of better, it stroked Adam's ego to know Toby had faith in his abilities to heal Tia's wounded heart. The fact her son thought she needed to be fixed caused Adam to be both humored and concerned.

"I'm sure your mama misses your father a lot," Adam commented, taking a sip of the hot coffee.

Toby shook his head. "I don't think so. Mama said my father was always busy with work and didn't spend much time with us. My uncle Roland was heaps of fun, though. I miss him. He died, too."

"I heard about that. I'm sorry, Toby. Your mama said he used to take you to the zoo. What was your favorite animal?"

Toby leaned his elbows on the table as excitement flooded his face. "The bears. Uncle Roland let me see them for as long as I liked. Grandfather took me once, but he didn't let me stay long. Grandfather does this a lot."

Toby crossed his arms across his chest, pushed his eyebrows together and scowled.

Adam had all he could do to hold back a laugh at the boy's comical expression. At his nod, Toby continued. "But Uncle Roland and I watched them and watched them. They look like this..." Toby held his arms over his head and curled his fingers like claws then opened his mouth wide and growled, swaying back and forth in his chair.

In his exuberant movements, he almost tipped out of the seat, but Adam grabbed him before he fell to the floor.

Toby clung to his arm then swung back onto his chair. "Thanks, Daddy. I almost splattered."

Adam chuckled and scooted Toby's chair a little closer to his, realizing he had much to learn about caring for a young child. "You are welcome. It would be a shame to have a splattered boy before we even eat our breakfast."

The waitress arrived with their food. Toby waited while Adam asked a blessing on the meal before picking up his fork and cutting into his pancakes. Adam placed a slice of bacon and a forkful of scrambled eggs on the child's plate before tucking into his food.

Toby ate most of his pancakes and another piece of bacon, surprising Adam by the amount of food he put away.

Glad to see the boy was a good eater, Adam finished his coffee while Toby drained his milk glass and wiped his face on his napkin.

"Shall we go for a walk before we head home?" Adam asked after he paid the bill and helped Toby put on his coat and hat.

The little boy tugged on his mittens as he glanced up at Adam. "May we? May we walk past Erin's house?"

"I think that can be arranged."

"Oh, goodie!" Toby pulled on Adam's hand as they stepped outside the restaurant. They sauntered to Arlan and Alex's house where Adam retrieved his hat while answering multiple questions from Toby.

"Is Mr. Arlan your brother?" Toby asked as they walked back out to the street. "He looks like you."

"That's right, Toby. Arlan is my brother, so that makes him your uncle and Alex your aunt."

"You mean I get a new daddy and an uncle and aunt?" Wonder filled the boy's voice as he stopped and stared at the big man beside him.

Adam swung Toby into the air and settled him on his broad shoulder as they resumed their jaunt through town. "You sure do."

"I've never had an aunt before. Will Aunt Alex like me?"

"She already likes you," Adam assured the child. In fact, he didn't think there was a child in town Alex didn't like. Although he'd noticed she had a few favorites like Percy Bruner, the son of the mercantile owners, the little Jenkins girl, and Tom Grove.

Despite the tales around town about Fred Decker being a holy terror, Alex seemed to have tamed the beast well enough. After Alex and Arlan helped send his outlaw father to prison, the boy and his mother had both settled down considerably.

"I like her, too. Mama said next year I'll go to school. I hope we live here so Aunt Alex can teach me."

"Everyone says she's a very good teacher."

Toby nodded in agreement. He bounced and thumped Adam on top of the head with his hand as he caught sight of Erin Dodd walking along the boardwalk with her father. "Oh, Daddy! It's Erin! Can we see Erin? Please?"

"We can if you settle down and quit beating my head." Adam crossed the street in a few long strides and set Toby down so he could give Erin a hug as she and the pastor approached them.

Adam shook hands with Chauncy and pointed to the two little ones, happily chattering with each other.

"Beautiful morning, isn't it, Adam." Chauncy smiled, glancing around him for Tia. "Where's your wife?"

Adam swallowed hard at the mention of his wife. He still hadn't quite come to terms with the fact he was not only a married man, but wed to the woman who'd haunted his dreams since he was a teen. "Yesterday was quite exhausting for her, so Toby and I decided to let her sleep in this morning."

"A long night?" Chauncy teased, elbowing Adam in the ribs.

Adam scowled at him. "It's not... it wasn't..." He released a sigh. "She needed her rest. Let's leave it at that."

"Whatever you say." Chauncy held out his hand toward his daughter. "Come on, sweet pea. We need to get going."

"But, Daddy," Erin whined. "Can't Toby and I play?"

"Not today, pumpkin. Maybe another day."

Erin's bottom lip rolled out in a charming little pout that would have softened the most hardened heart.

Her father appeared immune to her manipulative tactics as he took her hand and grinned at Adam. "We'll have to plan a play date another time."

"Sure, Chauncy. Just let us know. I'm sure Tia would be happy to have Erin visit." Adam tipped his hat to Erin and winked at her, turning her pout into a smile.

"Your new daddy is pretty, Toby." Erin giggled then skipped down the sidewalk with her father.

"I thought girls were pretty," Toby said as he took Adam's hand and they meandered toward the mercantile.

A disquieting feeling settled over Adam. He covertly glanced back over his shoulder to see Mr. Nivens sneaking along behind them. If the man thought he'd snatch Toby on Adam's watch, he'd better think twice.

Unobtrusively changing direction, Adam made his way to the bank. When he opened the door and ushered Toby inside, Luke and Arlan both stared at him in surprise.

"Good morning, Toby." Luke hunkered down and greeted the boy with a friendly smile. "Are you helping Adam today?"

"Yep. Mama's tired so we're letting her sleep. That's what nice mens do."

Luke choked back a laugh and waggled an eyebrow at Adam. "You're right. That is what nice men do, especially if they're the reason your mama is so tired today. The day after her wedding... to Adam... as his wife."

Adam glowered at Luke. "That's enough discussion about my wife. I was hoping the two of you could keep an eye on Toby for a minute."

Toby's little brow puckered into a frown. "Are you leaving me here? Aren't you having a good time with me?"

Adam picked up Toby and cuddled him to his chest, wondering how the boy had worked his way so thoroughly and completely into his heart in such a short time. "I'm not leaving you here, Toby. I saw someone outside I need to speak with and I don't want you to get cold while you wait. I thought you might like to visit Uncle Arlan and have him show you how he opens the big safe here at the bank."

"I can watch you open the safe?" Toby turned to Arlan, captivated by the idea.

"You sure can. Come on. I'll show you how it works." Arlan held out a hand to Toby.

The little boy hugged Adam then wiggled down and hurried over to his uncle. "I can't wait to tell Erin."

Luke walked Adam to the door, realizing something was amiss. "What's wrong?"

"Mr. Nivens, the judge's hired man, has been following us around town all morning. I thought he might

151

have left town. No one's seen him since the cat attacked him." Adam inconspicuously glanced out the window, seeing the man in question hiding around the corner of the building across the street. "Evidently, he hasn't given up yet."

"Do you need some help?" Luke asked, tipping his head in the direction Adam indicated.

"I think I can handle him, but I'm trying to figure out how to sneak up on him. If I walk out of here without Toby, he'll know something is up."

Luke pointed to the back of the bank. "Come on. I have an idea."

At the back of the bank, Luke pushed away a false wall, revealing a hidden door. At Adam's questioning look, Luke shrugged. "You never know when you're going to need an escape route."

Luke unlocked the heavy metal-lined door and slid it back, glancing both ways in the alley. No one was around so Adam stepped outside and kept to the alley until he made his way a block down the street.

Using a passing wagon for cover, he crossed the street and went down another alley, coming up behind Mr. Nivens. The idiot did a poor job of hiding in the shadows across from the bank.

Adam wrapped a hand around his neck and jerked him back before the man had time to react.

"Mr. Nivens, I have a message for you to give your employer. If he ever wants to see his grandson again, he will leave Tia and the boy alone. They will arrange to visit him when they are good and ready and not a minute before. He has no right to that child and he never will."

Adam gave the man a shake. "Is that understood?"

The man bobbed his head up and down as best he could with the stranglehold Adam had on his neck.

"Tia and Toby are under my protection now and I won't stand for any further interference from the judge.

You make that clear to him. If he tries anything, anything at all, they'll disappear and he'll never see that child again. Not ever." Adam turned loose of the man's neck and spun him around. "I better not see you around town again. If I do, you might live to regret it."

"You don't know who you're messing with," Nivens sniveled as he backed away from Adam. "The judge isn't gonna like this one bit. My orders are to come back with that boy and the judge doesn't particularly care how I get him."

"Unless you're deaf, I'm not repeating myself. Now haul your sorry backside out of town while you still have the opportunity to leave in something besides a pine box."

Adam pushed past the man and started back across the street when he heard a loud pop. Pain burned across his left side.

He glanced back as Nivens holstered a gun and turned away with a sneer. Adrenaline shot through Adam and he took three running steps, tackling Nivens before he could get away.

"I suppose I should thank you for being a terrible shot," Adam growled as he punched Nivens in the face repeatedly. A hand on his shoulder stopped him and he glanced up at Arlan.

"Stop, Adam. He's unconscious." Arlan stared at the man. "He won't appear quite the same with that broken nose."

"I don't rightly care." Adam staggered to his feet and fought a dizzy spell. When he swayed, Arlan noticed the blood dripping from his side.

"He hit you? Luke and I heard the shot, but thought he'd missed." Incredulous, Arlan started to wrap his arm around Adam, but his brother pushed him away.

"I'll be fine. Can you haul this piece of garbage down to the sheriff's office? I guess I should probably have the doc stitch this up before I head home. I don't get the idea my wife would appreciate the job."

Despite the situation, Arlan smirked. "I don't believe she would. Luke can get the sheriff while you and I go visit Doc. It'll just take…"

Arlan glanced up as the sheriff ran their direction along with a few of the townsfolk.

"What's going on out here?" The sheriff took in Adam's pale face and the blood-drenched snow around him as well as the man he'd searched all over town for twice after he attempted to attack Tia.

"I see you found Mr. Nivens. Mind if I take him off your hands?" The sheriff grinned at Adam as he motioned to Douglas from the livery to help him drag the man back to the jail. He studied Adam a moment and shook his head. "You better have doc take a look at that wound. You wouldn't want to make your new bride handle that mess."

Adam sighed as Luke hurried outside with Toby. He stopped to lock the bank door then followed the little boy as he raced over to Adam.

Tears streamed down the child's face as he studied his new father. "Are you going to die, Daddy?"

"No, Toby. I'm not going to die, but I do need to go visit the doc and have him fix this scratch. Do you want to come along?" Adam tried to offer the child a reassuring smile while he grew increasingly lightheaded.

"Sure!" With the morbid curiosity of youth, Toby brightened at the prospect of watching the doctor in action.

"Toby, you hang onto my coat while Mr. Luke and I help your daddy to the doctor's office," Arlan instructed as he got on one side of Adam and Luke took the other. Together, they half-dragged Adam to the doctor's office.

Since the office was empty, Doc ushered them into an examination room.

Luke tried to get Toby to go with him to the waiting area, but the boy refused to leave. "It's okay, Luke. Thank you," Adam said with a clenched jaw as the doctor helped him remove his coat and shirt.

"Try to stay out of trouble for the rest of the day," Luke grinned as he left, returning to the bank.

Arlan watched him leave then smiled at Toby. "You want to go with me to get Adam a shirt and coat."

"No. I'm going to stay right here with my daddy. He might need me." Toby crossed his little arms over his chest and widened his stance.

Arlan nearly choked watching him. Adam always made the same move when he stubbornly refused to change his mind. Amazed by the similarities between the golden-haired boy and his dark-headed brother, Arlan nodded his head.

"Okay, Toby. You keep a good eye on my brother until I get back."

Solemnly, Toby agreed. "I will, Uncle Arlan."

"Don't bother with a coat, Arlan. Just bring me something to wear home," Adam said, staring at his brother.

Arlan nodded his head then rushed out as the doctor studied Toby. "Young man, if you think you could climb up on that chair, you can help me stitch up Adam."

When Toby rushed to do as he asked, the doctor chuckled. "You better take off your coat and mittens first, son."

Toby yanked off his mittens and nearly ripped the buttons off his coat in his haste to remove it. When he'd tossed everything into a corner out of the way, he scrambled onto the chair the doc had moved near the examination table, yet out of his way.

While Toby removed his outerwear, Doc had cleaned the wound. Fortunately, for Adam, it grazed along his side. Although it had missed his ribs and hadn't hit any organs, the flesh wound wouldn't heal well without stitches.

"We better wash your hands first, Toby." The doctor helped him scrub his fingers and dry them before setting him back on the chair.

The doctor laid a pair of scissors, bandages, and gauze on a tray then handed it to Toby. "Can you stand right here beside me and hold that tray? It would be a big help, Toby."

"Yes, sir." Toby held very still, watching the doctor insert the needle and thread into Adam's skin and pull the edges of the wound together.

Adam sucked air through his teeth then glanced over his shoulder at Toby and winked at him. "This is quite an adventure for our first day as father and son."

"Only you could get shot the day after your wedding while taking a boy out for breakfast." Doc mused as he stitched the wound. When he'd made a dozen neat stitches, he knotted the thread and cut the end. He rubbed an ointment over the wound then covered it with gauze and wrapped a bandage around Adam's midsection to hold it in place.

Once he'd secured the end of the bandage, he took the tray from Toby and set it on the counter. He washed his hands then opened a drawer and removed a peppermint stick, handing it to the child. "You did a fine job, young man. Thank you for your assistance."

"Thanks for letting me help, Doc!" Toby jumped off the chair and stuck the candy in his mouth, sucking on the flavorful stick.

Doc turned back to Adam. "You make sure that bandage gets changed daily and if it feels hot or looks infected, haul your sorry self right back here."

"Thanks, Doc. I'll take care of it."

Doc ruffled Toby's hair as the boy picked up his coat and put it back on then sat down on the chair and twirled the peppermint stick around and around in his mouth.

Arlan reappeared with a new shirt for Adam then helped him put it on. "If I left it up to you, you'd either have worn your bloody clothes or gone home half naked." Arlan raised an eyebrow, daring his brother to argue.

"You know me well, brother. Now, help me off this table because I'm not sure my legs are gonna hold me."

"I can help, Daddy!" Toby volunteered, rushing around to Adam's left side.

"Thanks, Toby." Adam rested a hand on Toby's head as Arlan bore much of his weight on his right side.

"You boys stay out of trouble, you hear?" Doc cautioned as he held open the door and the three of them stepped outside.

"Do you want me to secure a buggy, Adam? Are you sure you can walk home?" Arlan's concern rang heavy in his voice.

"I'll be fine, Arlan, but I wouldn't mind a little help." Adam leaned on him for support while his hand rested on Toby's little head.

"If you pass out before we get there, I'm not lifting you up," Arlan warned.

"Wouldn't expect ya to." Adam's words started to slur.

Arlan hurried their pace as they turned the corner and made it up the steps to Tia's front door.

"Toby, can you open the door?" Arlan asked as the child pushed back the screen door.

"Sure, Uncle Arlan. Mama keeps a key right here." Toby fished into a crack between the porch floorboards and pulled out a key then inserted it into the lock. Unable to push it hard enough to open it, Arlan somehow managed to keep Adam upright while unlocking the door.

Toby rushed inside ahead of them. At the noise, Tia breezed out from the kitchen. Her warm smile turned to shocked dismay as she took in Adam's white face and Arlan's strained look.

"Where do you want him? He's about to pass out, Tia," Arlan warned as Adam started to lose his balance.

"Oh, gracious! Right this way!" She rushed down the hall and opened the door to Adam's room, hurriedly turning back the covers she'd just finished straightening not ten minutes earlier.

Arlan carefully moved until Adam collapsed on the bed.

"What on earth happened?" Tia glanced from her husband to her brother-in-law, waiting for an explanation.

Toby yanked on his mother's hand. "The bad man Crabby doesn't like shot my daddy."

Tia's hand fluttered to her chest and she gulped in air. "Good heavens!" Her frightened gaze turned to Arlan. "Will he be okay? What can I do?"

Arlan grinned as he carefully rolled Adam onto his back and removed his boots. "Just keep an eye on him. The bullet grazed his side, but it made a nasty wound. Doc gave Adam twelve stitches. He lost quite a bit of blood, mostly because this fool decided to tackle Nivens after he'd been shot and pummel the thug half to death."

All the color drained from Tia's face. Adam had been shot because of her, because of his involvement with her and Toby.

Arlan glanced over at her. "You don't look well, Tia. Do you need to sit down?"

Drawing a deep breath, she willed herself to calm down. "I'll be fine, Arlan. Thank you. Now, tell me what I can do to help my husband."

Chapter Thirteen

Adam thought he'd go mad from restless boredom before Tia agreed to let him get out of bed.

A wry grin spread across his face as he thought about his new bride keeping him in bed. Unfortunately, it was because of the wound in his side and not any ardent intentions on her part.

Since Nivens shot him, Tia had fussed over him until he thought he'd lose his mind.

Although he'd slept most of the day yesterday, he'd been eager to get up this morning. However, his wife insisted he stay in bed and rest one more day.

Every hour or two, she checked on him, bringing him a cup of tea or something to eat.

Every time she bent over the bed to straighten his covers and fluff his pillows, Adam tamped down the urge to pull her into his arms. Her luscious scent filled his nose while his fingers itched to reach out and unpin the rich, thick waves of her tea-colored hair.

The sunlight shining in the window revealed the fact it was a beautiful day. Thoughts of all he could be doing made Adam antsy to rise. He started to swing out of the bed, but stopped when Tia glared at him from the door.

"What do you think you're doing?" she asked, marching into the room as he pulled his legs back beneath the covers.

"Plotting an escape," Adam admitted.

Tia laughed and placed the back of her hand against his forehead. It felt pleasantly cool against Adam's warm skin.

Although he didn't have a fever from his injury, Tia's presence left him overheated.

"No fever." She smiled at him. "If you're a good boy, you may get out of bed tomorrow."

"I'll be dead before the morning if you don't let me get up and do something," Adam growled, shooting her a narrowed glare.

Laughter danced in her eyes as she shook her head. "No. I spoke with Doc myself and he assured me bed rest was the best and fastest way for you to heal." She glanced around and noticed the book she'd given Adam to read tossed onto the chair across the room.

After retrieving it, she set it on the bedside table. "I thought you enjoyed Mark Twain's stories."

"I do, I'm just not in the mood to read." Adam pointed toward the window. "It's a beautiful day out there. The sun's sparkling on the snow, yet you've got me hiding in here like some scared little school girl." He sighed and ran his right hand through his mussed hair. "You and Toby should have gone to church."

"Toby went with the Dodd family and stayed to have lunch with them. In fact, I should go fetch him soon." Tia glanced at the clock on the small table by the rocking chair beneath the window.

"I'll go with you," Adam offered and started to rise again.

Tia rolled her eyes and released and exasperated sigh. She pushed on his chest, forcing him to stay in the bed. "You will not get out of that bed, Adam Guthry. I mean it. It's my fault you were injured in the first place. The least you can do is to accept my ministrations with less fuss and bother than a cranky child." With her hands fisted on her hips, she appeared both serious and determined.

Amused by her anxious state, Adam flipped back the covers and wrapped a hand around her waist, pulling her onto the bed. "If you're so all-fired convinced I need to stay in this bed, keep me company. I can think of a few things that would take my mind off being stuck in here all day."

Air whooshed out of Tia as Adam held her against his chest. Warmth unlike anything she'd ever known seeped into her from the contact with his bare skin.

Forcefully turning her attention to the bandage wrapped around his middle, she wanted to make certain he hadn't injured himself with his tomfoolery.

Assured blood didn't ooze through the white cloth, she made the mistake of lifting her face to Adam's.

His blue eyes glittered like sapphires in the moonlight as he held her gaze, drawing her into a place where nothing but the two of them existed.

Mesmerized by the yearning in his eyes, the dimples teasing her in his cheeks, Tia leaned forward and pressed a kiss to his left dimple. The raspy feel of his whiskers against her soft skin thrilled her as his masculine scent invaded her senses.

Oh, how she longed to kiss him like she'd always dreamed of doing. To own his kisses and be owned by him.

For a moment, she considered what might happen if she mustered the courage to press her lips to his and pour out the love she kept hidden in her heart.

Tempted to find out, her mouth was only a breath of space above his when the front door banged open and Toby called to her.

Adam muttered under his breath as she scrambled to her feet and rushed out of the room.

Toby stood in the front entry removing his coat and hat while Chauncy Dodd held Erin's hand.

"You didn't need to bring Toby home. I was just getting ready to fetch him." Tia settled a hand on Toby's shoulder as he leaned against her legs.

"Erin and I thought we should check in on Adam and see how he's fairing." Chauncy smiled. "It must be a terrible burden to have to wait hand and foot on that big lug."

Tia grinned as the pastor winked at her. "It is. I'm practically worn to a frazzle." She motioned for them to follow her down the hall. "He'll be glad you came, Chauncy. And you, too, Erin."

When they entered the room, Toby started to run for Adam's bed then remembered at the last minute he wasn't supposed to bounce on it. Carefully, he climbed up then held out his hand for Erin.

"Come on, Erin. My daddy will show you his stitches." Toby grinned at Adam. "Won't you?"

"There's not much to see," Adam said. He folded back the covers just enough the two youngsters could gawk at the bandage.

"But I got to see it, Erin. Doc let me help. I'm gonna be a doctor when I grow up and marry you."

Erin giggled. "And we'll live on a boat with Aunt Filly and she'll make Turkish delight every day!"

Tia laughed and brushed a dark curl away from Erin's forehead. "My goodness. You two have everything all planned out, don't you?"

"Yep!" Toby hopped off the bed and tugged on Erin's hand. "Come on. Let's check on Crabby. He misses me when I'm gone."

The sound of their footsteps racing down the hall echoed into the room. Tia grinned at the sound of their chatter coming from the kitchen. "I better check on them and rescue the cat."

Chauncy watched her leave then turned his attention to Adam. The two of them visited for a short while then the pastor offered Adam a broad grin. "You sure don't seem like a man near death. From the way Tia talked, I thought you'd be writhing in pain, ready to meet your maker."

"That woman," Adam raised his right hand and pointed at the wall, indicating Tia in the kitchen, "has got it in her head she can order me around and expect me to obey." Indignant, Adam huffed. "I'll be danged if she isn't right."

Chauncy chuckled. "It must be quite a tribulation to have a lovely woman catering to your every whim while you laze the day away."

"You have no idea," Adam said, his mood darkening. If Toby hadn't arrived home at such an inopportune moment, he might be savoring the sweet flavor of his wife's kisses.

Instead, she'd jumped up from the bed and ran from the room like a scared rabbit.

"Oh, I've got a good idea. The same incurable malady once rendered me useless and hopeless," Chauncy said, backing toward the door.

"Really? I didn't know you'd been gunshot."

Chauncy chuckled. "I haven't been. But I know lovesickness when I see it."

Adam tossed a pillow at Chauncy. The pastor ducked and stepped into the hallway. "Get well, Adam. I'm sure we'll see you around town in a day or two."

"Thanks, Chauncy. And thanks for keeping an eye on Toby."

"He's a great little boy. We're happy to watch him anytime."

Chauncy disappeared and Adam listened to the sound of him leaving with Erin before Toby reappeared in the room.

"Want to share my candy?" He held out half a peppermint stick to Adam. "Mama said I could share it with you."

Adam smiled at Toby and ruffled his hair then accepted the broken stick. "Thank you, Toby. That's very generous of you. When I was a boy, I wasn't very good about sharing my candy with Arlan."

"Mama says I have to share because it teaches good lessons." Toby stuck his portion of the candy stick in his mouth and sucked on it. "I wish I could go to school and learn lessons with the other kids."

"You'll go next year. In the meantime, maybe I can help you learn a few things." Adam watched Toby's eyes light up in anticipation.

"You will?"

He grinned at the boy. "I will. In fact, if you can find a big string or a piece of rope, I'll teach you something right now."

"Oh, yes!" Toby jumped off the bed and started out the door. Abruptly stopping, he spun back around and handed Adam his sticky candy. "Hold this, please."

Adam took the peppermint and watched as Toby raced out of the room. He returned a short while later with a yard-long length of frayed rope. He handed the child back his candy and licked the sticky residue from his fingers then picked up the rope.

"Climb on up here, little man, and I'll teach you everything you need to know about tying knots like a real sailor."

Chapter Fourteen

Judge Cedric Devereux sipped from his cup of coffee, liberally laced with brandy. Content, he leaned back in his chair by the parlor fire, enjoying a tranquil evening.

Catherine, his wife, sat across from him, tediously working on another needlepoint chair cover. The woman had stitched so many of them, nearly every chair in the house bore the results of her efforts.

Cedric glanced over at her, proud she still appeared as lovely as the day they wed forty-four years ago. He'd not asked for more in a wife than for her to be well dressed, gracious, and provide a welcoming atmosphere for their guests.

She'd served him well and he held some affection for the woman, particularly since she bore him two sons.

Pain stabbed his heart as he thought about losing both his boys so senselessly. Patrick, his oldest and favorite son, died when a horse bolted, dragging a buggy behind it through the streets. Before it was brought under control it had injured a dozen people and killed one innocent bystander — his son.

Then there was Roland's death, still fresh and painful. Roland had never grown up, never wanted to. Catherine had coddled the boy and Cedric blamed her for his raffish, rascally ways. It would have turned into quite a scandal for Roland to end up dead in a saloon from a brawl over a soiled dove. That's why Cedric arranged for it to appear as if Roland had been defending himself during a robbery outside the sordid establishment.

Over the years, Cedric had availed the services of men of questionable character to carry out his wishes.

Even now, one of the men on his payroll was in Hardman, preparing to bring his grandson home in time for Christmas.

He hadn't mentioned his plans to Catherine. There'd be time enough to inform her once Tobias arrived with Mr. Nivens.

Smug with his successful schemes, Cedric took another sip from his coffee and picked up the book he'd been reading the previous evening.

He heard the bell ring at the front of the house and wondered who would call at that time of the evening. No one in their circle of friends would have been so unforgivably rude.

The clearing of a throat at the doorway alerted him to the presence of his butler.

"Yes, Charles?" Cedric motioned for him to step into the parlor.

The butler's face remained expressionless as he strode across the room with a silver tray carried in his gloved hands.

"Two telegrams arrived for you, sir." Charles held out the tray and Cedric snatched the messages from it.

"That will be all, Charles. Thank you."

Dismissed, the butler hurried from the room.

Cedric scanned the first telegram. When he finished, his face flushed an ugly shade of purple. He wadded up the paper and tossed it into the fireplace, muttering under his breath.

Startled, Catherine stared at him. "Whatever is the matter, Cedric?"

"That woman!" Cedric yelled, stabbing his index finger into the air above his head. "That woman has gone and married again!"

"What woman, dear?" Catherine leaned forward in her chair. "Of whom are you speaking?"

"Tiadora! That blasted, stubborn..." Cedric broke into a string of curses that caused Catherine's eyebrows to meet her hairline.

As he read the second telegram, he yanked at the collar of his shirt until two buttons flew off. He wadded the second telegram into a ball and threw it into the fire to join the first message.

"Cedric?" Catherine asked, frightened by his behavior and the murderous gleam in his eye.

"I need to attend to a matter, my sweet. Don't wait up for me." Cedric got to his feet and hurried from the room, bellowing for Charles as he rushed toward the door and shrugged into his coat.

"Have Ed bring the carriage around, Charles. I must leave at once."

"Yes, sir." Charles didn't wait for more instruction. He opened the front door and ran out to the carriage house.

Within minutes, the carriage rolled around by the front door. Cedric hurried down the steps and climbed inside as Charles stood in attendance.

"While I'm gone, I need you to get in touch with this man and ask him to meet me at my office first thing tomorrow morning." The judge handed Charles a slip of paper.

"Yes, sir. Right away, sir." Charles tipped his head to Cedric.

"And for heaven's sake, don't mention anything to my wife." Cedric barked as the carriage lurched forward and headed down the drive.

Three hours later, Cedric returned home. He'd made sure Nivens wouldn't be able to talk, tying any of his nefarious deeds back to the judge. No, that idiot would mysteriously disappear before he ever reached trial for shooting the milksop stupid enough to marry his former daughter-in-law.

Enraged Nivens hadn't followed his orders to the letter, obviously more had transpired than the man simply serving Tia with the papers he'd sent and encouraging her to return with Tobias to their home in Portland before he was forced to take legal action against her.

With her married, it would be nearly impossible for him to pursue custody of his grandson.

The only way to ensure the child became his was if Tia and her new husband were suddenly to perish.

Cedric was more than happy to arrange for that to happen.

Chapter Fifteen

"Where are you going?" Toby asked as Adam tugged on his boots then slipped on his coat.

"I've got business to attend to, but I'll be back in time for supper tonight," Adam said, wrapping a scarf around his neck.

Toby's lip puckered and his little brows knit together in a frown. "Don't you want me to go, too?"

Adam hunkered down and opened his arms to the boy. Toby lunged against his chest as Adam wrapped him in a hug. "I'll be out in the cold most of the day, Toby. Your mama would flay the skin right off me if I took you out and let you get a chill. Besides, Christmas is coming and I might have a few surprises that require some attention."

"Surprises?" Toby asked, leaning back as the sparkle returned to his blue eyes.

"Yes, surprises, little man." Adam set him down and tweaked his nose. "Promise to be good today and keep an eye on your mama and Crabby."

"I will," Toby said, his good humor restored. He handed Adam his hat and watched as the big man pulled on his gloves.

Tia strode into the room, carrying a stack of clean dishtowels. She set them down on the counter and raised an eyebrow at Adam. "Going somewhere, sailor?"

Adam grinned at her. "Yes, ma'am, I am. I promised Blake I'd help him set up for their skating party Saturday. I'll be out at his place most of the day."

"But, Adam, don't you think you should…" Tia gasped as Adam silenced her with a quick kiss. If Toby hadn't been watching, she wondered if it would have lasted longer than the time it took her to blink in surprise.

"Mrs. Guthry, you've held me prisoner in this house for days. I'm ready for some hard work and fresh air." Adam winked at Toby and opened the back door.

"I've done no such thing. Why, just yesterday you spent the day at the livery with Douglas doing who knows what and we had dinner with Arlan and Alex. How, exactly, is that holding you prisoner?"

Adam took a step closer to her and bent his head down until his warm breath caressed her ear. "I'll forevermore be a prisoner of your charms, Queenie."

A shiver of delight raced through Tia as Adam kissed her cheek then stepped outside.

The look he tossed back at her made heat churn in her belly. "Go on with you, and tell Ginny I said hello."

"I will. You two have a good day and don't forget to keep the doors locked. Even though Mr. Nivens is no longer a threat, I'm certain we'll hear from the judge again."

Tia nodded in understanding then watched as Adam strolled down the back steps and cut through the lawn to the front of the house. Crabby sat on a wooden stump and licked his paws, soaking up the sunshine that turned the snow into a glistening wonderland.

Unaware she studied the slight swagger to Adam's gait, the way his shoulders smoothly rolled with each step, she wondered what it would be like to be loved by a man such as Adam Guthry.

Saddened by the thought she'd never know, she forced aside her maudlin musings and pasted a bright smile on her face as she turned to face her son.

"Toby, I think it's about time for us to bring some Christmas cheer to the house. What do you say to that?"

"Hooray!" The little boy ran around in an excited circle before grabbing his mother's hand. "Can we hang garlands and string popcorn and bake cookies and..."

Tia laughed and scooped him into her arms. "Let's do one thing at a time, sweetheart. How about we start by making paper snowflakes for the windows?"

"May I make one for Erin?" Toby asked as he squirmed to get down.

Amused by his constant interest in Erin, Tia smiled. "Yes, you may."

"I'm surprised your wife let you out of her sight to help me today," Blake said. Adam helped him carry benches from the back of the wagon to set around the pond for the skating party taking place that weekend.

Blake had purchased the adjoining property in the spring so he could expand his horse breeding operation. Part of the new addition included a pond. As soon as Ginny saw it, she'd enthusiastically clapped her hands and informed Blake they simply had to host a skating party during the holidays.

Since the weather had been unreasonably cold, the pond had frozen several feet down, making it possible to carry out her plans for the event. To Adam's knowledge, Ginny had invited everyone in a ten-mile radius to attend.

Blake, Luke, Chauncy, and Adam had gathered to clear the snow off the ice and ready the area for the guests who would attend the event.

"Last time I checked, she practically had him hog-tied to the bed," Chauncy teased as he scooped snow into a pile.

Adam glowered at him as he lifted another bench.

"Aren't you apt to rip out those stitches?" Luke asked as Adam easily hefted the bench.

"Nah. I don't know why everyone made such a fuss. I've had far worse injuries at work." Adam glanced at his friends. "Although, when I get hurt on a boat, I don't have the luxury of lazing in bed while a beautiful woman checks on me every hour."

Luke thumped him on the back. "I'm sure that was a real hardship for you."

Adam grinned. "I somehow managed to suffer through her ministrations, and all the delicious food she insisted I needed to eat to regain my strength."

The other men chuckled.

Chauncy squeezed his shoulder. "We are glad you're fine, though, Adam. It's not every day there's a shooting in our town. Do you think you'll have any more trouble from Tia's former father-in-law?"

"I'm counting on it." Adam glanced around. "Speaking of counting, where is my brother? I assumed he'd be out here, too."

"Someone needed to keep the bank open," Luke said, lifting a shovel of snow. "It's a good thing your brother is much more interested in balancing the books and keeping up the accounts than me. It gives me time to enjoy a beautiful day like today."

Adam squinted up at the pale yellow sun brightening the winter sky. "It is a splendid day to be out, even if it's cold."

"What are you complaining about? Isn't it frigid on the river in the winter?" Blake asked, leaning on the handle of his shovel as he looked at Adam. "I've ridden a few ships down that river and thought I might freeze from the inside out before we reached the port."

Adam grinned. "It can get cold out there, bone-chillingly so, but I just add another layer of woolen underwear and go on with my day."

"Maybe you won't need those extra drawers this winter since you've got a new bride to keep you warm." Luke waggled his eyebrows at Adam.

Adam scooped a handful of snow and lobbed it at the banker. Luke ducked as he laughed and they returned to work.

When they finished, they ventured to Blake's house where Filly and Ginny had lunch ready for the men.

The hot beef stew and slices of warm corn bread filled their empty stomachs and warmed them from the winter's chill.

"Did you get everything set up?" Ginny asked as she refilled their coffee cups.

"We sure did, Ginny Lou," Luke said, winking at his sister.

She frowned at him then turned to pour more coffee into Adam's cup. "Are you feeling well enough, Adam?"

He suppressed a sigh of frustration. If one more person asked about his health, he thought he might explode. Instead, he pasted on a smile and nodded to Ginny. "I'm fit is a fiddle, Ginny, but thank you for asking."

"It was so brave of you to fight that nasty man while defending Tia and Toby," Ginny gushed, setting down the coffeepot on the stove. "You're like a heroic knight in shining armor."

Chauncy snorted while Luke chortled and Blake shook his head at his wife's theatrics. Adam rolled his eyes and caught Filly's grin as she looked at her sister-in-law.

The two women seemed such an unlikely pair, but from what he'd witnessed, they were close friends. Petite, fair-headed, and full of plans, Ginny's appearance was far different from Filly's mahogany hair, green eyes, and tall height. She was nearly as tall as Alex. Yet, the two women seemed to hold a deep affection for one another. He thought they balanced each other well. Ginny drew Filly into her fun and nonsense while Filly kept her sister-in-law from getting into too much trouble.

Adam leaned back in his chair and looked around the Stratton home. He remembered being in it a few times as a boy. From the outside, it didn't appear much different, but the inside looked vastly changed.

Recalling the humble furnishings that used to fill the home, it now boasted some of Blake's unique, expensive pieces. Ginny had added plush rugs and velvet-tufted chairs. She'd also insisted Blake add running water and build on a bathroom, since she was used to a life of luxury.

Surprised she seemed happy living out in the country with Blake, Adam mused that love could make any place a home.

Thoughts of Tia filled his mind as he sipped his second cup of coffee and ate a piece of the custard pie Filly set before him.

Although he'd offered her the option of staying in Hardman when he returned to Portland, Adam wanted Tia and Toby to go with him. In the few days they'd lived in the same house as a family, he'd grown accustomed to it, to having them both around. Selfishly, he didn't want to give that up when he went back to work.

If they'd agree to go with him, he might even look into a new job opportunity he'd been offered last month to captain a boat on day excursions. At most, he'd only be gone a few nights a month instead of several days out of each week. The new position would also be notably less hazardous.

As his mind worked through the possibilities, he partially listened to the conversation taking place around him.

"Has she given away any of her secrets, Adam?" Luke asked, with a probing glance.

"What?" Adam asked, confused. "Who?"

"Stop dreaming about your wife and pay attention to the conversation," Chauncy chided. "Luke is bound and determined to discover how Alex does all of her magic tricks. So far, he's only been able to get her to share the secrets for a handful of basic sleight of hand maneuvers that even the first-graders could figure out."

Luke glared at his best friend. "I don't see you getting any inside information either."

"Nope, but you are the one obsessed with prestidigitation, my friend." Chauncy winked at Filly and she nodded her head.

Luke turned his attention back to Adam. "Have you seen her do any tricks?"

Adam took a sip of coffee. "Not many. She's done a few simple tricks after dinner a couple of times. I'm looking forward to seeing her performance at the Christmas Carnival. Arlan showed me her magic wagon." Adam whistled. "Now that is what you'd call a unique piece of craftsmanship."

"That it is," Luke agreed. He rose to his feet and slapped Blake on the back. "We need to get back to town, but you know where to find us if you require assistance with anything else."

Blake shook his brother-in-law's hand. "No, you've all done enough. I appreciate your help preparing for the party. As long as it doesn't snow between now and Saturday, we should be all set."

"A blizzard wouldn't dare mess with my sister's plans for a party," Luke said, reaching out to muss Ginny's hair.

She ducked and stuck her tongue out at him, causing everyone to chuckle.

Filly gave the two of them an indulgent look. "You two will be old and gray, hobbling around on canes and still tormenting each other."

"I hope to goodness we are." Luke winked at his sister then held out Filly's coat for her.

Chauncy pulled on his coat and hat. "I've got some calls to pay to folks out this way before I head home. Thank you for lunch, ladies. Although I know Filly made the food, your coffee has vastly improved, Ginny. It no longer tastes like bitter mud."

Ginny wrinkled her nose at Chauncy as he chuckled and hurried out the door.

Adam soaked up the lighthearted heckling of his friends. He missed this, missed being part of a fun group of people who knew each other, cared about each other.

He'd made friends in Portland, but it wasn't the same as this bunch who shared his past.

Blake kissed Ginny's cheek then motioned to Adam. "Shall we get started on that project you mentioned?"

"That would be great, Blake, if you're sure you have time. I know you get bogged down with holiday orders." Adam smiled at Ginny before he followed Blake out the back door to his workshop.

As they stepped inside, the scents of various types of wood mingled with the furniture polish and varnish Blake used on his creations.

"This is impressive." Adam glanced around the large space, taking in the finished pieces, the works in progress, and the stacks of wood ready to be used for furniture and some of Blake's other projects.

The aromas of nuts, popcorn, and cherries, with hints of pine tantalized Adam's nose as they approached the stacks of wood. Adam leaned closer and breathed deeply of the faint aroma of roses.

"What's that wood?" Adam pointed to a fragrant, slightly pink-hued board.

"Rosewood. Smells good, doesn't it?" Blake lifted a piece of wood and handed it to Adam. He sniffed it again, enjoying the light fragrance.

While he laid it on a stack of wood, Blake picked up another board from a stack along the wall and handed it him. Adam took a deep breath and coughed, covering his nose. "That's awful. It smells worse than a sun-baked dead fish, and I've had plenty of experience with those."

"Red oak. It does not have a pleasant smell, but it is a beautiful wood." Blake took the board from Adam and set it back on the pile. "Now, let's talk about that project you want to work on."

Adam removed two pieces of paper from his coat pocket and smoothed them out on Blake's workbench.

"I want to make this for Toby." Adam tapped his finger on a drawing of a boat. He pointed to the second drawing. "And this other project will be a surprise for Tia."

"Let's do Tia's first," Blake said, studying the drawing. "I've got some cherry wood already cut that should work perfectly."

Adam nodded his head. "I appreciate your assistance with this, Blake. I could make them without your help, but since I'm short on time with Christmas approaching next week, I need to hurry up and get these finished."

"My pleasure," Blake said, setting several small pieces of cherry wood on his workbench. "I've never made a boat like the one you've planned, so it'll be an interesting challenge for us both."

With Blake's tools and talents they finished the surprise for Tia in an hour. After staining the wood and setting it aside to dry, they started working on Toby's boat.

Using oak for the frame and cedar for the planks, it quickly took shape.

Before he left for the day, Adam gave Tia's gift a coat of varnish then wiped off his hands. After thanking Ginny for lunch and Blake for his help, he walked the short distance back to town.

Whistling a holiday tune as he strode down Main Street, Adam took a moment to admire the festive atmosphere with so many of the businesses and homes festooned with wreaths, garlands, and bows.

Suddenly realizing Tia had yet to adorn the house for the holiday, Adam wondered if she had any decorations.

Rather than heading straight home, he made a detour by the mercantile. The bell above the door jingled, announcing his presence as he stepped inside the store. The scent of apples and cinnamon greeted him, and he took a deep breath.

"There's cider bubbling on the stove back there, Adam, if you'd like a cup." Aleta Bruner smiled at him as she walked out of the storeroom to stand behind the counter.

"It smells mighty good, Aleta, but I'll pass. I'm looking for a little Christmas cheer to take home to Tia and Toby." Adam smiled as Percy Bruner ran inside and slammed the door behind him.

"Son, how many times have I asked you not to slam that door?" Aleta shook her finger in the direction of the rambunctious boy.

"Probably almost as many times as you've told me not to run inside, whistle in the house, or snitch candy right before dinner." Percy grinned at his mother and doffed his hat. His bright red hair stood every which direction.

Adam hid a smile as Aleta threw her hands up in the air, piqued. "Run along upstairs, Percy, and finish your homework before supper."

"Yes, ma'am." Percy nodded to his mother then smiled at Adam. "Have a nice evenin', Mr. Guthry."

"You as well, Percy." Adam watched the boy start to run to the back room then slow to a walk when his mother loudly cleared her throat.

As Percy clattered up the stairs, Aleta sighed. "I swear, that boy of mine would deplete the patience of St. Peter himself."

Arlan chuckled. "He's a good boy, Aleta. Alex speaks quite highly of him."

Aleta beamed and nodded her head. "I know it, but sometimes..." The woman snapped her mouth shut and looked at Adam. "Now, you said you want to take home something with a bit of Christmas cheer?"

"Yes, ma'am."

Aleta stepped around the counter. "I've got just the thing. These arrived yesterday, but I've already sold three of them." She picked up a footlong sleigh, decorated with a lithograph of Santa driving two reindeer pasted to the side. Although simple, Adam knew Toby would love it.

"Can you fill that open section with nuts?" Adam asked as he nodded to Aleta.

"I certainly can. Would you like any type in particular, or a variety?"

"A variety, I think. Tia used to love almonds, but I'm not sure what Toby likes."

Aleta nodded and quickly filled the little sleigh with an assortment of nuts. Adam had her add a nutcracker, in case Tia didn't have one, then Aleta tied a bright red bow around it.

"That's perfect, thank you." Adam smiled as he paid her then tipped his hat. "Have a pleasant evening."

"You as well, Adam. Give Tia my regards."

"I will. Good night."

Adam hurried home from the store and stamped his boots twice on the back step before opening the kitchen door to a subdued Toby pouting at the table and Tia near tears.

The accusing glare she tossed at him brought Adam up short as he shut the door and set the sleigh on top of the icebox while he removed his outerwear.

"What's going on in here?" Adam picked up Toby when the boy ran over to him and lifted his arms.

Gently patting the child's back, he moved over to where Tia sat with Crabby on her lap. The cat growled as she tried to work out a knot tied in his tail.

A quick look around revealed Toby had spent the day practicing his knot-tying skills.

Chapter Sixteen

"Oh, Toby." Adam muttered, doing his best to hide his mirth.

"Mama hollered at me." The little boy buried his face against Adam's neck and sniffed. "Just 'cause I tied a little ol' knot in Crabby's tail. The kitty didn't care."

Tia glowered at Adam as she tugged on the knot and the cat growled at her again.

"Here, let me help." Quickly setting Toby down, he picked up the cat. Adam rubbed his hand over Crabby's head and scratched behind his ears. Once the cat started to purr, he turned so Tia could work the knot out of his tail.

"From now on, little man, no tying knots on living things, okay?" Adam gave Toby a stern glance.

The child sniffled again. "I didn't mean to be bad." A big tear rolled down his cheek, followed by another while his lips quivered. "I think I better go to bed without my supper."

"Let's not get carried away." Encouragingly, Adam smiled at Toby. "Did you learn your lesson?"

Tears filled his eyes as Toby nodded.

"You might have hurt Crabby by tying his tail in a knot, so you won't do anything like that again, will you?" Adam asked.

Toby rapidly shook his head.

"All right, then."

Toby pointed to Tia. "But I hurt Mama."

Adam glanced down at Tia as she worked the knot free. "Are you hurt, Tia?"

She shrugged as he set the cat in its box. "Crabby dug his claws in a few times, that's all."

Adam took her hands in his and examined them, but didn't see any scratches.

Toby pointed to Tia. "He scratched her legs, Daddy."

Adam shot his wife a devilish smile as he swept her into his arms. Before she could protest, he set her on the counter and pushed up her skirts.

"Stop that, this instant!" She swatted at his hands, making Toby giggle. When she leaned around Adam and pinned him with a frosty glare, the boy grew silent.

"You let me worry about those scratches, Adam Guthry." Tia smacked his hand again and jumped off the counter. She turned to her son. "As for you, young man, the only thing I better catch you tying knots in from now on is that old rope Adam gave you for practicing. Is that clear?"

Slowly, Toby nodded his head.

Tia waggled a finger in the direction of the hall. "Now go wash your hands and face while I get supper on the table."

When Toby left the room, Tia blew a breath of air between her lips and leaned against the counter before scowling darkly at Adam. "This is all your fault."

Adam slapped a hand to his chest and offered her a look of innocence. "My fault? What did I do? I've been gone all day."

"You..." Tia took a step forward and shook a finger in his face. "You, Mr. Guthry, taught him how to tie all those stupid knots. Just look what you've done!"

She pointed to the curtains by the kitchen sink that had been tied together in a basic knot. As Adam looked around the room, he noticed Tia had decorated for Christmas, yet the ribbons she'd draped around the doorway bore a series of knots as high up as Toby could reach.

"He tied my yarn into a jumbled mess, my dishtowels into a wad, and..." Tia huffed indignantly, "you should see what he's done to my silk stockings."

Adam entirely liked the idea of seeing Tia's stockings, especially if they encased her shapely legs.

"I'm sorry, Queenie. I had no idea he'd practice tying knots on everything within reach. If it makes you feel any better, he's done a bang-up job of it, though. He's tied a few knots better than some of the men I work with." Adam lifted one of the knot-ridden ribbons and admired the bowline knot.

A grunt of disapproval made him drop the ribbon and turn back to Tia.

"I promise Toby and I will set everything to rights after supper. May I help with anything right now?"

"Not until you go wash up." Tia waved a spoon at him. "And tell Toby to quit dawdling. He can set the table."

"Yes, ma'am."

Adam refrained from saying anything further to Toby about the knots as they ate.

As soon as they'd finished the meal and helped with the dinner dishes, he made Toby remove every knot he'd tied around the house.

"How come you didn't help your mama decorate for Christmas today?" Adam asked as they worked the knots out of the fringe on the mantle scarf.

"I did help her," Toby said, pointing to the paper snowflakes dangling from silver thread in the front windows.

"We made snowflakes, and put the garland on the fireplace, and hung a wreath on the front door. Mama said she'd ask you to climb up in the attic to bring down the rest of the decorations." Toby leaned closer to Adam and lowered his voice. "She's scared to go up there."

Adam grinned. Tia had never liked going into the attic of the house, convinced ghosts or spiders lived up there, just waiting to terrorize her.

One year, after Tia had read about Charles Dickens' ghosts, Adam and Carl snuck up to the attic and banged around. Of course, her grandmother was in on the ruse, asking Tia to run up there to bring down an old hatbox she needed.

With no small degree of trepidation, Tia slowly made her way up the attic stairs. Adam hid behind an old trunk while Carl ducked under a sheet covering a rocking chair with a broken back.

Stepping away from the safety of the stairs with great hesitation, Tia's eyes darted around the room, searching for the hatbox her grandmother wanted.

After unearthing a discarded fur coat that looked like it had been chewed on by a dog, Adam pulled it over his head and snuck around to the stairs while Carl set the rocking chair into motion.

The steady creak of the wood caught Tia's attention and she turned around, staring at the chair with eyes as wide as bread plates.

Adam bit his lip to keep from laughing when Carl rose out of the chair, shrouded with the sheet, making ghostly, ghastly sounds.

Tia spun around and nearly plowed right over Adam in her haste to get away from the ghost until she decided a bear had inhabited the space.

Screams cut through the dusty attic air. She somehow leaped past Adam and raced down the stairs, screeching like a banshee.

Carl and Adam tossed aside their coverings and laughed so hard they tumbled down the stairs, landing in a heap at the bottom.

Once Tia realized who had frightened her so badly, she pummeled them both until her grandmother finally made her stop.

Evidently, Tia had never recovered from her fear of the attic.

"Your mama always was scared of the attic. I'll bring the rest of the things down later." Adam smiled at the boy as they finished untying the last of the knots in the parlor. "Okay, little man. Anywhere else you tied knots today?"

Toby nodded his head and took Adam's hand, leading him down the hallway to Tia's bedroom. He pushed open the door then walked over to the bed. Silk stockings were heaped into a pile of twisted knots.

Adam picked up two stockings and admired the fine job Toby had done in executing a perfect sheet bend knot, looping them together. Proud of the child's skill, Adam tamped down his eagerness to praise Toby and instead studied the bit of silk in his hand. He worked the knot free, but in the process, the stocking had multiple pulls in it from his rough hands.

"You know what, Toby. I think we may have to buy your mama new stockings."

The boy's lip stuck out in a pout again. "I didn't mean to ruin Mama's things. I'm sorry." Toby sniffled and leaned against Adam's leg.

Adam picked up the child and rubbed his back. "You learned an important lesson you won't soon forget, though. Right? No more tying knots on anything except your rope."

"I won't forget, Daddy." Toby gave him a solemn look. "I promise."

"I trust you, Toby." Adam glanced around the room and held back a bark of laughter at the corset strings Toby had tied in a knot around the bedpost — with the corset still attached.

He set the boy down and quickly loosened the knots, then studied the pale green brocade garment in his hand. Curious what it would be like to see Tia wearing it and a pair of those silk stockings, his temperature climbed. He tossed the corset onto the bed and took Toby by the hand.

"Anything else you got into today?"

Toby shook his head.

"All right, then. It's off to bed for you."

Toby took a step toward his bedroom then glanced back at Adam. "Will you tuck me in and tell me another story about one of the boats you've been on?"

"I sure will, son. Hurry and get ready for bed."

The little boy rushed into his room to put on his nightshirt then raced down the hall to the bathroom to brush his teeth.

Adam supervised the process, although he didn't offer any help. Like his mother, Toby was incredibly independent and liked to do things for himself.

"I want Mama to tuck me in, too," Toby said as he ran down the hall toward the parlor.

Adam watched as Tia returned with Toby. She ignored him as she entered the child's room and tucked him into bed.

"You sit right there, Mama," Toby said, patting her hand. He pointed to the other side of his bed. "And you sit here, Daddy."

Adam moved inside the room and walked around the boy's bed, sitting on the opposite side of Tia.

When she looked over at him, he winked and the barest hint of a smile touched her lips. Adam studied the contours of her mouth, wondering if she'd taste like summer peaches — ripe and sweet.

Distracted by thoughts of his lovely bride, Adam felt a tug on his hand as Toby drew him back to the moment. "I'm ready for my story, now."

"Let's see, a story about a boat..." Adam appeared thoughtful as he rubbed his chin and stared at a painting on the wall of a boy pulling a boat by a string. He cleared his throat and smiled at Toby. "There once was a beautiful little boat. It was sleek, strong, and fast. It outran all the other boats on the river."

"What color was the boat?" Toby asked, settling deeper into his pillow.

"Blue, like the sky overhead." Adam smiled at the child, knowing that was his favorite color. "The beautiful little blue boat would speed through the water so fast, it looked like a streak of light as it passed the older, slower boats poking along. Sometimes the little boat teased and taunted the bigger slow-moving boats. One day, as the beautiful little blue boat rushed from one harbor to another, a big, ugly boat rammed into it on purpose. It broke the little boat, smashing it into pieces."

"Oh, no!" Toby sat up, eyes wide with fear. "What happened?"

Adam gently pushed Toby back down in the bed and brushed at the cowlick ever at odds with the rest of his hair. "Well, the pieces of the little boat drifted to the shore for miles. But a kind man, the man who built the little boat, carefully gathered each one. He hauled them all back to his workshop. He worked and worked until he'd rebuilt the little boat. When he finished, he painted it blue, with a bright red stripe down the side. He took the little blue boat back to the river. It bobbed in the water for a while, getting used to the feel of it again, before it once again raced down the river, happy as it could be."

"I'm glad the little blue boat could sail again." Toby's eyes drifted shut.

"Me, too, little man. Now go to sleep." Adam leaned over and kissed Toby's forehead.

"I love you, Daddy," Toby whispered.

Adam's heart clenched and he swallowed hard. "I love you too, Toby. Sleep well, son."

"Night, Mama."

"Good night, baby." Tia leaned over and kissed Toby's cheek before she stood and adjusted his covers. Adam joined her in the doorway as they watched Toby turn onto his side and fall asleep.

Quietly closing the door partway, Tia returned to the parlor. She sat down and picked up the knitting needles she'd set aside when Toby asked her to tuck him into bed.

Adam sat across from her in a chair by the fire and watched the needles clack back and forth, reflecting spears of firelight.

"What are you making?" he finally asked, fascinated by the speed with which her fingers flew. He didn't remember Tia ever sitting still long enough to learn any skills like knitting, crocheting or needlepoint when he'd known her before. The talents she acquired had to come after she'd wed Patrick Devereux.

"A scarf for Alex," Tia said, holding up dark red ball of yarn. "I already made one for Arlan. I wasn't sure what would be a proper gift to give them."

"They'll appreciate anything you make," Adam assured her, leaning back in the chair.

"Did I see you bring home something earlier?" Tia asked without glancing up.

"I did. I'll fetch it." Adam retrieved the sleigh from the kitchen and set it down on the low table in front of the couch.

"Oh, Adam, it's darling. It looks perfect right there. What a thoughtful gift." Tia set aside the knitting and dropped to her knees in front of the table.

Adam noticed her wince and put a hand on her back as he leaned down to look into her face. "What hurts, Tia? I know something did."

"It's nothing," she said, rising to her feet and wincing again.

"Nothing, huh?" It was obvious something pained her. He'd get an answer out of her sooner or later. "Let me take a look at those scratches from Crabby."

Tia shook her head and backed away from him. "No. I'm fine. However, it's time for me to go to bed." She reached back to untie her apron strings and jerked on them.

Like a dog chasing its tail, she went around and around in circles, furiously yanking on the strings until Adam pulled her to a stop.

"Looks like Toby got to your apron, too. How'd he tie it in a knot without you noticing?"

Tia stamped her foot in frustration. "He said he needed to fix my bow. Oh, that child has been utterly vexing today! He's never been so full of orneriness before and I can't imagine what's gotten into him now."

Her gaze turned to Adam as he worked the apron strings loose. Once he released the knot, she whipped off the apron and shook it at him. "In truth, the facts point to your influence as the cause for my troubles with Toby."

"Me?" Adam asked, perplexed. "All I did was show him how to fashion a few knots every man ought to know how to tie. You're the one who was home all day while he tied the house into knots."

Tia sank onto the sofa and covered her face with her hands. Adam couldn't tell if she was laughing or crying from the way her shoulders shook. Finally, she lifted her gaze to his. Although her eyes watered, the smile that brought apples to her cheeks made him grin at her mirth.

When she gained control of her laughter, she released a breath. "Honestly, Adam, I can't begin to explain what happened today. One minute he was helping me set out the holiday decorations and wrist-deep in my cookie dough. The next minute, I turned around to see knots everywhere. Toby told me he wanted to play in the parlor and I kept checking on him. Nothing seemed amiss. Since he played so quietly, I didn't think anything of it. I stepped outside to speak to Mrs. Ferguson for a moment, and he stayed in the kitchen. When I returned inside… knots everywhere." Tia leaned back and giggled. "Poor ol' Crabby. That cat would let Toby scalp him and not twitch an ear, but he sure didn't like me touching his tail. I'm surprised he let you hold him while I finished."

"Crabby knows a good guy when he sees one." Adam's lopsided grin charmed her.

Tia's face softened. "Yes, I guess he does."

"Now, Mrs. Guthry, I want to check those scratches. Arlan always claimed you could get more diseases from cat scratches than from eating candy you found in the outhouse."

Repulsed, she wrinkled her nose and he chuckled. She started to move but Adam blocked her in on the sofa.

Every inch she scooted back, he advanced forward until she'd wedged herself into the corner of the sofa and had nowhere to run.

"Come on, Tia. Let me see. You may need me to do some doctoring." The wicked smile he gave her did nothing to soothe her overwrought nerves.

Ever so slowly, he picked up one foot, worked off her shoe and let it drop to the floor. He repeated the process with the other. Gently, he massaged both feet, causing Tia to swallow back a groan.

When his warm, callused hand slid beneath her skirt and petticoats, she sucked in a gulp of air. "Adam! Stop it right now. That's enough."

He raised a heated gaze to her while his hand moved up her calf, over her knee and trailed across her thigh. "Oh, calm down, Tia. It's not like I haven't seen it all before."

Indignant, she glowered at him. "Swimming in our underclothes in the creek when we were nine is a lot different than you... than you doing... this!"

"And what is this, Tia?" Adam's voice dropped to such a husky level, she shivered in response to it.

In truth, she didn't want Adam to stop. She wanted to be his wife, his true wife, but not because of an obligation on his part to fulfill his duties as a husband. And certainly not because he was a virile man who found her attractive. She wanted Adam to want her out of love, out of his heart's need for her, just as she loved and needed him.

As the flame in his eyes cast a spell over her, he slid both hands up and down her legs. Gently, he pushed up her skirts and petticoats.

When he exposed her bloomers to the light, he gasped at the streaks of dried blood running down both legs.

"I'm gonna wring that cat's neck right now." Adam growled as he carefully lifted the fabric away from her skin.

"Oh, leave Crabby alone. It isn't his fault. If anyone is to blame for the whole mess, it's you." Tia knew the cat drew blood by the sting she'd felt when he'd sunk his claws into her leg, but she'd been too angry to pay any mind. Now, though, as Adam tried to pull the blood-crusted fabric of her bloomers and stockings away from her skin, it hurt.

A whimper escaped her as he touched a particularly sore spot.

His eyes found hers again. "I'm so sorry, Tia. I'm truly sorry for..."

She put a hand over his mouth to silence him. "It's just a few scratches, Adam. I'm not made of glass and I won't break. You seem to have forgotten I could outclimb, outrun, and outshoot you when we were young."

"I know, but you're a refined lady of society now, not that rough and tumble playmate from so long ago." Adam rocked back on his heels. "Why don't you remove those bloody clothes and let me see to those scratches? You really do need to be careful about them getting infected."

"If you think this is the first time Crabby and I have done battle, you would be sadly mistaken." Disappointed that Adam got to his feet and stepped back from her, Tia wished he'd take her in his arms, or at least tease her by saying outlandish things she had to pretend offended her.

"I'm going to take a hot bath. And I assure you, I can tend to the scratches on my own." Tia rose and picked up her shoes before crossing the room. She looked back at the sleigh full of nuts on the table. "Thank you for the thoughtful gift. I truly appreciate it. I also appreciate your help with Toby this evening. He adores you, you know."

"I really do love him, Tia. He's a special boy, even if he does tie you up in knots."

Grinning at his joke, she gave him one final glance then walked down the hall, conflicted. Part of her rejoiced that Adam loved her son. The rest of her possessed bitter jealousy that Adam didn't love her, too.

Chapter Seventeen

"Oh, just look at everyone!" Tia squeezed Adam's arm as they walked toward the pond where half the town skated. Others sat around the edges on benches visiting or stood close to the roaring bonfire, warming chilled hands and feet.

A large table held a variety of refreshments. Tia waved at Ginny and hurried over to give her a hug.

Adam set a gingerbread cake she'd made on the table then lifted Toby from where he'd ridden on his shoulder as they walked out to the farm.

Although Adam offered to borrow or rent a sleigh, Tia wanted to walk. Invigorated by the clean, fresh air and the sunshine overhead, she enjoyed sauntering down the road with the two males she loved the most.

Seeing Toby ride on Adam's broad shoulder made her heart ache with joy and sadness. At some point, when Adam decided he wanted out of their fake marriage, it would devastate Toby.

For her son's sake, she hoped Adam kept his promise to honor his vows.

Determined to enjoy the day, she chased away her sad thoughts and greeted her friends.

Toby located Erin among the throng and the two children raced around laughing and giggling.

Finally, Adam picked up Toby and strapped on his skates while Chauncy put a pair on Erin.

The two youngsters stepped onto the ice. Their feet slid from beneath them, leaving them on their bottoms.

Erin's lip puckered into a pout, but Toby giggled. "Come on, Erin, let's do it again!"

In light of her playmate's enthusiasm, the little girl worked herself upright and the two of them made it a few feet before falling to the ice again.

Tia sat down on a bench and put on her skates. She glanced over at Adam, pleased to see he strapped on skates as well. Ever since she was thirteen, she'd dreamed of him skating with her as a man who loved her, not as a boy who liked her as a chum.

Sixteen years later, she still wished that dream would magically come true. Unsteadily, she got to her feet and took a few tentative steps. Hampered by her long coat, she removed it and draped it over the bench.

Adam stood and pretended to wobble on his skates.

Tia laughed. "You were always a good skater, Adam. You're not fooling me." Slowly moving her feet forward, she stepped onto the ice.

"You weren't too shabby yourself," Adam said, gliding in a circle around her. "In case I didn't make mention of it earlier, Mrs. Guthry, you are perfectly charming today."

Politely, Tia tipped her head, pleased by his compliment. A black velvet brocade jacket topped her red plaid skirt, accented by the bright red gloves on her hands. She'd fastened a smart little black hat with a cluster of red satin roses on top of her head while a red scarf encircled her neck.

"In fact, wife of mine, you are charmingly perfect and astoundingly lovely in your skating outfit."

Adam skated another circle around her, offering her a grin so full of boyish appeal, for a moment she felt seventeen again.

"You don't look bad yourself, Mr. Guthry." Tia admired the way Adam's shoulders filled out his double-breasted navy pea coat. Rather than denims, as he often wore, he had on a pair of tan canvas trousers. He'd left his hat at home. His thick tousled hair drew her interest, as did the sparkling blue of his eyes, enhanced by the sapphire-hued scarf around his neck. "You've grown into a very handsome man, Adam."

He stopped skating and stared at her a moment. Flustered by his intent perusal that started at her head and went to the tips of her skates, she reached out a hand to him. "Since you're an old married man now, you're stuck skating with me today, sailor. Come on. Take me for a spin across the ice."

"I thought you'd never start making demands, Queenie." Adam winked then moved behind her, settling one hand on her waist while holding her hand with his other. They both slid their right foot forward, skating in unison around the pond.

"This is nice." Tia wasn't sure if he heard her over the noise around them, but his hand tightened ever so slightly on her waist and he pulled her closer against him.

Lost in dreams, she closed her eyes and allowed him to glide her around the pond. Unexpectedly, someone crashed into their legs and knocked their feet out from beneath them.

"Sorry, Mrs. Guthry, Mr. Guthry. I'm not very good at this yet." One of Alex's students struggled to get to her feet.

Adam stood and gave Tia a hand, making sure she was uninjured before assisting the girl. He offered Tia an inquisitive glance, seeking permission to help the teen. Tia nodded, impressed Adam had sought her approval.

"Here, let me give you a few pointers," Adam said, taking the girl's hand in his and showing her how to glide instead of trying to walk on her skates. He took her for a spin around the pond then returned to Tia as she made her way over to her son. Toby and Erin continued to take a few steps and fall on their rumps.

"At this rate, our boy won't be able to sit down for a week," Adam mused as he watched Toby take another spill.

Tia's heart filled to overflowing at Adam's reference to Toby as "our boy." He cared for her son as he would his own.

Adam grabbed her hand and tugged her along behind him. "I've got an idea." After snatching two of the pillows Ginny had placed on a bench for some of the older women to sit on, he secured them to Erin and Toby by tying a thin rope around their waists.

"But, Mama, this is dumb," Toby whined as Adam tied Erin's rope.

"Oh, just give it a try, son," Tia encouraged.

Resigned to wearing the ridiculous cushion, Toby took a few faltering steps and fell backward onto the pillow. As it cushioned his fall, he grinned at Erin.

"It's fun, Erin! Give it a try!"

The little girl took a few faltering steps and fell, giggling as she bounced on the pillow.

Adam placed his hand on Tia's waist and bent down by her ear. "Should we give them some skating lessons or just let them play."

"For today, let them play. We can teach them another time when there aren't so many around. With the skating rink open in town, this shouldn't be such a novelty," Tia mused as Adam guided her back onto the pond.

As their blades cut across the ice with a smooth *whoosh, whooshing* sound, Tia smiled. It reminded her of the many times she, Carl, and Adam had skated together.

Only Carl wasn't the one she wanted to hold her hand or her heart. Always and forever, it had been Adam.

Beneath the shadow of her long eyelashes, she glanced up at her husband. The firm outline of his jaw, strong chin, and the puckish look of his face when he grinned filled her with admiration.

As long as she could remember, Tia had loved the dimples in his cheeks. His smile made him appear so lovable and playful. Yet, as she studied him, she admitted Adam possessed raw, rugged masculinity.

Bliss settled over Tia — pure, sweet bliss at skating around the pond on a wintery afternoon with the man she wholeheartedly loved.

"You're awfully quiet, Miss Queenie. What's rattling around in that pretty head of yours?" Adam asked, turning her in his arms so he skated backward and could see her face.

"According to what you and Carl always told me, a bucket full of beans with a few rocks thrown in for good measure." Tia grinned as Adam chuckled.

"We did tease you a lot, didn't we."

Tia rolled her eyes. "All the time. In fact, I'm not certain the two of you were ever serious."

"Oh, we had our moments." Adam turned again, skating beside her as he held both her hands in his. "Do you remember the spring social when you wore that peach-colored dress?"

Heat filled Tia's cheeks as she recalled one of the most embarrassing moments of her life. "How could I forget?"

"Well, you did make an impression on everyone there." Adam laughed as memories washed over him. "Tell me again how it all transpired."

"You know good and well what happened, and it was partially your fault," Tia accused, shooting Adam a reproachful glare.

"Aw, come on and tell me anyway," he coaxed, kissing her cheek.

Distracted by Adam's kiss, she almost lost her footing, but he held her steady. She glanced over her shoulder at him and he offered her a rakish grin. "Go on, Tia, tell me the story."

"Fine," she huffed. "I wanted a new dress for the spring social and Grandma told me I had to make it myself. You know how much I hated sewing."

Adam smirked. "Almost as much as you hated losing a contest to me or Carl."

"Exactly. Anyway, she helped me cut out the pattern and offered suggestions as I sewed that blasted dress, but she didn't make a single stitch on it. That was a year or two before she bought a sewing machine so every single seam had to be sewn by hand. I worked on that thing for two weeks. I ripped out the seam in the back so many times, I thought I might wear out the fabric. The day of the social, I still hadn't finished it so I decided it wouldn't hurt anything to run a quick basting stitch through the last few seams instead of sewing it properly. Out of pity, Grandma sewed on the lace trim and ribbons while I took a bath and got ready."

"And you were as pretty as a just-picked summer peach when you walked into ol' man Luther's barn. I thought I was gonna have to wallop every unmarried man there, from school boys to adults, for the way they ogled you." Adam leaned a little closer to her ear. "There wasn't a thing in this whole world sweeter than the way you looked strolling into that barn, standing near the door in a ray of afternoon sunshine. Your hair was pulled back with a matching ribbon and I could have kissed the living daylights out of you."

Shocked by Adam's confession, Tia glanced over her shoulder to see if he was joking. The sincerity on his face and the glow in his eyes told her he spoke the truth. "I had no idea, Adam."

"How could you not know, Tia? It was pitiful how infatuated I was with you back then. Carl hounded me about it all the time."

Tia could easily picture Carl tormenting Adam. "He did not."

"He did. That's the truth. Ask Arlan if you don't believe me." Adam squeezed her waist again. "Now, go on with the story, if you please."

"Where was I...? Oh, so Grandma sewed the trim on the dress while I got ready then hurried out to Mr. Luther's farm. You and Carl were both in fine form, dancing me around the barn, teasing me mercilessly, flirting with every girl there."

"I did not!"

"You did, too, and you know it." Tia giggled. "I wanted to snatch all the other girls bald-headed for flirting back. Anyway, you and Carl both decided to dance with me at the same time. Rather than take a turn, you each pulled on an arm and the sleeves ripped right out of my dress. You two fell back, and my flimsy seams gave way. The bodice dropped forward and there I was, in that barn full of people, in my ruined dress with my chemise showing. You and Carl stood there like two idiots, staring at the dress sleeves you held in your hands while I thought I might die of humiliation."

"I came to your rescue." Adam guided her around three teen boys who'd fallen in a heap.

Tia giggled. "You grabbed an old horse blanket and wrapped it around me. Even if I'd wanted to repair the dress and wear it again, which I didn't, it smelled like Mr. Luther's old nag."

Adam laughed. "But it was a memorable dance."

"No doubt about that," Tia said, releasing a breath in the frosty air. "The spring social was the last time I wore anything in that color, too."

Unhurried, he leaned forward until his breath brushed across her neck. In a deep tone that made shivers of pleasure trickle over her, he whispered in her ear. "Maybe you should rethink that decision, Queenie. That color was made to be worn by you."

She glanced back at him and he nodded, flashing his dimples at her. "I'm not saying all your fancy gowns don't look nice, because they absolutely do. However, the next time you need a new dress, consider that color. Or..." Adam paused and quirked an eyebrow suggestively, "you could just wear your underthings. In fact, I'd be happy with nothing at all."

A blush started at her neck and seared across her cheeks at his flirtatious and somewhat scandalous words.

Before she could scold him for being so outrageous, Toby skated toward them with Erin.

"Hi, Mama!" Toby grinned broadly. "See us! See us skate!"

"I do see you, sweetheart. Are you having fun?"

Erin took a tumble, landing on her pillow-covered bottom. Toby managed to stay upright and held out his hand to help her.

Adam smiled at Tia, proud over the boy's nice manners.

"I'm ready for some of those refreshments," Adam said, pointing to the table where women served cake, pie, cookies, and hot cider.

"Me, too," Toby agreed, taking hold of Adam's hand while Erin clung to Tia's. The two children wanted cookies and clomped through the snow on their skates to eat them with their friends.

Adam chose a generous slice of the gingerbread cake Tia brought while she took a piece of chocolate cake Filly had made.

"Umm, this is good." Adam pointed to the moist, spice-laden cake with his fork. "I'm partial to any sort of spice cake. I almost asked if you'd let me lick the bowl this morning when you mixed up the batter."

Amused, Tia smiled at her husband. "You should have asked. I would have let you. Toby isn't fond of cinnamon, so I generally make something he prefers, but I'm glad you told me it's something you enjoy. I recall you used to hog all the cinnamon cookies when Grandma made them."

"I'd forgotten about her cookies." Adam's face held an endearing, imploring grin when he looked at her. "I don't suppose you have her recipe."

"I may." Tia gave him an impish smile. "And if you can behave yourself and not get into any mischief for at least one whole day, I might even make some for you."

In mock dismay, Adam took a step away from her. "Are you implying I'm anything but good and can't stay out of trouble?"

Tia pretended to consider his question and tapped her gloved finger against her chin. "Hmm. Let's review your past week, shall we? You were shot, had a dozen stitches, and taught my son to tie knots in everything including poor Crabby's tail. You've teased me without mercy. And don't think I don't know who ate the last piece of the toffee Filly gave us."

Unaffected by her list of his transgressions, Adam winked at her. "Is that all? I thought you possessed real evidence that I'd been up to no good."

Tia released a long-suffering sigh and ate the rest of her cake in silence. She'd just taken the last bite when Luke and Filly walked up to them.

"Are you two having a good time?" Filly asked, hugging Tia around the shoulders.

"Yes, we are." Tia smiled at her friend. "Where's Maura today?"

"Ginny asked some of the older girls to take turns watching the little ones in the house. Maura didn't seem to mind all the extra attention and since the girls are taking turns, none of them miss out on all the fun with the rest of us." Filly winked at Tia and leaned closer to her as Adam and Luke engaged in a conversation about the booming businesses of hauling freight up and down the Columbia River. "I couldn't help but notice you and Adam seem to be having a wonderful time. You skate together so well, it almost looks like you practiced."

Tia shook her head and set aside her plate. "No, but we used to skate together when we were younger. Adam, Carl, and I spent a lot of time in the winter sledding, skating, and building snow forts."

A deep voice spoke beside her, startling her. "While hiding from his dashing and much smarter younger brother."

Filly and Tia smiled at Arlan. Tia placed a hand on his arm and offered him a sympathetic smile. "We were ornery to you, Arlan. I'm sorry. I never realized how much it must have hurt your feelings to get left behind so frequently."

Arlan grinned. "Truthfully, if I wanted to come along, I would have. Adam just made it sound like I wanted to go and he wouldn't let me because I preferred to stay home and study. He didn't think it would help my already bookish reputation if word got out I'd rather sit by the fire and work through a math equation than tag along with you three rabble-rousers. Anytime I asked to go, Adam never said no."

The more she learned about Adam, the more she respected, appreciated, and loved him. Despite his teasing ways and reckless tendencies, he had to be the biggest-hearted, kindest man she'd ever encountered.

Esteem for her husband filled Tia's smile as she looked to his brother. "It's a relief to know we never purposely ignored you or cheated you out of fun."

Alex nudged her husband's side. "To hear Arlan tell it, Adam had to practically drag him out of the house after they moved to town. If it wasn't for Adam's insistence he needed outdoor stimulation, this one would have turned into a wrinkled prune and withered away."

"Now, dear lady, nothing as dire as that would have transpired." Arlan kissed his wife's cheek. "You remember how hard it was when Dad died, Tia. Mother didn't know what to do and took ill. She never was the same after his death. Even though Mother insisted we both finish our schooling, Adam had to grow up quickly and take over many things."

"I remember," Tia said with a wistful hint of sorrow. When Mr. Guthry had been killed in a tragic accident, his wife and sons sold their small farm a few miles outside town and moved into Hardman. While they managed well enough, Adam seemingly left behind his childhood overnight to become the responsible adult in the family. Oh, he still tended to be a tease and prankster, but nothing like he was before his father passed away.

Adam noticed Arlan and Alex next to Tia and reached out to thump his brother on the shoulder. "I haven't seen you out there showing off your footwork on the ice, little brother."

"And you won't. You know I never learned to skate as well as you. In fact, Toby and Erin do better than I could." Arlan pointed to where the two youngsters managed to go several feet before landing on their pillows. "That's a clever idea. I wish someone had thought to tie a cushion on me as a child. It sure would have saved me some lumps and bumps."

"Come on, Arlan. Bring your lumpy, bumpy behind with me and I'll show you how to skate," Alex smiled coquettishly at her husband and playfully batted her dark eyelashes at him.

Arlan winked at Tia. "Be prepared to watch a grown man make a complete fool of himself because a pretty girl flirted with him."

Tia laughed as Alex tugged on his hand, pulling him onto the pond. Despite Arlan's statement that he couldn't skate, he did quite well on the ice. Tia recalled him skating with her, Adam, and Carl several times as children.

She glanced over at Filly. "I adore your skating costume. The green in the plaid sets off your eyes and hair so well."

Filly smiled. "And I love your outfit, Tia. The red gloves are the perfect accent, especially against this backdrop of unending white."

"We have had more than our share of snow this year, haven't we?" Tia observed.

"I'd complain about it, but it is so pretty. I just hope there aren't any big storms between now and Christmas Eve. Luke's parents are traveling with Blake's parents and should be back December twenty-third as long as nothing holds them up."

"I'm sure everything will be fine," Tia said, reaching out to squeeze Filly's hand.

Several members of the community band assembled, including Arlan, to play music for a while, until they grew cold.

"Come on folks! Grab your best gal and take her for a waltz across the ice." A jolly-faced man led the band in playing *Blue Danube.*

"Guess that means you have to dance with me now, Queenie-pie." Adam took Tia in his arms and swept her around the ice. Several other couples joined in the skating as the youngsters and older folks watched.

"How is it a man as big and brawny as you can be so graceful on the ice?" Tia asked as Adam flawlessly skated across the frozen pond.

"Are you hinting that I'm generally an overgrown oaf?" A mischievous light gleamed in his eyes, made even bluer by the winter sky overhead.

Tia could have easily fallen into the pools she saw there and never found her way out again. Instead, she tipped her head and studied him. "I wasn't hinting at it, I'll tell you that to your face." At his shocked, wounded look, she grinned. "I'm just teasing, sailor. However, I have wondered any number of times in the last few weeks, how a man of your size can move with such elegant ease. You truly are pleasing to watch, Adam."

As the words left her mouth, Tia wished she could stuff them back in. With no idea what had come over her, what possessed her to speak so openly to Adam, she looked into his face. Relief calmed her racing pulse as he smiled at her and inclined his head in a polite nod.

"Thank you for your kind words, wife. It gladdens my heart to know you think me slightly more civilized than a wild beast turned loose in a tea shop."

Her laughter chimed around them and Adam drew her closer in his arms, fully aware of how much he'd missed her the last eleven years, how much he still wanted her.

The sounds of the ice beneath their skates blended into the background with the hum of other voices and the music from the band. Obsessed with tasting Tia's mouth, he neared desperation to savor her sweet lips.

He forgot all about the waltz, about being on the middle of a pond with half the town around them, as he cupped her chin and tipped her head back slightly. With limited self-control, he slowly lowered his head toward hers. Their lips would have connected if Toby and Erin hadn't chosen that moment to scream as if Beelzebub himself chased them onto the ice.

Adam jerked back and grabbed Tia's hand, speeding across the pond to the children.

Erin sobbed while Toby's wide-eyes appeared as if they might pop right out of his head.

Tia placed a comforting hand on Erin while Adam knelt before Toby and held his arms in his hands. "What happened son? What's wrong?"

"Me and Erin saw tracks in the snow. I thought it was a bunny. We followed them over there." Toby pointed to a cluster of trees on the far side of the pond. "A bad man tried to grab me. Erin kicked him with her skate. I poked him in the eye when he bent over then we runned back here."

By this time, Chauncy and Abby Dodd as well as several others had gathered around the two distraught youngsters.

Luke and Blake hastily removed the skates from their boots and took off running in the direction of the trees with the sheriff. Chauncy picked up Erin while Adam lifted Toby into his arms.

"You two were very, very brave. I'm proud of you," Adam said as Toby squeezed his neck in a tight embrace.

"He was a scary man, Daddy. His face looked all smooshie." Toby leaned back from Adam with tears swimming in his eyes.

Adam turned to Tia to interpret Toby's description. She reached out and grasped Toby's hand in hers. "What do you mean by smooshie, sweetheart?"

Toby appeared thoughtful then he looked to his mother. "Member the clown Grandfather bought for me. The one I didn't like?"

"Yes, baby. I remember." Tia had hated the toy. It had a creepy face and painted eyes that followed her every move. She didn't scold Toby when he set it against the stove and ruined it.

"'Member when it melted, Mama? When his face went like this?" Toby dragged a hand down one side of his face, mimicking the melted appearance of his clown.

"The bad man had a melted face, is that what you're saying Toby?" Tia asked as Adam tried to make sense of their conversation.

"Yes! One side of his face was smooshie. The other side had a scar, right here." He drew a line down from the outer corner of his eye to his cheek. "Do you think I broke his eyeball? It squished when I poked it."

In spite of the frightening circumstances, Adam held back a chuckle. "I'm sure you didn't break it, Toby. It'll probably hurt him for a while, though."

"Good," Toby said, seemingly pleased at inflicting some damage to the man. "He scared me and Erin."

"I'm sorry about that, Toby."

The little boy stared at Adam. "It wasn't your fault, Daddy." The child shrugged. "He's just a bad man."

"In light of the current circumstances, it's probably best if we head home." Adam glanced at Tia and she nodded in agreement.

The incident put an end to the party as the guests departed. While Tia and Adam removed their skates, Toby stayed close to Erin and her parents. Several of them helped clean up, waiting for Luke, Blake, and the sheriff to return.

When they finally appeared, they walked over to where Adam and Tia helped Ginny and Filly pack up the refreshment table.

"What happened, Blake?" Ginny asked, placing a hand on her husband's chest. "Did you find the man?"

Blake shook his head. "No, love. We found a set of tracks where Toby indicated, but we lost them in the trees."

The sheriff looked to Adam. "For now, let's all go home."

Adam offered Tia an encouraging look. "Tia, why don't you and Toby help Ginny carry those baskets back to the house. I'll be right there."

She gave him a slightly perturbed look, aware he wanted to speak to the sheriff without her hearing the conversation. Rather than voice her disapproval, she handed Toby a basket and gave him a nudge toward Ginny's house.

When she was out of earshot, Adam took a step closer to the sheriff. "Toby said the man's face looked like it had been melted on one side and he had a scar running from the corner of his eye to his cheek. Without seeing him, I can't tell you for sure, but there's a thug for hire who loiters at one of the ports in Portland. He'd as soon slit someone's throat than give them the time of day. With Tia's father-in-law intent on taking Toby, it wouldn't surprise me if he sent another degenerate to steal the boy."

"I was thinking along those lines, too. I didn't want to worry you or Tia, but I received word that Mr. Nivens disappeared before he ever made it to the jail in Portland." The sheriff had contacted a U.S. Marshal to transport the man to Portland to stand trial since they weren't equipped for anything like that in Hardman. "Somehow, after leaving the train in Portland, the U.S. Marshal ended up dead and Nivens disappeared. No one seems to know if he's dead or alive. My gut says whoever hired him didn't want him to talk and made sure his body wouldn't be found."

Adam struggled to digest this bit of news. "Maybe I should take Tia and Toby and leave. Just leave without any word about where we're headed."

The sheriff shook his head. "You and I both know people like the judge have contacts everywhere. He might not find you tomorrow or next week or even next year, but you can't live your life looking over your shoulder."

Adam knew the man spoke the truth. "I don't know what to do to keep them safe."

"Keep an eye on them. I'd hoped the judge would give up, now that Tia has you. Evidently, he's more persistent than we thought." The sheriff put a hand on Adam's shoulder and gave it a squeeze. "Don't frighten the boy, but just make sure you or Tia never leave him alone or let him out of sight until we get a handle on this. If we can catch the man who tried to snatch him today and connect him to the judge, this nightmare will be over."

"And if you don't catch him? Then what?" Adam asked as he and the sheriff helped load benches into Blake's big wagon.

"We'll worry about crossing that bridge when we get to it. What did you say that man's name is, the one with the scarred face?"

"Bass. His name is Beauregard Bass."

The sheriff looked at Adam and grinned. "You are pulling my leg."

"No, sir. That's his name. And you don't want to shorten it either. I once saw him run an Arkansas toothpick into a man for calling him Beau."

"Thanks for the warning," the sheriff said, nodding toward Ginny and Blake's house. "Go collect your little family and get on home with them before it turns dark."

"I will, Sheriff. Thanks again."

209

Chapter Eighteen

After spending what seemed like hours tossing and turning in bed, Tia finally gave up on sleep.

She buttoned her dressing gown and slid her feet into slippers before leaving her room.

Quietly making her way to Toby's room, she checked to make sure he was safe. In the light from the small lamp she'd set on a shelf in the hall, she noticed a smile on his face as he slept.

With devoted motherly affection, she lightly brushed the hair back from his forehead and placed a kiss there before leaving the room.

Satisfied Toby was well, she picked up the lamp and ventured to the kitchen where she stoked the stove, trying not to make any noise. When she turned around with the teakettle to make a cup of tea, she almost dropped it as Adam rushed into the kitchen brandishing a pistol in his hand.

"What are you doing?" she hissed in a whisper. Hastily plunking the kettle down on the stove, she pressed a hand to the pulse pounding so rapidly in her throat, she thought her heart might explode right out of her chest. "You scared the waddin' out of me."

Adam set the gun on the table and offered an apologetic grin. "I heard a noise and wanted to make sure everything was fine. I bet you haven't said the word waddin' since you moved to Portland."

"Once, and I was severely reprimanded for my primitive speech." Tia added more wood to the stove then washed her hands. "From then on, I thought it, even if I didn't say it. I can't help it that Grandma shared her southern dialect with me. The esteemed Devereux family were appalled by some of my word choices and made sure I knew Grandma's favorite phrases wouldn't be tolerated."

Adam stepped around the table and wrapped her in his arms. "You can use them all you want around me. I always enjoyed listening to your grandma talk. It put me in mind of those big southern plantations I've heard about, and mint juleps, and those flowering trees. What did she call them?"

"Dogwoods," Tia said, recalling how much her grandma loved to tell stories about her growing up years in North Carolina.

"Why did you let them take so much from you, Tia? It's like they picked away at your spirit until there wasn't much left." Adam rubbed his hands comfortingly along her back.

Tia sighed and wrapped her arms around his waist, relishing the security and acceptance she found with him. "What else could I do? I couldn't leave Patrick, couldn't come back here. I made my choice and had to stick with it. Grandma would have said something about making my bed and having to sleep in it."

Adam chuckled. The deep rumble felt achingly familiar against Tia's cheek as she pressed against the warm skin of Adam's bare chest.

"I think a better saying of hers would have been the one about getting fleas from lying down with dogs."

She sighed. "I can't argue against that." With her weakened defenses, Tia knew she should step away from Adam, away from the comfort and care he so willingly offered. But she was tired and lonely, fearful and pensive. Rather than put distance between them, she snuggled a little closer and trailed her fingers across the broad expanse of his back.

Adam groaned and drew her more fully against him. With unwavering clarity, Tia knew where she belonged. Home was right there in Adam's arms.

Her thoughts trailed back over the time they'd spent together enjoying the skating party with their friends. Up until that horrid man had tried to snatch Toby, Tia thought it was the most wonderful day she'd had for years and years.

Adam had charmed her, wooed her, teased her, and romanced her. Yet because she'd been so caught up in her love for him, a crazy man had nearly snatched her child and made off with him.

Conflicted by her longing for Adam, her desire to be loved by him, and her need to protect her son, Tia battled to keep her emotions in check. Fear would drive her away from the man she loved if she wasn't careful.

Perceiving her struggle, he picked her up, sat down on a kitchen chair, and held her on his lap. He rocked back and forth, like he would with a child, whispering words of encouragement.

"It'll all be fine, Tia. I won't let anyone take Toby and I won't let anything happen to you. I promise." Adam kissed the top of her head. "Everything will be just fine."

The soothing tone of his voice combined with the comforting shelter of his presence calmed her. Fully relaxed against him, she allowed herself the pleasure of enjoying the moment, of the decadent luxury of resting in his powerful arms.

Suddenly, Adam tipped her chin up to look at him. "Do you remember how your grandma used to go on and on about the peaches she enjoyed, right off the tree in the summer? How those peaches were the sweetest, juiciest fruit she'd ever tasted?"

Tia smiled. "I remember. She made them sound like the most delicious thing that would ever touch your lips."

Adam released a choked sound. "Every time I see a peach, I think of you, Queenie. I think of you and those luscious lips of yours and how much I want to taste them."

Tia tipped her head back and gaped at him. If it hadn't been for the craving for her burning brightly in his eyes, she would have been sure he jested.

"Tia..." Adam whispered her name in a husky tone that made threads of desire and longing weave throughout her entire being.

His tempting mouth rested mere inches from hers. Before anything else could happen to delay the kiss, she tugged his head down until their lips met.

Adam let her kiss him, softly at first. He held perfectly still as she pressed timid, hesitant kisses to his lips.

His only response was to trail his thumb along the column of her throat.

Emboldened by his touch, her kisses grew more demanding. As she moved closer against him, drove her hands into the tousled richness of his hair, he deepened the kiss, taking control of the sizzling passion snapping between them.

Fiery embers of yearning that had remained banked in the recesses of their hearts burst into flame. Tia knew nothing would satisfy the hunger in her except Adam. Always and forever Adam.

"Tiadora, are you sure?" Adam asked as he fumbled with the buttons on her dressing gown.

Unable to draw enough breath to speak, she melded her lips to Adam's again, desperate to hold him closer, to love him with abandon.

His hand slipped inside her gown. The heat of his fingers seared her skin as he worked to unfasten the top buttons of her nightdress.

Full of eager anticipation, Tia screamed when a weight dropped onto her shoulder and bounced off her lap, using Adam's head for a springboard before speeding off in a blur of white.

Startled, Adam jumped to his feet, dumping Tia onto the floor as he frantically reached for the pistol he'd left on the other end of the table. Sudden realization that their attacker was only Crabby forced a growl out of his throat. He set the pistol back down and ran a hand through his hair.

"I swear, Tia, I'm going to find that cat and turn it into a pair of fuzzy mittens!" Adam's chest heaved as he glanced around, frustrated and angry the cat had disturbed their amorous interlude.

Tia sat on the floor, watching the impressive form of Adam's chest rise and fall as the situation went from frightening to entirely humorous.

The hand she clapped over her mouth did nothing to stifle her giggles.

When Adam reached down to give her a hand, she jerked him off balance until he sat on the floor beside her, shoulders shaking with silent hilarity.

Finally, neither of them could hold back any longer. They both broke into uncontrollable laughter.

"Oh, Adam, you should have seen your face when Crabby jumped off your head," Tia said between gasps of air and more giggles.

"Me? Your eyes were as wide as dinner plates when he landed on your shoulder. You looked like the grim reaper's hand had reached out and grabbed you." Adam snorted with glee.

Awakened by all the noise, Toby shuffled into the room, dragging a blanket behind him. "Why are you sitting on the floor? What's funny?"

Tia reached out to him and settled him on her lap, kissing the top of his head. "I'm sorry we woke you, baby.

Adam and I were just, um..." She searched for an appropriate response. "We were merely engaged in a meaningful interaction when Crabby offered his opinion on the matter."

A fresh round of laughter assailed Adam, causing Tia to break into peals of uncontrollable giggles.

Toby stared at them as if they'd lost their minds. Finally, he got up and took a few steps away from the two adults sitting on the floor, behaving like deranged lunatics.

"I'm going to bed. Try to be quiet, please. I need more sleeps." Toby frowned at them before marching back down the hall to his room.

Adam was the first to recover enough sense to get to his feet. He helped Tia to hers. Together, they tucked Toby back into bed then returned to the kitchen. Every time they looked at each other, Tia giggled and Adam chuckled, so they agreed it was best to turn in for the night.

Tia settled into the soft comfort of her bed with a smile in her heart and the dark, scrumptious flavor of Adam's kisses on her lips.

Chapter Nineteen

The knob on the back door rattled as Adam unlocked it then stepped inside. Tia glanced up from where she rolled out sugar cookies on the counter and offered him a brief smile before returning her attention to the flour-coated dough.

Toby sat at the table with crayons and a paper tablet, coloring pictures. Adam stepped beside his chair and studied the drawing the boy had made of what he assumed had to be Santa Claus. A red blob stood by two brown blobs. "Is that ol' Saint Nick?" he asked the boy.

"Yep!" Toby looked up at him and grinned. "It's Santa with his reindeer."

Adam ruffled the child's golden hair. "You're doing a great job coloring, little man."

Toby beamed with pleasure and picked up a green crayon, drawing something that might have been a tree.

Entertained by the boy's fascination with the upcoming holiday, Adam removed his coat, hat and scarf, leaving them on hooks by the back door.

After washing his hands at the sink, he snitched a piece of cookie dough and popped it into his mouth.

"Mmm. That's good dough, wife." He stuck his finger back in the bowl for another piece but Tia smacked his hand.

"Stay out of my dough."

"Aw, come on, Queenie. I worked hard this morning shoveling walks and chopping firewood. Don't I deserve a little treat?" Adam took a step closer to her, flashing his dimples as he stuck his fingers back into the bowl and swiped another bite.

Lost in the warmth of his gaze, Tia absently nodded her head.

"I think I need a little sugar, too." Adam licked the last bit of dough from his index finger then traced it across Tia's bottom lip. She opened her mouth to protest at the same moment Adam bent down and captured her lips with his, enfolding her in his arms.

Toby giggled and ran over to them, tugging on Tia's apron. "What are you doing?"

Adam lifted his head, keeping his gaze fastened to Tia's unsettled one as he answered the boy. "I'm kissing your mama, Toby, and I plan to do it every day, so you better get used to it."

Toby wrinkled his nose and returned to the table. "Erin says her daddy gives her mama slobbery kisses."

"Good for the pastor," Adam mumbled, tracing his finger over Tia's lip again.

Addled from his attention to her mouth and the splendor of his kiss, Tia scooped a glob of dough from the bowl and dropped it in Adam's hand, hoping to distract him.

He winked at her and ate the dough.

Under the assumption he'd find something else to do beyond torment her with his enticing smile and mouth-watering kisses, she glanced over as he removed his shirt.

Her eyes widened as she watched him remove his undershirt and lay it along with his shirt over a chair. Adam's broad shoulders, brawny chest and muscled arms made her fingers itch to explore all that wonderfully exposed skin.

Disconcerted by the direction of her thoughts, she frowned as he lifted his left arm. He tried to look at the stitches on his side, twisting this way and that.

Unable to see them, he scratched at his side until Tia wiped her hands on her apron and stepped over to grab his hand in hers.

"Stop that, Adam. You're worse than a child." She released his hand and examined the healing wound. A shudder rolled over him as she lightly ran her finger around the gash. Her fingertips burned from the slight touch. "You ought to have Doc take those stitches out. I think they're ready."

"Do you have a pair of sharp scissors?" Adam asked, tugging upward on the skin above the wound, trying to study it.

"If you're planning to cut them out yourself, then the answer is a resounding no."

Adam narrowed his gaze. "Either I do it myself or you can do it for me. I'm not going to bother Doc with something this simple."

Tia took a step away from him, appalled at the idea of removing his stitches. She'd never been squeamish, but thoughts of touching Adam's skin, being that close to his bare upper body, left her completely rattled.

As much as his presence affected her, she wasn't convinced she could keep her hand still enough to pull out the stitches without causing him undue agony.

Adam glanced at her again and shook his head. "You want to help me, Toby? You did a great job helping when Doc put them in."

Tia scowled. "No! Toby will not be the assistant to your idiotic plans."

Resigned to helping Adam, she set a small pan of water on the stovetop to boil then disappeared down the hall. Only a minute passed before she returned with a sharp pair of scissors and a pair of tweezers. Carefully, she dropped them into the hot water.

While they boiled, she hurriedly cut out the cookie dough, dropping shapes of stars and trees onto baking sheets and shoved one into the oven. After cleaning the counter and washing her hands again, she motioned to Adam.

"Sit on the end of the counter so I don't have to bend over to do this." Tia lit a lamp while Adam took a seat on the counter where she indicated.

"Are you sure you can handle it, Queenie? I can have Toby help me." Adam knew he goaded her, but he needed a distraction from his all-consuming need to own her, to love her.

She scowled at him and set the lamp beside him then opened a cupboard near the door. Unable to reach what she wanted, she pulled over a chair from the table and stood on the seat, taking down a bottle from the far back of the top shelf.

Adam's eyebrows rose at the sight of the whiskey bottle she set near the lamp. "If I find you tipsy one evening, I'll know the cause. What else is in that cupboard over there?"

Affronted, Tia huffed. "I'll have you know the only liquor that's touched these lips was the time you and Carl talked me into sampling that bottle of vile hooch Mr. Luther concocted."

Adam chuckled at the memory. "I can't speak for Carl, but that stuff cured me from ever wanting another drink."

After soaping a cloth and wiping it over the wound then rinsing it, Tia poured whiskey onto a clean cloth and swabbed it over the stitches.

Adam watched her work. "Might I assume you keep that for medicinal purposes?"

"You might assume correctly." Tia finished cleansing the area on his side then took the scissors and tweezers from the pot of boiling water.

Interested in the proceedings, Toby pulled over the chair Tia had stood on and climbed onto the seat, leaning against Adam's knees.

"Are you sure you want to watch this, sweetheart?" Tia looked to her son.

Briskly, he nodded his head. "If I want to be a doctor someday and marry Erin, I should watch."

Tia looked at Adam. He hid a smirk, but she saw the humor in his eyes. Afraid she might hurt him, she gingerly used the tweezers to lift the first knot in the thread and snipped it. Slowly, she pulled it loose. Her gaze lifted to Adam's and he smiled at her, offering a look of assurance.

"You're doing fine, Tia."

In fact, if she kept touching him so gently, he'd forget about the stitches and Toby's enthusiastic presence, and plunder her pretty mouth with kisses right there in the kitchen.

The blood in his veins heated and his temperature climbed with every soft brush of her hand until Adam thought he might combust.

He tried chasing his thoughts another direction, to work up some worry about the man out to grab Toby, or how they'd work things out when it was time for him to return to Portland. Try as he might to focus on something worrisome, he kept coming back around to how much he enjoyed Tia touching his skin, how much he wanted her to touch him all over.

He'd thought about stopping by the doctor's office earlier that morning when he was shoveling the boardwalk, but he decided he'd much rather have Tia remove the stitches.

During their childhood, she'd always liked to doctor the scrapes and cuts he and Carl sustained in their daily rough and tumble play. She'd never once turned away from a wound, no matter how much it might make other girls squirm.

Right now, though, Adam was the one who felt like squirming. If she didn't finish and fast, he shouldn't be held at fault for anything that might happen. The idea of resuming where they'd left off the other night before the cat scared them both half to death held a great deal of appeal.

Adam glanced over at Crabby napping in his box near the stove. The cat had pranced around the house the morning after he used Adam's head as a jumping off point as though he'd done nothing wrong.

Perhaps divine intervention had caused the cat to make his presence known at such an inopportune moment. If he'd had even a few more uninterrupted minutes with Tia, Adam knew he wouldn't still be sleeping alone in the guest room. Instead, he'd be cuddled up close to the beautiful woman worrying her very kissable bottom lip.

Raw hunger for her filled him as she smoothly pulled out the last of his stitches.

Relieved when she finished, Adam patted Toby on the head and allowed the boy to examine the holes left behind in his skin before Tia attempted to place a bandage over it.

He slid off the counter and pushed her hand away. "It'll be fine, Tia. Thank you for doing that for me."

On his way out of the kitchen, Adam grabbed his clothes and sauntered down the hall.

A short while later, he reappeared dressed in a fresh shirt and a clean pair of canvas trousers. He carried Toby's boat book and two yard-long lengths of rope, leaving them on the small bench by the door.

At Tia's perplexed look, Adam tipped his head toward Toby. "Alex asked if I'd speak to the students this afternoon about what it's like to be a pilot on the Columbia

River. I wondered if you and Toby would like to go along."

"Oh, yes, Mama! Please? May we go?" Toby ran across the kitchen and tugged on her apron as she placed the last sheet of cookies into the oven.

"I suppose that would be fine," Tia smiled at Toby then glanced at Adam. "Are you sure we won't be in the way?"

"Not at all. In fact, Alex was the one who suggested Toby might like to visit the school." Adam lifted a hot cookie from the baking sheet Tia had just removed from the oven and juggled the cookie in his hand until it was cool enough to take a bite.

Toby started to reach for one and Adam realized he'd have to be more careful about what he did since the child mimicked his every move.

"Here, son, let's share this one," Adam said, breaking the cookie in half and handing part of it to Toby.

Tia glared at him then released a sigh. "You'll spoil his lunch."

"Oh, I don't think part of one cookie will do him any lasting harm." Adam placed a hand on Toby's shoulder and gave him a slight nudge toward the door. "Why don't the two of us go outside while your mama finishes baking her cookies?"

"Okay!" Toby grabbed his coat and ran out the door while Adam gathered the child's mittens, hat and scarf.

He winked at Tia as he opened the door. "If we stay out of your hair for a while, will you let me snitch more cookies after lunch?"

"Only if you're a good boy." Tia waved her mixing spoon at him as she washed a few dishes.

"I'm always good, Mrs. Guthry. And if you give me the chance to get you alone, I'll show you just how outstandingly amazing I can be."

Shocked by his words, Tia blushed as Adam shut the door.

After lunch, Adam kept an eye on Toby while Tia changed her dress and combed her hair. When she breezed into the parlor, he gave her a long once-over before nodding his head in approval. He held her coat as she slipped it on, letting his fingers caress her neck and linger on her shoulders much longer than necessary.

While he helped Toby put on his hat and mittens, Tia pinned a fashionable hat on her head that matched the dark green of her coat.

Adam smiled and offered his arm to her as the three of them walked down the front steps and headed through town toward the school.

As they strolled along, Adam bent his head down and stirred the tendrils of hair she'd left dancing around her ear. "You are quite ravishing, Tia."

She turned to smile at him and discovered his face remarkably close to hers. "Thank you, kind sir. You are quite handsome."

Tia loved the rugged appearance of her husband. His navy coat only accentuated his tall, solidly built form. As she'd come to expect, he'd left his hat at the house, but he wore a scarf at his throat although he hadn't slipped on his gloves.

His tanned face and white teeth created a mesmerizing contrast when he smiled a smile made for charming softhearted women. She fought down the urge to taste the dimples in his cheeks and linger over that square chin.

Disturbed by her thoughts, Tia turned her attention back to her son. He held onto her other hand and chatted non-stop about Erin, the Christmas program at church, the Christmas Carnival, and pondering if Santa would bring him what he wished for.

"Do you know what he wants for Christmas?" Adam whispered as Toby waved to Aleta Bruner when they entered the mercantile.

"He wouldn't tell me, just said he sent his wishes to Santa Claus. I'm not even sure what he meant by that." Tia replied as she turned to greet Aleta.

Adam picked up a box Aleta had ready for him, thanked her, and ushered Tia and Toby back outside.

Tia stared at the box in his hand, but didn't ask what was in it as they finished the walk to the school.

Adam opened the door and waited while Tia and Toby stepped inside out of the cold. The three of them stood at the back of the classroom while all eyes turned their direction.

Alex smiled and hurried toward them. "Oh, I'm so glad you came." She hugged Tia and Toby then placed a hand on Adam's arm. "I've been telling the students about your work, Adam. They are quite interested to hear more about it from you."

Adam helped Tia remove her coat then took off his, leaving them on hooks by the door. He picked up the things he'd brought along and followed Alex to the front of the room.

"Class, please welcome Mr. Guthry. I think most of you know him. For those who do not, Adam is my husband's brother." Alex smiled at him and motioned for Adam to take a seat at her desk.

He shook his head and remained standing in front of it. "Hello, students."

"Hello, Mr. Guthry." The class smiled at him, eager to discover more about his work.

Adam talked about how he came to be a pilot on the river, about the dangers involved, and the long hours he worked. He used Toby's picture book to show them the different types of vessels he guided from the bar on the coast to Portland and ports further inland.

"Have you ever been in a shipwreck?" Tom Grove asked from his seat at the back of the room.

"I have, Tom. Experience doesn't make it any easier."

"Did you get hurt?" A little girl in the front row asked.

Adam smiled at her and nodded his head. "I sure did."

"Did you get any scars?" Percy Bruner asked from his seat beside Anna Jenkins.

"I've picked up a few," Adam said.

Tia had noticed several scars Adam didn't have as a young man. She assumed the nasty scar on his back and the long, thin line that crossed his mid-section, as if something had attempted to gut him, came from his work. However, she never imagined he'd been in a shipwreck.

"Can we see one?" another boy asked.

"Class, I don't think..." Alex stepped forward but Adam gave her a look that let her know he didn't mind their questions.

Adam rolled up his shirtsleeve to reveal his bicep and showed them a jagged scar across the flesh.

"What happened?" Anna Jenkins asked with round eyes.

"The steam engine blew up in a ship I was on. I woke up in the hospital a little worse for wear, but happy to be alive." Ready to change the subject, Adam picked up the two lengths of rope he'd brought along and showed the students how to tie several knots. He invited Toby to the front of the room and asked the little boy to demonstrate his knot-tying skill.

Toby beamed with pride as Adam complimented him on tying a perfect knot.

"Many times, the boats I pilot carry cargo from faraway places," Adam said, digging into the box he picked up at the mercantile. He'd asked Aleta to fill it with a variety of imported spices. He lifted a stick of cinnamon. Closing his eyes, he held it beneath his nose and sniffed, then handed it to one of the children in the front row to pass around the room.

"One of my favorite things about the cargo ships is being able to smell the spices. Did you know cinnamon comes from a type of evergreen with a soft bark? It is originally from a small island near India, but the Egyptians imported cinnamon from China. Ancient Romans held cinnamon sacred. I've even read that Emperor Nero burned a year's supply of cinnamon at his wife's funeral."

Engaged by the story, the students passed around the cinnamon while Adam lifted a knobby root from the box.

"Ginger was first cultivated by the Chinese and growers in India. It was one of the spices that led to the opening of spice trade routes." Adam passed around the root then lifted out a few star-shaped spices. He held them in the palm of his hand as he walked around the room. "Star anise is the fruit of a small tree native to China. The seedpods give the fruit its distinctive shape."

He showed them nutmeg, cloves, and bay leaves then grinned as he pulled a peppermint stick from the box. "Peppermint is a cross between watermint and spearmint. The plant is indigenous to Europe and the Middle East, although it can grow most anywhere. Mint leaves can be used for tea or to garnish a fancy meal." Adam looked at Tia and winked. "The oil from the leaves can also be extracted and used for a number of purposes. My favorite use is peppermint sticks."

Adam passed around a tin of candy and each student received a peppermint stick.

He nodded to Alex and she stepped beside him. "Well, class, wasn't that wonderful of Mr. Guthry to bring you all a treat?"

"Thank you, Mr. Guthry," the students said in unison.

"You're welcome." Adam picked up Toby's book and the rope he'd brought along. "A word of caution — do not practice tying knots on anything but a piece of old string or rope. You might end up out in the woodshed if you do. Toby and I discovered that the hard way."

Tia blushed as he stared at her and the older students laughed. Adam helped her on with her coat, tugged on his own then waved to Alex and the students as they stepped outside.

Toby skipped along beside them, sucking on his peppermint stick.

"Where's your candy, Mrs. Guthry?" Adam asked as they strolled toward the center of town. He popped a piece from a broken peppermint stick into his mouth.

"I didn't take a piece, but it was so kind of you to buy candy for the class, Adam." A saucy grin highlighted her high cheekbones as she glanced at her husband. "I'm sure Alex will appreciate all those sticky hands and faces. You certainly know how to endear yourself to the relatives, don't you?"

Adam sucked on the candy in his mouth. "Don't you remember how hard it was to sit in class and pay attention the week before Christmas. We would have welcomed any kind of interruption, especially one that involved candy."

"Agreed." Tia squeezed his burly upper arm with both hands, unsettled by the strength she felt through his coat sleeve. Hastily shifting her thoughts away from his physique, she smiled at Toby as he ran ahead and glanced back at them. "Where did you learn so much about all those different spices?"

"Oh, you pick up tidbits here and there," Adam said, waving for Toby to draw closer as the boy raced ahead of them. "When I'm not out on a boat, I do a little reading."

"I have a hard time picturing you quietly sitting in a parlor reading a book. I don't think you can sit still for that long."

Adam grinned. "Maybe I don't have quite as many ants in my pants now that I'm all grown up."

"And who says you've finally grown up?" Tia teased. "From what I've seen, you're only marginally more mature than you were at sixteen."

"Is that so?" Adam's look held an appealing mixture of mischief and mirth, causing Tia to be instantly wary of him. She started to pull away, but he stopped on the boardwalk and wrapped his arms around her. Much to her surprise, he licked her cheek with his candy-coated tongue.

Thrilled by his playfulness but unwilling to show it, she grimaced and tugged a handkerchief from her pocket, scrubbing at her sticky cheek. "My word, Adam. Must you?"

"I must, Queenie," he said, winking at her as he took her arm and they continued on their way.

Toby spied Erin waving from the window of her mother's store across the street and skipped that direction.

Before Adam or Tia could tell him to be careful, a man darted from around the corner of the building and snatched Toby, turning to run back down the alley.

Tia screamed while Adam took off running after him.

Not one to stand around in hysterics, she picked up her skirts and ran to the sheriff's office. The door banged against the wall as she rushed inside, terrified and out of breath.

"That man," she gasped, forcing herself to speak between gulps of air. "The one from the skating party. He took Toby."

The sheriff lunged to his feet and grabbed his coat, yanking it on as he hurried out the door with Tia right behind him.

"Which way did he go?" he asked as they crossed the street.

"Down the alley by Abby's shop." Tia watched as the sheriff sprinted past the store and around the corner. Abby ran out and put her arms around Tia, holding her as she cried.

"He took my baby, Abby. He took my baby."

"It'll be okay. Adam will get him back. Come inside and wait."

Tia tried to pull away, but Abby guided her inside the warmth of her store.

When the sound of gunshots rattled the windows, Tia and Abby both raced outside. Abby stood by her door with Erin clinging to her skirts while Tia ran toward the sound.

Around the corner and down several blocks she sped, heedless to her skirts trailing in the snow or the hairpins falling from her head.

By the time she reached a crowd gathered around a prone form, her hair tumbled around her shoulders and down her back, with the hat she'd worn lost somewhere along the way.

Fearing the worst, her heart stopped then resumed beating when Adam broke away from the group with Toby in his arms. The little boy clung tightly to his neck and Adam kept a protective hand on his back as he held him close.

Upon seeing his frantic and fearful wife, Adam gathered her into his arms and held them both.

"That man, he almost... he might have..." For Toby's sake, Tia held back her sobs as she took her son from Adam and cuddled him close. "Oh, baby. Are you okay? Did he hurt you? Is..."

Adam put a hand on her back and she glanced at him. He shook his head and frowned slightly, warning her not to add to Toby's fright.

Tia rained kisses across her son's cheeks and forehead.

He leaned back from her and sniffled. "I was scared, Mama, but I 'membered Daddy promised he'd take care of me." Toby reached out to Adam. The big man took the little hand in his. "And you did, Daddy. Just like you said. You didn't let the bad man take me."

The three of them watched as the sheriff and Douglas from the livery hefted Beauregard Bass as the man howled in pain from a bullet to his knee and one to his thigh.

The sheriff stopped in front of Adam. "As soon as we get him patched up at Doc's place, he'll spend Christmas in jail. Unlike Mr. Nivens, I'll make sure he doesn't disappear before he can testify against the judge."

Adam nodded his thanks and took Toby from Tia then draped his arm around her shoulders. The crowd dispersed about the time Arlan and Chauncy ran up the street.

"What happened?" Chauncy panted, as though he'd run a long distance and had yet to catch his breath.

Adam looked to the pastor then his brother. "That was the man who tried to take Toby Saturday at the skating party. He was bold enough to grab him while we watched and tried to run off. I chased after him while Tia fetched the sheriff. We caught up to him about the same time. While he had his eye on the sheriff, I grabbed Toby. He put up a bit of a fuss, but the sheriff made certain he couldn't run off, at least for a good long while."

Tia noticed blood at the corner of Adam's mouth and a bruise forming on his cheek. When she reached up to wipe away the blood, he jerked his head back. "No need to soil your gloves, Tia. I'm fine. Thank goodness, we're all just fine."

Adam rested his forehead against Toby's for a moment. "I think I've had enough excitement for one day. How about we head on home?"

"If you don't mind, I'll come along with you," Arlan said, falling into step beside Adam and Tia.

Tia looked ready to drop, so Adam handed Toby to Arlan and put his arm around her waist, lending her strength and support. "We'll be there in no time, Queenie."

She nodded her head, remaining silent as they made their way home. Arlan shifted Toby so he clung to his back, enjoying the ride his uncle gave him.

At the house, Adam opened the door and ushered Tia inside while Arlan followed with Toby.

"Thanks for the ride, Uncle Arlan. That was fun." Toby grinned at the tall man as he backed up to the sofa and let him drop to the soft cushion.

"You're very welcome, Toby." Arlan ruffled his hair. "I'm happy to give you a ride anytime."

"Be careful what you say or you might become Toby's personal pack mule," Tia said, smiling at Arlan. She helped Toby remove his coat and hat along with his mittens and boots. "Go wash your hands and face and then we'll have a snack."

"Okay, Mama."

Toby raced out of the room with all of his usual enthusiasm, unaware of the tension and turmoil still coiled around the adults.

"That was a close one," Adam said, helping Tia out of her coat and motioning for Arlan to take a seat. His brother shook his head.

"I need to get back to the bank, Adam, but I wanted to make sure you all were fine." Arlan moved closer to the door.

"If we aren't, we soon will be. Thanks for checking on us, Arlan. It's appreciated." Adam thumped his brother on the back as he walked him to the door.

"Why don't you join us for dinner tonight? I'm sure Tia doesn't feel like fixing supper and I promised to take Alex to the restaurant. You three might as well join us." Arlan gave his brother a hopeful look.

"That's a fine plan, Arlan. Meet you at the restaurant?"

"At six." Arlan nodded his head then hurried out the door.

Adam closed it behind him then returned to the parlor. Tia remained unmoving where he'd left her standing near the fireplace.

Quickly stoking the fire, Adam wrapped his arms around her from behind then pulled her against his chest, rubbing his hands up and down her arms. She shivered.

Uncertain if it was from the cold or her fears, part of him hoped it was from the pleasure of his touch.

"It's all over, Tia. Mr. Bass isn't going anywhere and with the confession he'll no doubt give the sheriff, the judge won't bother you anymore."

Unexpectedly, Tia turned to face him, throwing her arms around him and burying her face against his chest. "Thank you for saving my baby. You are such a good man, Adam Guthry. Don't ever forget it."

He tipped her chin up so she could see his face and offered her a roguish grin. "I guess I better keep you around to remind me from time to time."

She worked up something that resembled a smile, wiped away a few tears lingering on her lashes and pulled herself together as Toby raced into the room.

"Mama, may we please have hot chocolate and cookies?" Toby asked, tugging her toward the kitchen.

"I think that can be arranged." Tia tapped his nose with her finger and gave him a tender glance. "Why don't you check on Crabby? He'd probably like to come in and warm up by the stove for a while."

Adam gave her a speculative glance as she poured milk into a pan and took chocolate out of the cupboard. "Are you sure that demonic ball of fur deserves to come inside?"

"How can you talk about Crabby that way?" Tia pointed her knife at him as she cut chocolate to melt for their drinks. "He's just keeping an eye on things."

Adam leaned one elbow on the counter and smirked. "Then I guess I better figure out how to make that cat a pair of blinders because sooner or later, I have every intention of having my way with you."

Chapter Twenty

"Sir, there is someone here to see you." Charles stood in the doorway of the parlor, his face an expressionless mask, perfected from years of working for the judge.

Cedric Devereux snapped the newspaper in his hands closed and glared at the butler. "Well, show him in, man. Don't just stand there in the doorway like a post."

"I believe, sir, given the nature of his, um… business, you might prefer to carry on the conversation elsewhere." Charles tipped his head toward Catherine. The woman sat in a chair near the fire engrossed in a book.

"Very well," Cedric huffed, rising to his feet and following Charles back to the foyer. A man of questionable appearance and an even more questionable reputation waited. Cedric approached him with a hateful glare and motioned for him to follow him down the hall into the library.

Angrily pushing the button on the wall to bathe the room in light from the electric lamps, Cedric marched over to his desk and took a seat. "I thought I made it perfectly clear, Mr. Smith, that you were to never come to my home, regardless of the nature of the matter."

Mr. Smith sneered at Cedric and leaned back in the chair. "Ya might 'ave mentioned that a time or two, but I figured ya'd want to hear this news straight away."

Cedric leaned forward, resting his arms on the top of the desk. "And what news might that be?"

"The news that Mr. Bass won't be bringin' back yer grandson. Seems he tried to snatch him in broad daylight and got hisself shot in the kneecap then thrown in the hoosegow for his trouble. He ain't gonna be too happy about that. None too happy at all. And if ya think Mr. Bass is gonna be as easy to get rid of as Mr. Nivens, ya might want to reconsider that line of thinkin'."

Cedric stood and marched around his desk. "I've heard all I need to out of you this evening. In the future, send one of the messenger boys, but don't show up here at my home again."

Slowly, Mr. Smith rose to his feet and gave Cedric a long, calculating glance. "I reckon if ya want to be bossin' me, it's gonna cost ya. Either that, or I can waltz into yer fancy parlor down the hall and tell yer purty wife how ya got to be a powerful and mighty judge, cause it sure weren't due to yer honor or hard work."

Silently fuming, Cedric opened his desk drawer and withdrew a bag of coins, tossing them to Mr. Smith.

After opening the small bag and inspecting the contents, Mr. Smith tipped his head to Cedric. "Reckon I can show myself out just fine. Merry Christmas, Judge."

Cedric waited until he was sure the man had departed then hurried down the hall. He found Charles in the entry foyer, mopping up the mud Mr. Smith had tracked onto the marble tiles.

"Charles, I need a ticket on the next train heading East. Send Ed to secure it while you pack a bag for me. Unfortunately, there is a nasty piece of business I need to attend to in some backwater town."

"But, sir, it's nearly Christmas." Charles gaped at his employer.

The man never, ever dirtied his own hands. For him to decide to leave town either meant the law was about to catch up to him or he was up to no good. Truthfully, Charles didn't care what caused the judge to leave. The prospect of a reprieve from Cedric's demanding presence, even for a few days, filled him with a sense of relief.

"I don't care. Get me that ticket and my bag!" Cedric shouted then stalked off in the direction of the parlor, inventing a story to tell his wife.

There was no time to waste if he planned to return home by Christmas with his grandson in hand.

Chapter Twenty-One

"Tell me again why we're out here, freezing our feet before it's even light out?" Adam asked as he, Arlan, Chauncy, Luke, and Blake trudged through the drifts of snow behind Luke's house where trees grew abundantly on the surrounding hills.

"Because we won't have time to cut down these trees later, that's why. Between the Christmas Carnival, Christmas Eve services, and the folks arriving today, this is the last opportunity we'll have to cut down Christmas trees," Luke explained as they plodded on through the cold and dark.

Each of them carried a lantern. They'd left the horses and a wagon at the bottom of the hill. Although the rest of them had no idea where they were heading, Luke led the foray. He and Filly had walked out in the early autumn and marked a group of trees she thought would be perfect for festooning their homes for Christmas.

"Are you sure we aren't walking in circles?" Adam asked as Luke guided them over a ridge.

"Positive," Luke said, lifting his lantern higher and pointing to a dark shape in the distance."I'm pretty sure that's the stand of trees over there."

"Too bad the girls are unable to join us," Blake mused as he followed his brother-in-law.

"Someone would have needed to stay behind to watch the little ones and none of the girls would appreciate traipsing through this knee-deep snow before the sun has even touched the sky," Chauncy said. He grinned at Arlan. "With the exception of Alex the Amazing, of course. No doubt, she'd enjoy it."

"She would. In fact, she would have come along except she's trying to finish numerous details for the last day of school before the holiday break and get ready for the carnival tomorrow." Arlan turned to his brother. "You've probably noticed Alex is more of an outdoorsy girl than most. She's even ridden Blake's stallion, Romeo, bareback."

Adam had admired the huge, spirited horse when he'd been at Blake and Ginny's place. "Somehow, that doesn't surprise me. How is it you managed to make her fall in love with you?"

Arlan smiled. "I wielded all the charm I learned from watching you. And a little Christmas magic didn't hurt, either."

Adam chuckled as Luke stopped near a stand of fir trees. He walked around them and tugged a blue ribbon off a head-high branch.

"This is it. Filly marked the one she wanted, so feel free to choose whatever tree strikes your fancy," Luke said, setting the lantern on a stump. He took a handsaw out of the pack on his back.

"Let's wait until the sun at least rises so we can see what we're chopping. It should be up shortly," Blake said, leaning on the handle of the ax he carried. "I know Filly sent along a tin of cookies, Luke, so let's have at them."

"Tia made hot chocolate," Adam said, removing a flask from his coat pocket. "Even if it is only mildly warm by now."

"According to my daughter, Tia makes the 'bestest chocolate in the world,'" Chauncy said, affecting a falsetto as he spoke.

The rest of them laughed and accepted the cookies Luke passed around. Adam took a drink from the flask then handed it to Arlan.

As they visited and ate the cookies, the sun peeped over the horizon, waving streamers of pink and gold across the morning sky.

"Now, that's the way to start a day," Adam said, breathing in the pine scented air and gazing at the sky overhead, painted by the Creator in an array of glorious colors.

The men set to work cutting down trees for their homes and one for the church.

After dragging them down the hill to the wagon, they rode into town.

Adam thought Toby might bounce himself silly as he hopped from one foot to the other, watching out the window as he and Arlan unloaded the tree and carried it to the back door. After trimming a few branches along the trunk, Arlan helped him carry it inside and set it in the parlor where Tia directed.

"Oh, it's so lovely, Adam, and it smells divine." Tia clapped her hands together and sniffed the aromatic air.

"Santa can come! We have a tree!" Toby cheered, jumping around the room with unbridled joy.

Tia swung him into her arms before he sent something crashing to the floor in his excitement.

"I need to get to the bank," Arlan said, grinning at his nephew. "Toby, you keep these two out of trouble today."

The little boy giggled. "I will, Uncle Arlan."

Arlan smiled at Tia and nodded at his brother before departing. Adam went to the kitchen and removed the old coat he'd worn to keep from getting sap all over his pea coat. He was surprised the chore coat he'd left in his room at Arlan's still fit him, although it was a little snug through the shoulders and chest.

Even though he'd worn gloves, he still managed to get sap all over his fingers. As he stood at the kitchen sink scrubbing them with soap, they seemed to get stickier and stickier.

The stream of water stopped as Tia turned it off and took a tall, thin bottle from a cupboard.

"What's that?" Adam held his hands over the sink as she poured the liquid over his fingers and into his palms.

"Olive oil. I use it for cooking, but it might take off the sap. Just scrub it into your hands and I'll let you know when you're ready to wash them off." She returned the bottle to the cupboard.

"You're a bossy little thing, aren't you?" Adam winked at her as he scrubbed.

"Don't forget it," she said, fighting her attraction to him with every breath she took. Bent over the sink, scrubbing his hands, she watched the muscles play along his shoulders and arms. He smelled like leather and pine with a hint of chocolate from the drink she'd made early that morning before he left on the tree-hunting expedition.

Perhaps Adam wasn't the most debonair or refined gentleman, but he was kind, caring, brave, and strong. And he was hers.

Whether he admitted it or not, she knew his heart. Knew he still cared for her or he never would have married her.

At least, she hoped that played a part in his decision to become a husband to her and a father to Toby.

The little boy ran into the room, clearly enthused about the tree in the parlor. He flopped down on the floor by Crabby, telling the cat all about the tree and the pretty decorations that would go on it, and hanging a stocking by the fire.

"Is tonight the night when Santa comes?" Toby asked, glancing at his mother.

She shook her head. "Not tonight, sweetheart. Tomorrow. Rather than wait until tomorrow to decorate the tree, we should do it this evening."

"That's a fine plan," Adam agreed, still rubbing the oil into his hands.

Tia leaned over to look at his fingers. "Keep scrubbing."

He held up his oily hands and pretended to reach for her but she squealed and spun away, causing Toby to laugh.

"You're silly," the little boy said, pointing to them both.

Tia made a funny face, making Toby laugh even harder.

"Someone has a bad case of the giggles today," Adam said, glancing over his shoulder at Toby. "What do you think would cure it? Some castor oil?"

Toby stared at Adam, unsure if he was serious or not. When his stepfather grinned, Toby resumed laughing.

"Peppermints, and gingerbread, and building a snowman with Daddy, and skating with Erin would fix it." Toby's face held an impish look as he rattled off his list.

"Oh, you think you're being clever, don't you my little giggle box?" Tia picked up Toby and tickled his tummy, swinging him around in her arms.

When she finally set him down, Toby wrapped his arms around her waist and hugged her tight. "I love you, Mama."

"I love you, too, baby." Tia playfully swatted his rear. "Go wash your hands and we'll eat breakfast."

Tia turned on the water and handed Adam the soap. "You may wash your hands now."

He tipped his head to her with a solemn expression. "Yes, your highness."

"That's Queenie to you," she said, bumping his thigh with her hip and casting a saucy smile his direction.

Desire heated the blue of his eyes as he grinned at her. "You keep doing that, Queenie-pie, and you might get yourself into more trouble than you can handle."

Later that evening, she and Adam sat in the flickering light from the parlor fire. As they shared memories from their past and drank cups of spicy tea, Tia didn't want the evening to end.

After decorating the tree, they tucked Toby into bed with promises of a busy day awaiting him tomorrow.

By unspoken agreement, Tia and Adam returned to the parlor and sat together on the sofa, admiring the tree and enjoying their time together.

Suddenly, Adam set down his teacup and shifted so Tia rested against his side with his arm around her.

More content than she could ever recall feeling, she sighed and relaxed against him.

"This is nice, Adam. Thank you."

"For what?" he asked, watching the firelight dance through her hair. His fingers itched to remove her hairpins and bury themselves in the waves, but he bid his time.

"For bringing home such a lovely tree, and making the day so memorable for Toby. I'm not sure how he'll get through tomorrow, as wound up as he was tonight."

"You remember how exciting it was when you still believed in Santa Claus and the hope of what he might bring."

"Who says I still don't believe?" Tia lifted her head and looked back at Adam, grinning.

"What is it you want Santa to leave for you, little girl?" Adam asked in a deep rumbling voice, causing shivers of delight to wash over Tia.

"If I tell you, Santa might not bring it." She took another sip of her tea.

"Let's play a guessing game and I'll figure out what it is you want."

"Nope. It never mattered how hard I tried, you always beat me at those games. I'm not playing." As she took another sip of the spicy tea, she settled closer against him. "What do you want for Christmas, Adam? What's the one gift you'd like to receive Christmas morning?"

You.

A vision of Tia with all that magnificent hair spilling around her in his bed made his muscles tense while his blood heated in his veins.

Adam cleared his throat. "If I listened to what you've said the past few weeks, I haven't been a very good boy, so Santa will most likely leave a lump of coal for me."

Tia turned around and gazed at him, studying the stubbly growth of whiskers on his jaw and chin, the hint of the dimple in his cheeks, the tousled mess of his hair that she adored.

"Please, Adam? Tell me what you'd like for Christmas."

Purposefully ignoring her pleading, he changed the subject. "Why did you leave?"

"Leave?" Tia asked, baffled by his question. "I only ran to the mercantile for a few minutes to get more baking chocolate before supper."

"Not today." Adam sat up and leaned his elbows on his knees. "Why did you leave Hardman?" *Why did you leave me?*

The moment she set eyes on Adam at Carl's funeral, she knew she'd eventually have to tell him the truth. The last thing she wanted to do this evening, though, was have that painful conversation.

Still unsure of his feelings for her, she was afraid to tell him why she left, why she settled for Patrick.

"Why did you go away, Tia?" Adam asked in a voice that betrayed the anguish she'd caused. "I thought you'd be back in a few weeks and we'd plan a future together. Two weeks turned into a month then your grandmother broke the news to me that you'd wed some attorney twelve years older than you. I just don't understand why, Tia."

Carefully returning her teacup to the saucer in her hand, Tia set them aside and took a deep breath. "I left, Adam, because the only thing in this world I wanted at that time was you. I wanted to marry you, to be your wife, to have your babies, to spend every moment of every day making you happy."

Although his face remained impassive as he stared at her, his eyes expressed his shock. "I don't believe you."

"It's true, Adam." Tia placed her hand on his arm, needing to touch him. "I waited all spring for you to ask me to marry you. When graduation came and went without you saying a word... Grandma thought it might do me good to get away for a week or two and see something new. She was mostly tired of my moping around, convinced you didn't love me, at least not the way I loved you."

Both of their glances turned to the opal on her finger, glittering in the firelight. "Adam, if I'd known about the ring, known you planned to propose, I never would have left. I didn't know you loved me."

"How could you not know, Tia? Every person in town knew I was head over heels in love with you." Adam raised both his voice and temper.

Tia held a finger to his lips. "Shh. You'll wake Toby."

He dropped his voice to barely above a whisper. "Even if I didn't say the words, you should have known by my actions."

What Adam said was true, but she'd needed to hear him say it, to confess his feelings for her — and he never had. Perhaps he never would.

Adam sighed and ran a hand through his hair, making it stand up on end. "So you went off to Portland without the intention of staying and fell madly in love with Patrick Devereux."

"No."

He frowned at her.

She took another deep breath and held his gaze. "I planned to come back after a few weeks. Grandma was sure by the time I returned, you'd be over me or you'd realize how much you loved me and be ready to do something about it. The afternoon before I'd planned to come back, I went for a walk in the park near Aunt Lorraine's home. I met Patrick there. He was quite a bit older, but so charming and handsome with his golden hair and light blue eyes. Quite suddenly, he'd asked me to marry him and I agreed because you didn't want me."

Tia took a moment to compose herself before continuing. "You didn't want me enough to come after me and you didn't love me enough to write me a single letter while I was gone. I married Patrick, not because I loved him, but because he promised to treat me like a princess. For the most part, he did. I was something he showed off and bragged about then tucked away in the house when he had no use for me. But no matter how much I regret leaving without telling you my feelings, no matter how much I wish things were different, I wouldn't trade the experience for anything, because it gave me Toby."

Although he understood, it didn't make it any easier for him to hear. She'd loved him, would have married him if he'd just worked up the courage to ask her before she left.

"Why'd you come home?" he asked, nervously fiddling with a thread he plucked off the carpet beneath his feet.

"Initially, to bury Grandma, and pack up my memories here. Once I came back, once I stood inside this house, I couldn't leave." Tia brushed at a tear then pinned him with her gaze, her eyes as dark and gray as a stormy winter sky. "Do you want to know why, Adam?"

He didn't move, waiting for her to continue.

She got to her feet and looked down at him with regret oozing from every pore. "I couldn't leave, because of you. Because you were in the memories of this house and this town, and I couldn't let them go. I didn't want to let them go."

"Tia…" Adam stood and reached for her, but she backed away.

Her hands clenched at her sides and tears filled her eyes, but she took a deep breath and finished what must be said. "I've loved you since I was six years old, Adam. I've never stopped loving you. Not a single day has gone by that I haven't thought of you. The only reason I agreed to marry you is because I love you, not because you promised to save Toby from Cedric. It's because I've always and forever loved only you."

Before he could take her in his arms, before he could confess his love for her, she spun away and ran down the hall. The click of her door shutting, locking him out, echoed through the stillness of the house.

Adam sank onto the sofa, holding his head in his hands and praying for wisdom.

There had to be some way to convince his wife he loved her, had always loved her.

He'd been so young and foolish when he let Tia leave all those years ago. Suddenly, he wondered if he'd outgrown it. Instead of pretending he felt nothing for Tia, he should have professed his love for her from the start.

No matter what it took, he would convince her she was wanted, needed, and so deeply loved.

Chapter Twenty-Two

Adam tried to hide his awe as he cupped Tia's elbow in one hand and held the handles of a basket with his other. Together, they walked up the steps to Dora and Greg Granger's impressive house.

The home the senior Granger couple had built the previous year looked like an elaborate gingerbread house Adam had seen a few years ago in Portland.

Snow sprinkled the shakes of the roof and sifted across the peaks and gables as though an artistic baker had dusted the whole thing with powdered sugar and piped white frosting along the edges.

Pine garlands and red bows bedecked the porch. Two matching wreaths hung on the big front entry doors while the sounds of holiday music trickled outside. The scents of cinnamon and apples mingled with the fragrance of pine and fir, wafting around guests with a pleasant aromatic welcome.

"This is quite the house," Adam whispered into Tia's ear as they walked up the steps.

"It's exquisite," she said, smiling up at him, admiring the light shining in his brilliant blue eyes, matching the shade of the scarf wrapped around his neck. Earlier, when he'd walked into the kitchen in the suit he'd worn to their wedding, Tia almost dropped the chocolate pie she'd held in her hands.

Adam Guthry was a unique cross of rugged handsomeness and kind gentlemanliness that made her heart flutter and any number of inappropriate thoughts dash around in her head.

Tia noticed a few young women eyeing him as they stepped inside the foyer, greeted by Dora and Greg Granger.

Even if Tia hadn't known them, she would have picked up on the family resemblance between Dora and Ginny. Dora still looked young enough to be a sister to her daughter, rather than her mother.

"Tia and Adam! We're so sorry we missed your wedding." Dora gave them each a hug. "And, Toby... how nice to see you."

Greg shook Adam's hand then thumped him on the back. "Good for you marrying this lovely girl before someone else took a notion to claim her."

Adam grinned and helped Tia remove her coat. Toby yanked his off and handed it to the servants gathering wraps, coats, and hats in the large entry.

"Please go right on in. If you brought something for the potluck luncheon, it goes in the dining room, there." Greg indicated the first door down the hallway.

Adam took Tia's hand and led her into the dining room where she set out two chocolate pies, a gingerbread cake, and a chicken casserole.

Filly gave her a hug then bustled back to the kitchen where she and a handful of volunteers ensured all the attendees at the second annual Hardman Christmas Carnival would have plenty to eat and drink.

Toby tugged on Tia's hand, capturing her attention. "Come on, Mama. I want to find Erin."

"And I want to listen to Arlan play his trumpet," Adam said, lifting Toby in one arm and offering the other to Tia. She took it with an indulgent smile and they proceeded to the large parlor where the community band played and most people gathered, waiting for lunch.

Arlan acknowledged them with a wink as he performed. Adam set Toby down and watched as the boy ran over to where Erin perched on her father's knee, listening to the festive music.

Adam led Tia across the room to a chair near Chauncy's and motioned for her to take a seat while he stood behind her, leaving his hand on her shoulder.

Since their discussion the previous evening and her admission that she loved him, had always loved him, she'd acted hesitant around him. At breakfast she barely spoke, and remained quiet as she worked in the kitchen preparing food to contribute to the potluck.

Adam decided not to press her, at least not until later when they were alone. Neither of them would get any sleep until things between them were resolved, even if they stayed awake the whole night to do it.

If Adam had his way, there wouldn't be any need for him to continue sleeping in the guest bedroom. He'd waited long enough to make Tia his own and one more night seemed far too many.

Forcefully returning his thoughts to the Christmas event they attended, Adam gazed around the room full of neighbors and friends. Arlan had explained Alex and Ginny came up with the idea for the celebration the previous year. Since everyone enjoyed it so much, the community decided to make it an annual event.

Adam noticed Ginny flitting in and out, overseeing Blake and Luke as they carried in more chairs.

A tall figure at the door dressed in an elaborate red and black costume caught his attention. He bent down so he could whisper in Tia's ear. "It appears sister Alex is the star of the show."

Tia nodded her head in agreement. "She's so striking, such a beautiful woman. I love her costume."

In truth, Adam was a bit surprised to see Alex wearing black pants tucked into knee-high boots. The ruffled white blouse and black damask waistcoat embroidered with delicate red rosebuds beneath her red velvet topcoat highlighted her feminine appearance despite her pants.

A black top hat, adorned with a red feather and a bit of holly, sat at a jaunty angle on top of her head while dark hair cascaded around her shoulders and down her back.

"I don't see how a bookish ol' banker like Arlan convinced Alex to marry him," Adam teased, secretly proud of his brother and his lovely wife.

Tia glanced up at him and grinned. "It's that Guthry charm you and your brother both seem to possess."

The band stopped playing when Greg stepped to the front of the room and thanked everyone for coming. He invited them to eat, as soon as Chauncy asked a blessing on the meal.

After lunch, an auction of various art projects, crafts and unique items created by Alex's students raised funds for a local charity.

Once the auction ended, the crowd trailed upstairs to watch Alex's magic performance.

Slightly disappointed he wouldn't get to see her perform out of her wagon, Adam still looked forward to her show.

Several people in town had talked about how entertaining the performance had been the previous year.

Arlan sat beside Adam as they watched Alex go through her routine with Tom Grove serving as her assistant.

Tia smiled at Toby as he sat one row up with Chauncy, Abby, and Erin Dodd. From the corner of her eye, she thought she saw a face she recognized, one that gave her a moment of pause.

Carefully studying the crowd, she decided her imagination had somehow conjured an image of her former father-in-law.

The last place Judge Cedric Devereux would be caught on Christmas Eve was a magic show in the town of Hardman.

Chastising herself for her overactive imagination, she gave herself a mental lecture.

"Everything okay, Tia?" The warmth of Adam's breath caressed her neck while his deep voice tantalized her ear.

"Yes, I'm fine," she whispered, giving him a brief glance before returning her attention to Alex's show.

Enthralled with her sister-in-law's ability to make objects appear and disappear, cast illusions, and draw the crowd into a web of light-hearted magical fun, Tia clapped as enthusiastically as anyone when the show ended.

"Oh, she's marvelous, Arlan!" Tia leaned around Adam and grinned at her brother-in-law. "It's a shame she doesn't have the opportunity to perform more often."

"I know. She misses being on the road doing shows, but most of the time she is perfectly content with her work at the school."

Tia reached out and squeezed his hand. "And it's obvious she's crazy about you. The lure of magic wouldn't hold a candle to the love in her heart."

Arlan gave her a pleased smile and nodded his head. "That's what she keeps telling me." He stood as the crowd began to wander back downstairs for cider and dessert. "If I ask nicely, can you help me haul her props downstairs, Adam?"

"I'd be happy to." Adam kissed Tia's cheek. "As long as the queen doesn't mind."

She rolled her eyes at him and fluttered her hand toward the stage. "Go on, but you better hurry or I can't promise there'll be any gingerbread cake left for you."

"Save me a piece, Queenie. Please?" Adam winked at her and followed Arlan behind the stage.

Tia glanced around and saw Toby skipping out the door, holding hands with Erin Dodd.

Satisfied he behaved himself, she grinned when Ginny looped arms with her. The two of them descended the stairs, talking about their plans for the following day when they'd gather at Luke and Filly's home for Christmas dinner. In addition to the Granger and Stratton families, Arlan and Alex, Adam, Tia and Toby, the Dodd family, and the Bruner's would all meet at Granger House to celebrate Christmas together and enjoy a holiday feast.

As she reached the bottom of the stairs, Tia once again thought she caught a glimpse of the judge in the milling crowd, but knew her mind had to be playing tricks on her. She rubbed her temple and sighed.

"Are you unwell, Tia? You look a little pale." Ginny place a hand on her shoulder and glanced at her in concern.

"I'm fine, Ginny, but thank you for asking. It's probably just all the excitement of the day."

"It is an exciting day, isn't it?" Ginny smiled at her then waved to her mother-in-law. She excused herself to help Filly and some of the other women pour coffee and cider.

Unreasonably unsettled, Tia looked around until she located Toby and Erin sharing a sugar cookie and giggling together in the parlor with a group of children.

Relieved to see her son having such a wonderful time with his little friends, she turned into the dining room and cut a large slice of gingerbread for Adam and a small piece of pumpkin pie Alex had brought.

She visited with some of the women from church as she ate the pie then went to check on Toby.

The boy was not in the front room with the other children, although Erin was there. Mindful the two youngsters generally stayed together, she set Adam's piece of cake on a side table and approached Erin.

"Erin, have you seen Toby?"

The little girl nodded her head and swallowed the bite of cookie in her mouth. "He said he needed to use the necessary."

"Thank you, sweetheart." Tia cupped her chin and gave her a warm smile. "And thank you for being such a good friend to Toby."

Tia left the front parlor and strode down the hall toward the bathroom. The door stood open so she returned to the dining room, hoping to find Toby there, snitching more cookies.

He wasn't among those in the room, so Tia rushed into the kitchen and asked if anyone had seen Toby.

"I haven't, Tia, but he's got to be around here somewhere," Filly said, cutting a sheet cake into squares and placing the slices onto plates. "Have you asked Erin?"

"She said he went to the bathroom, but he wasn't in there. I checked the front parlor and the dining room." An impending sense of panic made Tia's breath come in short gasps as she knotted her hands at her waist.

Filly quickly wiped her hands on a dishtowel then reached out and grabbed one of Tia's hands. "Come on, we'll find him."

Together, they checked the library, the guest rooms on the main floor of the house, even the linen closet and didn't see Toby.

As they hurried down the hall, they ran into Arlan, Adam, and Luke as they returned from carrying Alex's props outside to her magic wagon.

Immediately, Adam stepped forward and grasped Tia's arms. Concerned by the fear in her eyes and the grim set of her mouth, he gave her an imploring glance. "What happened? What's wrong?"

"I can't find Toby. He was eating cookies with Erin one moment and the next, he was just gone." Tia leaned against Adam, drawing strength from his presence. "What if the judge sent someone else to try and take him? What if…"

Adam shook his head. "The sheriff wired the U.S. Marshal's office in Portland yesterday. They were going to arrest him based on the confession from Mr. Bass."

"But Adam, if nothing's wrong, where is he?" Tia clutched the lapels of his coat in her hands and gave them a frantic shake. "I can feel it, Adam. Something's happened."

"Then we'll find him." Adam turned to his brother and his friends. They agreed to search the house as well as outside.

Alex sent one of her older students to fetch the sheriff who'd already returned to his office.

Arlan and Adam pulled on their coats and gloves. Tia started to reach for hers, but Adam shook his head. "Stay here, Tia. If Toby is in the house, you need to be here for him."

"But, Adam…" Tia blinked to keep the tears pooling in her eyes from spilling down her cheeks.

"I'll find him, Tia. I promise." Adam kissed her full on the mouth. It wasn't a kiss borne of passion, but one shared from love and apprehension. "You know I always keep my promises."

She nodded and squeezed his hand. "Hurry, Adam. Please hurry."

Arlan and Adam raced outside with Luke and Blake.

"Let's spread out and go through town a street at a time," Luke suggested. "Blake and I'll take the north half if you two take the south."

"Good idea," Adam said, turning and walking down a block with Arlan beside him. "If you were trying to get a child out of town without being seen, where would you go?"

"The livery," Arlan said and took off running with Adam hot on his heels.

Together, they raced into Douglas McIntosh's livery and blacksmith shop. The man looked up from the counter where he did his paperwork and smiled. "What can I do for the Guthry brothers today?"

"Have you seen any strangers, Douglas?" Adam asked as a feeling of dread made knots form in his stomach.

"Sure have. He left about half an hour ago. Man had a rented sleigh from Heppner and said he planned to make the train this evening. He came in this morning and paid me a tidy sum to feed and water the team of horses, and to keep them ready to go this afternoon."

"Did this man have anything with him when he returned?" Adam asked, desperate to know if Toby had in fact been abducted.

Douglas removed his hat and thoughtfully scratched his head. "Come to think of it, he was carrying a small trunk. He seemed to struggle with it, like it was heavy, but when I offered to set it in the sleigh, he insisted on taking care of it himself."

"Was there anything strange in the sleigh?" Arlan asked. "Anything at all?"

"He had two heavy lap robes, a jar of peppermint sticks and a few children's books." Douglas looked from Arlan to Adam.

The two brothers nodded at each other in silent agreement. Adam ran out the door to let Blake and Luke know they were riding after whoever had snuck into town and back out again in the rented sleigh.

"We're going to need our horses, right now." Arlan hurried to saddle his horse, Orion, while Douglas saddled Adam's rented horse.

The sheriff caught up with Adam and agreed to ride along while Luke and Blake stayed in town, continuing to search for Toby.

"Do you think the judge sent someone else after Toby?" Adam asked as Arlan approached riding his horse and leading Adam's.

The sheriff shook his head as he mounted his own horse. "I didn't want to worry you on Christmas Eve, but I received a telegram this morning that the judge wasn't home when they went to arrest him. His wife said he had business out of town and planned to be back sometime Christmas Day."

"Then we better catch him before he makes it to Heppner and gets on that train." Adam swung onto the back of his horse, racing out of town.

An hour later, they topped a rise and saw a sleigh gliding along the snow-covered road ahead of them.

"That's got to be them," the sheriff said to Adam as they spurred their horses forward. In minutes, they overtook the sleigh.

A pompous, richly dressed man scowled at them as Adam and Arlan rode on either side of the sleigh, tugging the team to a stop.

"What is the meaning of this?" the man demanded, glaring at them. "I'll have you arrested for detaining me if you don't release the horses this instant."

"Oh, I don't think that'll be necessary," the sheriff said, pointing to the bronze star pinned to his coat. "These gentlemen are helping me with a problem. See we've got a little boy missing back in Hardman and heard you might know something about that."

The man scoffed and waved his hand toward the back seat of the sleigh. "As you can see, there are no children in my sleigh. Now, get out of my way, I have a train to catch."

The sheriff shook his head. "Might I assume you're Judge Devereux?"

"Yes. Have you heard of me, even out here in this backwater territory?"

"Oh, we've heard of you all right." The sheriff watched as Adam swung out of his saddle and stepped next to the sleigh, looking for any sign of Toby.

A small trunk, just big enough to hold a child rested on the floor in the back of the sleigh. He reached out to lift it and the judge turned on him, cracking the whip he held across Adam's arm.

Before the judge hit him again, Adam jerked the whip out of his hand and tossed it to the ground.

Quickly working the latch free on the trunk, he lifted the lid and gasped, gaping at Toby bound hand and foot.

Adam growled in rage and punched the judge in the face so hard, it knocked him off the seat of the sleigh into the snow.

"What have you done to my boy?" Adam untied Toby's hands and feet then tenderly lifted the child out of the trunk, terrified by his limp body and shuttered eyes.

The little chest rose and fell, so Adam knew Toby still breathed, but he remained unconscious.

"It's just a little chloroform," the judge said, holding a handkerchief to his bloody nose as he sat in the snow. "That boy isn't yours, he's mine. I intend to raise him in the manner I see fit."

"Well, now, that's going to be a little hard since you'll be spending the rest of your life in prison." The sheriff dismounted and locked handcuffs around Cedric's wrists. "Where we come from, what you did is called kidnapping. Most law enforcement officials and judges who aren't in the pockets of criminals take offense to that." The sheriff shoved Cedric into the sleigh then tied his horse to the back of it. "With the full confession your friend Mr. Bass gave us, including the details about the disappearance of Mr. Nivens and your involvement in any number of crimes through the years, you can plan on never again seeing the light of day as a free man."

Finally grasping the fact that his carefully plotted world crashed around his ears, the judge lost his bravado and began to plead for mercy.

The sheriff looked to Adam and tipped his head toward the judge. Adam reached out with one clenched fist and hit Cedric's chin with just enough force, his head snapped back and knocked the man senseless.

"Thanks, Adam. I wasn't looking forward to listening to his whining all the way back to town. I suppose I could take him on to Heppner, but my wife has a nice meal planned this evening and I'm not of a mind to miss it." The sheriff turned the sleigh around while Adam continued to hold Toby in his arms.

Arlan snatched one of the heavy robes off the seat as the sheriff drove past him then walked over to where Adam stood with Toby. Carefully, he tapped the child's cheeks while Adam tried to coax Toby awake.

"Come on, now, Toby, time to open your eyes so we can go back to your mama and have a merry Christmas. You don't want to miss out on the Christmas festivities at the church. How will Pastor Chauncy make it through the program without you there to be one of the shepherds?"

Toby's eyelashes fluttered and Adam gave Arlan a hopeful glance.

"You can do it, son. Open those eyes and give me a peek." Adam knelt on one knee in the snow, shifting Toby so he sat on his bent leg with his arm supporting his back.

The child's head listed to one side and Arlan tapped his cheeks again. "Come on, Toby. If you wake up, I promise Aunt Alex will show you a special magic trick."

"She will?" Toby mumbled as his eyelashes fluttered again.

Arlan grinned. "She sure will."

Toby released a ragged breath and slowly his eyes opened. Although he seemed somewhat dazed and foggy, he didn't appear any worse for wear.

"What happened?" Toby asked, as Adam hugged him tight and kissed his forehead.

Rather than answer his question, Adam handed the boy to Arlan while he mounted his horse. He held his arms out for his son. Between the two brothers, they got the heavy blanket wrapped around the boy as Adam cradled him in one arm in front of him.

"What do you remember, Toby," Adam asked as they started back toward town.

"Erin and I were eating cookies with our friends and I had to use the necessary. Mrs. Granger has such a nice one, doesn't she?" Toby asked.

"She certainly does," Adam agreed, eager to find out how Cedric had managed to kidnap Toby right beneath their noses. "Then what happened."

"Well, after I went to the potty, I wanted another cookie, one for me and Erin, so I went to get one. Then I saw Grandfather. He had my coat and hat and said Mama asked him to walk me home. Grandfather picked me up and carried me outside. That's all I member."

"That's good, Toby," Adam said, offering the child a reassuring smile.

"Did you see my Grandfather?" Toby asked, sitting up a little as he came more fully awake.

"I did, Toby, but he had to leave and I don't think you'll see him for a long, long time."

Toby released a relieved sigh. "That's good. Mama said we had to be polite to Grandfather and Grandmother, but they aren't much fun." Toby wiggled a hand free from his blanket cocoon and reached up to pat Adam's cheek. "I'm glad you're my daddy."

Adam swallowed down his emotion. "Me, too, son. Me, too."

Arlan and Adam urged the horses to hurry home, passing the sleigh halfway back to town. The judge remained knocked out on the seat beside the sheriff and Adam grinned at the lawman as he and Arlan rode past him.

The sheriff touched the brim of his hat and snapped the lines on the rumps of the team, eager to return to the warmth of his home and his own Christmas Eve plans.

Adam rode straight to Greg and Dora's home. Before he had a chance to pull the horse to a full stop, Tia raced down the front steps. Adam swung out of the saddle with a sleeping Toby in his arms. Before he handed the boy to her, he spoke in a hushed tone. "He doesn't know what happened, Tia. Don't scare him. The judge dosed him up good with chloroform. All he knows is that his grandfather won't be back for a long time."

"Oh, you saved my baby." Tears streamed down her cheeks as she took Toby from him and softly kissed her son's cheek. "I can't thank you enough, Adam, and you too, Arlan." She glanced to her brother-in-law as he stood nearby. "Thank you for bringing him home."

Adam gave her a tender smile. "He's my son, too, Tia. I promised to bring him back to you, and I did."

"And I promised him my wife would show him a magic trick, so I think I better warn her to have something planned for later." Arlan kissed Tia's cheek and patted Adam on the back before taking the reins of the two horses and walking off in the direction of the livery.

Adam squeezed Tia's hand. "Let me get your coat then I'll take you home. Once I get you and Toby settled, I'll let everyone know to call off the search." Adam turned to go inside, but Tia held onto his hand. He glanced at their joined fingers then lifted his gaze to her face. "Thank you, Adam." She placed a soft kiss to his cheek with Toby cradled between them.

The boy chose that moment to awaken and squirmed. "Ew! Don't slobbery kiss on me."

Adam chuckled and Tia dropped her head, raining kisses on Toby's cheeks, making him giggle.

"Hi, Mama." Toby reached up and patted her face. "May I have another cookie? I didn't get one earlier."

"Yes, baby." Tia rubbed her nose against his. "Let's go inside."

Chapter Twenty-Three

"He's snoring." Adam's soft chuckle made Tia smile as he returned to the parlor after checking on Toby.

Hesitant to set the little boy's gifts beneath the tree and fill his stocking, they first made certain he was sound asleep.

"Under normal circumstances, he'd sleep in late and give me a chance to catch up on my rest. However, I have a feeling Toby will be up bright and early, ready to discover the gifts Santa left for him."

"Who can blame him?" Adam asked as he placed an orange in the toe of Toby's stocking then filled it with foil-wrapped chocolates, peppermints, and a bag of shiny marbles.

Tia smiled at him from where she set a wooden sled, painted bright red, beneath the tree along with a few other packages wrapped in shiny red and silver paper.

"That's quite a sled." Adam picked it up and admired the sleek curves of the metal runners.

"Douglas made it for me. I asked him to do it as soon as I knew we'd be here for Christmas," Tia said, excited for Toby to find it beneath the tree. He'd mentioned several times how much he wanted his own sled.

"He'll love it, Tia." Adam set the sled beneath the fragrant branches of the tree then disappeared down the hall to his room.

He returned carrying a wooden boat, complete with a sail, and set it beneath the tree. Not big enough Toby could fit in it, the boat did look like a miniature of his favorite in the picture book.

"Oh, Adam. He'll be so thrilled." Tia sank to her knees and ran her hand over the smooth wood side of the boat. "Where on earth did you get it?"

Adam hunkered down beside her. "I made it, with Blake's help. If it hadn't been for his knowledge and tools, I might not have gotten it finished in time for tonight."

"This will be Toby's favorite gift. As you know, he absolutely loves boats." Tia stood and took a seat on the sofa.

Adam sat beside her, wrapping his arm around her. He maneuvered Tia around until her back rested against his broad chest. Together, they looked at the tree in the light from the fire.

The flames on the candles they'd lit earlier on the tree had already been doused. After attending the Christmas Eve service at church, they'd illuminated the tree for Toby's enjoyment then blew out the candles before tucking him into bed.

Adam thought back to the sermon Chauncy delivered, leaving nary a dry eye in the congregation as he talked about the best gifts in life.

The children performed in a program, reenacting the birth of the precious baby in a manager. Toby stood to the side with Erin, both dressed as shepherds, watching as Percy Bruner and Anna Jenkins revised their roles of Joseph and Mary.

Now that Toby slept and evening settled over them, Adam planned to woo his wife.

Slowly, he ran his hand along her arm and lifted her hand in his. The opal ring on her finger glittered in the firelight. Iridescent shards of light danced across the room like tiny fireflies.

With unhurried movements, he brought her hand to his mouth and kissed the tip of each finger, hearing a satisfied hum from Tia as she relaxed against him.

"Do you know what I was thinking the day I purchased this ring?" he asked in a low voice.

"I have no idea," Tia whispered, turning her face to look at him.

"I was thinking..." He tipped his head down and kissed her forehead. "That you were the most beautiful..." A kiss to her nose. "Funny..." A kiss to her temple. "Smart..." A kiss to her cheek. "Perfect-for-me girl in the world."

"Really?" Tia asked, closing her eyes and inhaling Adam's enthralling masculine scent.

"Really. The reason I didn't ask you before graduation, before you left town, is that I was afraid you'd tell me no."

Tia opened her eyes and started to sit up, but he splayed his hand across her mid-section holding her in place.

"I loved you with my whole heart and soul, Tia, and I never stopped." Adam trailed an index finger along her neck, gently traced the outline of her ear. "The moment I saw you at Carl's funeral, all those feelings I'd buried, all the love I pretended never existed, nearly knocked me to my knees."

He picked up her hand again and studied the ring. "When I asked you to marry me, I tried to convince myself it was for Toby, to keep him safe. That wasn't the real reason, Tia. I asked you to marry me because I can't live without you. Every word I spoke to you, every vow I promised when I slipped that ring on your finger, I meant."

Tears filled her eyes, but he continued. "I've loved you for so long, Tia, and I always will. From the day you walked into church and sat in the pew behind me with those beautiful sad eyes, you've held my heart in your hands."

"Adam..." Tia started to speak, but he abruptly rose to his feet and pulled a box from beneath the tree.

He handed it to her and she sat up, untying the red ribbon wrapped around it and removing the lid.

She lifted out a wooden jewelry box, one of the finest she'd ever seen. "Did you make this, too?"

"I did, with help from Blake." Adam watched her face. "Open it, Queenie."

Carefully tipping back the lid, she reached inside the box and lifted out a silver necklace. Holding the chain up to catch the light of the fire, she admired a knot made of silver in the center of the chain.

"What is this, Adam?" she asked, running her finger over the intricate design. "It's beautiful."

"It's called a True-Lover's knot." Adam dropped to one knee in front of her. "The knot is strong, nearly impossible to break once those two strands have been woven together into one." He took the necklace from her hand, dropped it into the box, and set it aside. "You and I are like that knot, Tia. Our hearts are tightly tied together, bound by love, and they always will be."

The tears she'd held back spilled down her cheeks. Adam sighed and brushed them away with his thumb.

"I love you Tiadora Elizabeth Guthry, I've loved you for so long. I'll love you until and with my last breath. Would you do me the honor of being my wife? My true wife?"

"Yes, Adam. Yes!" She wrapped her arms around his neck and pulled him close, thrilled as his lips tantalized hers in a fervent kiss full of hope and promises.

Suddenly, Tia pulled back and gave him a panicked look. "Oh, Adam, you're going to be so disappointed when you open your gifts tomorrow. Nothing I got you compares to this." She pointed toward the jewelry box sitting on the table.

Adam stood and lifted her to her feet. With a dimpled grin, he pulled the pins from her hair and watched it tumble in silky waves around her shoulders and down her back.

"Ribbons and shiny paper don't matter to me, Queenie. There's not a single thing you could buy for me that's any better than this." Burrowing his hands into the thick tresses, he nuzzled her ear, pressing close against her. When she moaned, he lifted her in his arms and kissed her so tenderly, she lost the ability to think of anything beyond her love for Adam.

He kissed her with a passion unlike anything she'd ever known, unlike anything she'd ever imagined.

Finally, he pulled back and held her gaze, allowing the warmth in his eyes to envelop her. "Wrap me in your love, Tia. That's all I want for Christmas — to take you in my arms and love you like you've never dreamed of being loved."

In response, she tugged his face down, capturing his mouth with hers as their hearts, at long last, connected.

"I love you, Adam Guthry. Only and forever you."

Epilogue

"And you promise you'll come to visit?" Erin Dodd asked as Toby pulled her on his new sled while their parents said goodbye.

"I promise, Erin," Toby said, glancing back at her with sparkling eyes and a charming grin. "I'm a Guthry now and we always keep our promises."

Suddenly, Erin jumped off the sled and wrapped her little arms around Toby, giving him a hug. "I don't want you to go."

"I know." Toby hugged her back, and then took her hand as they walked together to where Tia and Adam waited with Chauncy, Abby, Arlan and Alex.

Arlan had borrowed Luke's big sleigh and team to take Adam and his little family to Heppner to catch the train.

Before they left, they'd taken Toby to say his farewells to Erin.

"You'll come visit us in the spring, won't you?" Tia asked Abby as they stood with arms linked together.

"Yes. Chauncy needs a little time off from work. It will do us good to get out of town, and it will be fun to visit you."

"Maybe we can work in a little shopping," Tia said, causing the men to groan.

"Mama likes to shop," Toby whispered to Erin so loudly, everyone could hear.

"Come on, son, time to go." Adam place a hand on Toby's shoulder and gave it a gentle squeeze.

Toby handed Erin the rope tied to his sled. "You take care of my sled for me, Erin. Daddy said there's no snow in Portland, so I can't use it there, but we can play with it when we come next year for Christmas."

"I'll keep it safe," Erin said, her little lip puckering.

Toby turned away then spun around and gave Erin a kiss on her mouth. Before she could blink, he ran over to the sleigh and climbed into the back seat. He stood up and shook a finger Erin's direction. "And don't you go marrying anybody while I'm gone."

Erin waved at him then buried her face against her mother's skirts.

"We'll miss you all so much," Tia said, hugging Abby one last time before allowing Adam to help her into the back of the sleigh. Arlan assisted Alex in climbing beside her then he took a seat in the front, lifting the reins in his hands.

A loud snarling sound emanated from the crate beneath the back seat where Crabby awaited a release from his confines. After all the cat had done to protect Toby, Adam agreed they wouldn't leave him behind when they returned to Portland.

Adam shook hands with Chauncy and waggled his eyebrow at him. "Never imagined myself having a preacher in the family, but if Toby and Erin carry through with their plans, it looks like we'll be in-laws someday."

Chauncy chuckled and slapped his back. "She couldn't pick a finer family to belong to than all of you." He waved at Toby and grinned. "You take good care of my future son-in-law and his beautiful mother."

Adam kissed Tia's cheek, settling a blanket over her and Toby's laps before taking a seat beside Arlan. "I vow to do that very thing, Chauncy."

Gingerbread Cake

Adapted from an old recipe, this spicy, moist cake is a flavorful blast from the past. Serve with ice cream or cinnamon-laced whipped cream for an extra-special treat.

Gingerbread Cake
1 stick butter, softened
½ cup brown sugar, packed
1 egg
¾ cup molasses
½ cup applesauce
2 ½ cups flour
1 ½ teaspoons baking soda
2 ½ teaspoons cinnamon
2 ½ teaspoons ground ginger
1 teaspoon ground cloves
½ teaspoon salt
1 cup hot water

Preheat oven to 350°F. Grease and flour a large loaf pan.

In a large bowl, cream together brown sugar and butter. Beat in egg, molasses, and applesauce. The molasses will easily pour out of a measuring cup if you swirl a little oil around the inside or spray with non-stick cooking spray.

In a medium bowl, whisk together dry ingredients – flour, baking soda, cinnamon, ginger, ground cloves, and salt.

Add dry ingredients to wet ingredients one cup at a time, stirring gently between additions until all of the dry mixture is blended into the wet mixture. At this point, add the cup of hot water and stir to incorporate.

Bake for 50-60 minutes. A toothpick inserted into the center of the loaf should come out with a few moist crumbs attached.

Author's Note

I won't ramble on about the ghost town of Hardman and how it came to be the center of this series, but I thought I would share a few little fun details with you.

When I was researching board games popular in the Victorian era, I kept coming back to one in particular: Bulls and Bears — The Great Game of Wall Street.

The financial panic of 1873, the worst before 1929, inspired the board game. The Bulls and the Bears (the speculators) are depicted fleecing the sheep (the public). The images used on the game board were derived from cartoons by Joseph Keppler and Frederick Burr Opper, meant to point fingers at "robber barons" Jay Gould, W.H. Vanderbilt, and Russell Sage. Their cartoons appeared in the illustrated weekly magazine "Puck." Apparently, today this is ranked as one of the rarest of all nineteenth century American board games. If you find one lurking in the back of Great-Aunt Myrtle's closet, you might have a small gold mine on your hands.

As I've looked into events and happenings for my historical romances, one thing that has fascinated me is old zoos. For this story, I discovered the Portland Zoo began in 1888 with a donation of a grizzly bear from a Portlander's private menagerie to the city. From those humble beginnings, the zoo grew to house more than 300 animals in 1894, mostly from North America. One of the most famous residents of the zoo was Packy, the first elephant born in the United States in forty-four years when it arrived in 1962. The elephant drew more than a million visitors to the zoo.

As a sailor, Adam had to know how to tie knots, which meant I needed to read up on them. My dad taught me a few knots when I was a young girl, but I've forgotten most of them except the square knot and a half hitch. Realknots.com has some easy to understand knots.

For those of you unfamiliar with the <u>Columbia River</u>, it is the largest river in the Pacific Northwest. The river rises in the Rocky Mountains of British Columbia, Canada. It flows northwest and then changes direction into Washington State. Meandering south, it turns west to form most of the border between Washington and Oregon in a river route known as the Columbia Gorge before the river empties into the Pacific Ocean.

The gorge is a canyon ranging up to 4,000 feet deep and stretches for more than 80 miles as the river winds through the Cascade mountain range toward the Pacific Ocean. It provides the only navigable water route through the Cascades and the only water connection between the Columbia River Plateau and the Pacific Ocean. It holds a protected status as a national scenic area and is a popular recreational destination.

Ships coming inland from the ocean and those traveling down the river to reach the ocean face a treacherous area known as the Columbia Bar. The jaws of the mighty Columbia River empty into the ocean at the bar where gushing water combined with hurricane-force winds can create twenty- to forty-foot swells roaring off the Pacific. Eerily nicknamed the "Graveyard of the Pacific," this stretch of the coast lives up to the moniker.

Since 1792, there have been approximately 2,000 ships sunk in the area and more than 700 deaths. Water, weather, and geography combine to make the bar deadly. In 1846, after numerous shipwrecks, the Columbia River Bar Pilots organization formed to ensure the safety of ships, crews, and cargoes crossing the bar. The men and women who belong to this organization must hold an unlimited master's license (meaning they are licensed to pilot vessels without limits on size, power, or geographic location) and have served a minimum of two years as master of oceangoing vessels.

All vessels engaged in foreign trade are required to employ a Columbia River Bar Pilot licensed by the State of Oregon when crossing the Columbia River Bar. The standard of licensing for the bar pilots is one of the highest in the nation.

The pilots board the vessels and assume navigational control, using their experience and knowledge to safely navigate the restricted channels of the Columbia River and over the bar both coming and going from the sea.

Another organization, the Columbia River Pilots, provide maritime pilotage services to all ports on the lower Columbia and Willamette Rivers once ships have crossed the bar. These pilots are charged with safely and efficiently piloting vessels in all weather conditions, at all hours of the day and night, 365 days a year. Headquartered in Portland, the group has a station located in Astoria where pilots await inbound ship assignments.

This organization gave me the idea for Adam's line of work in the story.

And there really is a fun children's book by Frances Browne called <u>Granny's Wonderful Chair</u>.

I hope you enjoyed another visit to Hardman and meeting a few new characters along the way.

What characters would you like to see in future Hardman Holidays stories?

The Christmas Bargain (Hardman Holidays, Book 1) - As owner and manager of the Hardman bank, Luke Granger is a man of responsibility and integrity in the small 1890s Eastern Oregon town. When he calls in a long overdue loan, Luke finds himself reluctantly accepting a bargain in lieu of payment from the shiftless farmer who barters his daughter to settle his debt.

The Christmas Token (Hardman Holidays, Book 2) - Determined to escape an unwelcome suitor, Ginny Granger flees to her brother's home in Eastern Oregon for the holiday season. Returning to the community where she spent her childhood years, she plans to relax and enjoy a peaceful visit. Not expecting to encounter the boy she once loved, her exile proves to be anything but restful.

The Christmas Calamity (Hardman Holidays Book 3) - Dependable and solid, Arlan Guthry relishes his orderly life as a banker's assistant in Hardman, Oregon. His uncluttered world tilts off kilter when the beautiful and enigmatic prestidigitator Alexandra Janowski arrives in town, spinning magic and trouble in her wake as the holiday season approaches.

The Christmas Vow (Hardman Holidays Book 4) - Adam Guthry returns home to bury his best friend and his past, never expecting to fall in love with Tia Devereux, the woman who destroyed his heart.

Pendleton Petticoats Series

Set in the western town of Pendleton, Oregon, right at the turn of the 20th century, each book in this series bears the name of the heroine, all brave yet very different.

Aundy *(Book 1)* Aundy Thorsen, a stubborn mail-order bride, finds the courage to carry on when she's widowed before ever truly becoming a wife, but opening her heart to love again may be more than she can bear.

Caterina *(Book 2)* - Running from a man intent on marrying her, Caterina Campanelli starts a new life in Pendleton, completely unprepared for the passionate feelings stirred in her by the town's incredibly handsome deputy sheriff.

Ilsa *(Book 3)* - Desperate to escape her wicked aunt and an unthinkable future, Ilsa Thorsen finds herself on her sister's ranch in Pendleton. Not only are the dust and smells more than she can bear, but Tony Campanelli seems bent on making her his special project.

Marnie *(Book 4)* - Beyond all hope for a happy future, Marnie Jones struggles to deal with her roiling emotions when U.S. Marshal Lars Thorsen rides into town, tearing down the walls she's erected around her heart.

Lacy (Book 5) -   Bound by tradition and responsibilities, Lacy has to choose between the ties that bind her to the past and the unexpected love that will carry her into the future.

Bertie *(Book 6) - The next adventure in the Pendleton Petticoat Series - coming in 2016!*

Crumpets and Cowpies *(Baker City Brides, Book 1)* - Rancher Thane Jordan reluctantly travels to England to settle his brother's estate only to find he's inherited much more than he could possibly have imagined.

Lady Jemma Bryan has no desire to spend a single minute in Thane Jordan's insufferable presence much less live under the same roof with the handsome, arrogant American. Forced to choose between poverty or marriage to the man, she finds herself traveling across an ocean and America to reach his ranch in Oregon.

Thimbles and Thistles *(Baker City Brides, Book 2)* - Maggie Dalton has no need for a man in her life. Widowed more than ten years, she's built a successful business and managed quite well on her own in the bustling town of Baker City, Oregon.

Aggravated by her inability to block thoughts of the handsome lumber mill owner from her mind, she renews her determination to resist his attempts at friendship.

Full of Scottish charm and mischief, Ian MacGregor could claim any single woman in Baker City as his own, except the enchanting dress shop owner who continues to ignore him. Not one to give up on what he wants, Ian vows to win Maggie's heart or leave the town he's come to love.

Corsets and Cuffs *(coming spring 2016)*

The Christmas Cowboy *(Rodeo Romance, Book 1)* - The Christmas Cowboy (Book 1) - Saddle bronc rider Tate Morgan can ride the wildest horse on the circuit, but he has no idea how to handle feisty Kenzie Beckett.

Wrestlin' Christmas *(Rodeo Romance, Book 2)* - Shanghaied by his sister and best friend, former steer wrestler Cort McGraw ends up on a run-down ranch with a beguiling widow and her silent son.

Capturing Christmas *(Rodeo Romance, Book 3)* — Life is hectic on a good day for rodeo stock contractor Kash Kressley. Between dodging flying hooves and babying cranky bulls, he barely has time to sleep. The last thing Kash needs is the entanglement of a sweet romance, especially with a woman as full of fire and sass as the redheaded photographer he meets at a rodeo.

If you enjoyed *Capturing Christmas*,
don't miss out on ***The Cowboy's Christmas Plan***,
Book 1 in the Grass Valley Cowboys Series!

Grass Valley Cowboys Series

Meet the Thompson family of the Triple T Ranch in Grass
Valley, Oregon.
Three handsome brothers, their rowdy friends, and the
women who fall for them are at the heart of this
contemporary western romance series.
Book 1 – ***The Cowboy's Christmas Plan***
Book 2 – ***The Cowboy's Spring Romance***
Book 3 – ***The Cowboy's Summer Love***
Book 4 – ***The Cowboy's Autumn Fall***
Book 5 – ***The Cowboy's New Heart***

The Women of Tenacity Series

Welcome to Tenacity!

Tenacious, sassy women tangle with the wild, rugged men who love them in this contemporary western romance series.

The paperback version offers a short story introduction, *A Prelude*, followed by the three full-length novels set in the fictional town of Tenacity, Oregon.

Book 1 – ***Heart of Clay***
Book 2 – ***Country Boy vs. City Girl***
Book 3 – ***Not His Type***

The Coffee Girl - On the eve of her thirtieth birthday, Brenna Smith has a few goals in mind:

* Introduce herself to the hunky construction guy she runs into every morning at the coffee shop.

* Slap the smug smirk off the face of her detestable boss right before she quits.

* Open a bistro.

* Find the man who haunts her dreams.

Handsome and charming Brock McCrae owns a successful construction company and enjoys time spent with friends. However, he still has a few items on his to-do list:

*Find a place to call home.

*Get a dog.

*Work up the courage to ask the quirky woman he knows only as the Coffee Girl out on a date.

Will the two of them connect over more than a cup of java?

The Christmas Crusade — Levi Clarke is on a crusade to create a merry Christmas for the patrons of Center for Hope community center. He'll do whatever it takes to make it happen, even if it means seeking a sponsorship from Kat Kingsley, the woman too stubborn to realize she's still in love with him.

(If you enjoyed reading _The Coffee Girl_, this sweet novella continues the story.)

__Learnin' The Ropes__ - Mechanic Ty Lewis is out of options. Homeless and desperate to find work, he accepts a job in the tiny community of Riley, Oregon. Resolved to embrace a new adventure with an elusive boss, he leaves behind everything he's ever known in Portland to live in the middle of nowhere.

Lexi Ryan, known to her ranch hands and neighbors as Lex Jr., abandons her corporate career to keep the Rockin' R Ranch running smoothly after the untimely death of her father. It doesn't take long to discover her father did many crazy things during the last few months before he died, like hiding half a million dollars that Lexi can't find.

Ty and Lexi are both in for a few surprises as he arrives at the ranch and begins learnin' the ropes.

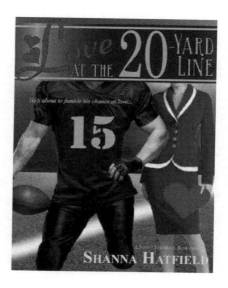

Love at the 20-Yard Line - Haven Haggarty is woefully inept when it comes to men and matters of the heart. Successful in her job as an image consultant with an up-and-coming company, she wishes she could enjoy as much triumph in her dating efforts. When she falls hard for a handsome wide receiver, Haven realizes she needs to tackle her fears or miss the opportunity to experience once-in-a-lifetime love.

Brody Jackson lives and breathes football. As a wide receiver for a popular arena team, he's determined to make it back to the NFL. Cocky and confident, he doesn't have the time or energy to be bothered with a serious relationship until he's blindsided by a sweet, naive girl who breaks through his defenses. He has to decide if he'll let go of his dreams or fumble his chance to win Haven's heart.

The QR Code Killer - Murder. Mayhem. Suspense. Romance.

Zeus is a crazed killer who uses QR Codes to taunt the cop hot on his trail.

Mad Dog Weber, a tough-as-nails member of the Seattle police force, is willing to do whatever it takes to bring Zeus down. Despite her best intentions, Maddie (Mad Dog) falls in love with her dad's hired hand, putting them both in danger.

Erik Moore is running from his past and trying to avoid the future when he finds himself falling in love with his employer's daughter. Unknowingly, he puts himself right in the path of the QR Code Killer as he struggles to keep Maddie safe.

From the waterfront of Seattle to the rolling hills of wheat and vineyards of the Walla Walla Valley, suspense and romance fly around every twist and turn.

Fifty Dates with Captain Cavedweller - When a hopeless romantic with a bit of a sarcastic attitude falls in love with an introvert who dreams of living in a man cave, they plan to live happily ever after. The only problem is that life seems to get in the way.

Waking up one day to discover they'd gone from perpetual honeymooners to a boring, predictable couple, author Shanna Hatfield and her beloved husband, Captain Cavedweller, set out on a yearlong adventure to add a little zing to their relationship.

This G-rated journey through fifty of their dates provides an insightful, humorous look at the effort they made to infuse their marriage with laughter, love, and gratitude while reconnecting on a new, heartfelt level.

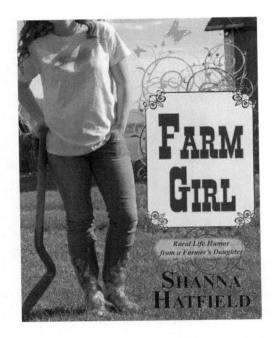

**Farm Girl** - What happens when a farmer who's been wishing for a boy ends up with a girlie-girl?

Come along on the humorous and sometimes agonizing adventures from a childhood spent on a farm in the Eastern Oregon desert where one family raised hay, wheat, cattle and a farm girl.

"Great read! I found myself laughing out loud quite a few times!"

Amazon Reviewer

<u>Savvy Entertaining Series</u>

Discover seasonal ideas for decorating, entertaining, party themes, home décor, recipes and more from Savvy Entertaining's blogger!

ABOUT THE AUTHOR

SHANNA HATFIELD spent ten years as a newspaper journalist before moving into the field of marketing and public relations. Self-publishing the romantic stories she dreams up in her head is a perfect outlet for her lifelong love of writing, reading, and creativity. She and her husband, lovingly referred to as Captain Cavedweller, reside in the Pacific Northwest.

Shanna loves to hear from readers.
Connect with her online:
Blog: shannahatfield.com
Facebook: Shanna Hatfield's Page
Pinterest: Shanna Hatfield
Email: shanna@shannahatfield.com

If you'd like to know more about the characters in any of her books,
visit the Book Characters page on her website
or check out her **Book Boards** on Pinterest.

38575131R00161

Made in the USA
Middletown, DE
21 December 2016